D0341137

fP

Other Books by John McNally

FICTION

The Book of Ralph

Troublemakers

ANTHOLOGIES

Bottom of the Ninth: Great Contemporary Baseball Short Stories

Humor Me: An Anthology of Humor by Writers of Color

The Student Body: Short Stories About College Students and Professors

High Infidelity: 24 Great Short Stories About Adultery

A Novel

JOHN MCNALLY

Free Press
NEW YORK LONDON TORONTO SYDNEY

FREE PRESS
A Division of Simon & Schuster, Inc.
1230 Avenue of the Americas
New York, NY 10020

This book is a work of fiction. Names, characters, places, and incidents either are products of the author's imagination or are used fictitiously. Any resemblance to actual events or locales or persons, living or dead, is entirely coincidental.

For information about special discounts for bulk purchases, please contact Simon & Schuster Special Sales at 1-800-456-6798 or business@simonandschuster.com

DESIGNED BY PAUL DIPPOLITO

Manufactured in the United States of America

10 9 8 7 6 5 4 3 2 1

Library of Congress Cataloging-in-Publication Data Control Number: 2006040525

ISBN-13: 978-0-7432-5626-1
ISBN-10: 0-7432-5626-3

To America's Iago,

Ann Coulter,

for rewriting history to suit her own nefarious purposes

Are there no stones in heaven
But what serves for the thunder? Precious villain!

—SHAKESPEARE, *OTHELLO*

Contents

PART ONE

The Test, 1995 3
Spring 2004 7

PART TWO

The Teeth, 1997 85
Summer 2004 91

PART THREE

The Hunt, 1995 165
August 2, 2004 171
August 3, 2004 192
August 4, 2004 209

PART FOUR

The Lycanthrope, *2004* 231
Two Days Before Election Day 237
One Day Before Election Day 248
Election Day 259

When a girl leaves her home at eighteen, she does one of two things. Either she falls into saving hands and becomes better, or she rapidly assumes the cosmopolitan standard of virtue and becomes worse.

—THEODORE DREISER, *SISTER CARRIE*

Part One

The Test

1995

Without fail they arrive every year. Dozens of men in black suits unfurl themselves from white panel vans parked in front of Jacqueline Bouvier Kennedy Grade School. The mornings they arrive are usually overcast, sometimes rainy—typical fall weather for this southwest Chicago suburb. There are five men to a van, and each man carries a heavy box into the school. Together, they wait in the lobby for the principal to greet them. These men are test administrators sent by the United States government, and they will spend the entire day here, distributing thick booklets and then, every half-hour or hour, imparting new information for yet another test. These tests, which will be evaluated at secret locations across the nation, will reveal critical information about the education of our country's children. How, for instance, does one state stack up against another state? How do entire regions of the country compare to other regions? How are our country's children doing this year compared to four years ago? This test is America's Report Card—a massive, ongoing project that costs millions, if not billions, of dollars. What's at stake is the nation's future.

And this is exactly what Jainey O'Sullivan's third-grade teacher, Mrs. Rutkowski, has told her students: that if they don't do well on the test, the Russians will take over, and if not the Russians, then the Chinese. If they think life is tough now, just wait until the Chinese take over. When the Chinese take over, Mrs. Rutkowski says, there will be no more Art class, no more Music, nothing fun, and all of the boys will have to join the Army. "No more cheeseburgers," she says. "No more pizza." Furthermore, they will no longer be allowed to speak English. They will have to learn a new language or suffer the consequences. Have they ever heard Chinese or Russian spoken? It's no cakewalk, she tells them. It's no day in the park.

Jainey sits quietly at her desk, ten perfectly sharpened Number 2 pencils lined before her. Her palms are as moist as her tongue. Jainey watches a lot of reruns on TV with her father, and the men who come to her school remind her of the men on Dragnet. *This year, the man assigned to her classroom, who looks like the man who came to her second-grade classroom last year (and who could very well be the same man, for all Jainey knows), heaves his heavy box onto Mrs. Rutkowski's desk. He tells the students that they should relax, that there are no winners or losers, but how can Jainey relax, knowing that if she gives the wrong answer, the Russians or the Chinese will bomb the country and take over? Furthermore, the man in the black suit doesn't look relaxed himself. Beads of sweat appear on his forehead, and Jainey can smell his sour breath each time he walks by.*

Jainey is a good student—not the best student but better than most—so why is it that she doesn't understand most of the questions on the test? The reading passages are too long to read within the time permitted. The questions for each reading passage are even more troublesome. Often, every answer seems to be right. For other questions, none of the answers appears correct. She can't remember if leaving the answer blank is better than filling in a bubble for something she clearly doesn't know. The Math test is even harder. Nothing looks familiar except for the numbers themselves. Why are there tiny numbers sitting on the shoulders of larger numbers? Why are there letters where there should be numbers? Jainey is so angry at her Math teacher for not teaching her what she needs to know that she breaks the tip of her pencil while filling in one of the bubbles.

Not until near the end of the day does she realize that she made a mistake early in the morning and has been filling in the wrong bubbles throughout the test. For question number eight, she has filled in bubble number nine. For question number nine, bubble number ten. For ten, eleven. For eleven, twelve. And so on. By now, only thirty minutes before the end of the school day, she has incorrectly filled in hundreds of bubbles.

Jainey tries erasing her filled-in bubbles, but she realizes that this is a futile task, that this would mean retaking the entire test, which she began at eight-thirty this morning. She flips through the thick booklet, turning back to tests that she has been warned not to look at anymore. She needs to look at those sections, though, to see where she made her first mistake. Where? Where? The pressure inside her head builds, as if her eyes are being gently squeezed between forefingers and thumbs, but she manages to keep most of her tears at bay. Still, her vision blurs over, and her ability to concentrate surges, going in and out, everything swirling, a sensation not unlike being tossed head-first into the deep end of a pool on a moonless night.

She is not sure when they came over, but here they are, Mrs. Rutkowski and the test administrator, both staring down at her. Jainey's hands are smeared with lead. Her test booklet is open to the first test. Half of her pencils are on the floor. But all Jainey can think about are the Russians and Chinese, bombs whistling down from warplanes, life as she's known it coming to an end, everything new and awful about to begin, and all of it is her fault.

Spring 2004

AFTER FINISHING HIS MASTER'S DEGREE, CHARLIE WOLF decided to remain in Iowa. Why not? He had no job, no prospects, nothing lined up. It wasn't uncommon in university towns to find such people—students or visiting professors who arrive for what should be a finite period of time but then stay on an extra year, an extra two years, sometimes never leaving at all. Often, these were the same people who, upon their arrival from New York or San Francisco, found the locals too provincial, the selections of restaurants and bookstores frighteningly limited, the landscape flat, depressingly spare. But then something would happen. They'd fall into the rhythms of life in a small prairie town, slowly warming to it all, only to wake up one day and realize that fifteen years had come and gone, and here they still were: *Iowa! Of all places!*

Well, Charlie wasn't going to be one of *them*—he wouldn't be here fifteen years from now—but what was wrong with hanging out for a year? Or two? Besides, his girlfriend didn't have any plans, either. They could get part-time jobs. They could continue spending lazy afternoons on the couch watching B movies. They could do what they did best—*loaf.* It would be a much-needed break—a break from everything—before diving back into the uncertain murk and sludge of real life. And what was wrong with that? At twenty-three years old, their entire lives were ahead of them.

Iowa City was a town full of large, drafty turn-of-the-century houses, and Charlie lived in a rambling Victorian that had been divided into twelve apartments. You could rent a room barely large enough for a futon and a coffee table, or you could rent a three-bedroom with bay windows and a roaring fireplace surrounded by a marble mantle. Charlie's apartment fell somewhere in between—one bedroom but no fireplace, a small kitchen but no dishwasher, a claw-footed tub but no shower. He liked its shoddy charm, the pocked hardwood floors, the spiderwebbed cracks along the ceiling, the way the faucets creaked when he turned them on or off. It was exactly how he'd fantasized life would be in graduate school, a kind of shambling, just-above-the-poverty-line existence, a world where the life of the mind overshadowed everything else.

And Petra was exactly the sort of girlfriend he'd always hoped for. Some days he wondered if he had conjured her out of the muggy Iowa air, this pale, dark-haired daughter of Russian immigrants, this feisty and beautiful young woman who could quote Gorky without blinking, but who also knew verbatim entire episodes of *Hogan's Heroes,* who at parties smoked cigars and drank vodka straight from the bottle, glug-glugging two or three shots' worth, who had taught Charlie a thing or two in bed ("No, no, twist your hip to the right and put your left foot right there, *yes,* right *there!*"), and who, wearing her father's tall fur cap, the kind of cap that Siberian soldiers wear, inspired everyone in a bar or a restaurant or a movie theater to turn and smile, an entire room full of men and women falling instantly in love with this girl they'd never before seen. Petra Petrovich. It was as though she'd stepped from the pages of a thick Signet-edition classic, a Russian character in full bloom, smelling of cold, frosty air and, faintly, of brittle pages from a mildewing book. Petra Petrovich. He whispered her name into her ear, over and over, and on those nights she didn't spend with him, he whispered her name alone, again and again, until he fell headlong into the knotted fist of his own unconsciousness, into a sleep so strange and woolly, he often woke up sweating and out of breath, the too-bright sun punching through the mini-blinds, the new day already begun.

America's Report Card

JAINEY O'SULLIVAN, seventeen years old and a senior at Reavis High School in the southwest Chicago suburb of Burbank, had been hearing about America's Report Card all year long, but what her teachers failed to understand was that none of her classmates gave two shits about the test. There was too much else going on in everyone's lives right now. In the past few years alone, Jainey's body had gotten hairier, she'd grown nearly a foot taller, her voice became weirder, more cartoonish, she was having to buy, along with her boxes of tampons, condoms at Walgreen's from the old guy with liver-spotted hands and a huge spongy nose, her shoes never fit anymore, she dyed her hair new colors, like purple and green, her body gave off odors that were sometimes interestingly foreign and sometimes outright revolting, pimples appeared on her face like thugs crouching in a dark alley, jumping out of nowhere and scaring the piss right out of her, her navel seemed eerily deeper as of late, she possessed too many creepy facts, like how many square feet of skin covered her body, she was no longer sure what she thought about God, she pierced herself places no one could see unless she took off her clothes, boys wanted to fuck her and she sometimes wanted to fuck them, she had started experimenting on herself with the handle of her hairbrush *(whoa!)*, she knew the quadratic formula by heart but had no idea what the hell it meant or what it could be used for, and terrorists—*suspected* terrorists, she reminded herself—were not infrequently arrested at the 7-Eleven around the corner from her house. She had all of these new things to contend with, and *more.* The world as she knew it, the planet from which she couldn't escape, was splitting at the seams. So why the hell should she care about some stupid test? Why? She *didn't* care—that was the problem—and so she came to a clear and definitive decision on her own. She would quit going to school. She had been a good student, a *model* student, so who could possibly blame her for slipping up with only a month to go before graduation? *No one,* she thought. *That's who.*

• • •

On the first official day of her truancy, Jainey tooled around Burbank in her brother's piece of shit car. She called it the Turd. The tires were bald. The rearview mirror hung from the windshield like a limp wrist. The cloth interior drooped onto her head. There were so many speckles of rust on its body, the car looked as though it might be harboring some contagious disease. But the Turd still ran, so Jainey couldn't complain.

When Jainey finally came home, it was well after midnight. She padded softly through the dark house and, after touch-feeling her way into the kitchen, flipped on the light. There sat Ned, her brother, holding a penlight in one hand, a spoon full of Cheerios in the other. A thick book with gold-leaf edges lay open next to his cereal bowl.

Jainey's heart pounded so hard, she could hear the *whoosh* and *thump* of blood against her eardrums, but she tried acting nonchalant. She cleared her throat and said, "Mom's car is taking up too much of the driveway, so I parked the Turd on the street."

Ned lowered the spoon back into his cereal bowl. "You parked a *what* on the street?"

And then Jainey remembered that she hadn't told her brother she'd given his car a nickname, let alone started driving it. Ned was six years older than Jainey and lived in the attic. He never left the house anymore; in fact, he rarely emerged from his upstairs lair. Entire months slipped by without Jainey even laying eyes on him, and only when she heard groans of heavy metal music pulsing through the air ducts did she think, *Oh yeah: he still lives here.*

"What're you reading?" Jainey asked. "Looks like the frickin' Bible or something."

"It *is* the Bible," Ned said. "So what." He stared at her, his eyes milky from the low-grade fever he always complained about. He blinked a few times. He pointed to a letter on the table. "Mail," he said.

Jainey never got mail, nothing, not even junk mail. Dubiously, she tore it open. "Dear Jainey," it began.

I'm giving away some of my things, and I'd like for you to come over Friday night to see if there's anything you want. I hope this finds you in good spirits. Yours, Mrs. Grant.

Mrs. Grant had been Jainey's grade school art teacher, the only teacher ever to encourage Jainey to pursue anything. Jainey had had a knack for drawing, and Mrs. Grant had instantly recognized it. "If you have a talent, you need to do something with it," Mrs. Grant had said, and Jainey did. In fact, Jainey had recently begun a new comic strip—her best yet—called *Lloyd the Freakazoid.* Lloyd had bulging eyes and a tongue too big for his mouth. He groped girls half his age and drank vodka straight from a bottle. He yelled inappropriate things in public like, "Hubba-hubba!" and "Mama mia!" and his fly was never zipped. Each comic strip had its own subtitle, such as "Lloyd Rides a Girl's Bike for the First Time," or "Lloyd Discovers a Salt Lick."

It was in Mrs. Grant's class in the seventh grade that Jainey came to the conclusion that there existed two versions of every person: the real version and the cartoon version. Whenever she met someone, she pictured their cartoon version, and then she imagined what the cartoon version would say and do. With only one exception, the cartoon version was always more interesting than the real person. That exception was Mrs. Grant.

Jainey tucked the letter into her back pocket, filched a granola bar, and walked out of the kitchen.

"The light!" Ned yelled. "Turn off the light!"

Jainey, already halfway up the stairs, pretended not to hear.

THE DAY BEFORE graduation, as the town bloated with parents bearing gifts, Charlie received a phone call.

"Charlie Wolf?" a man said.

"Is this a solicitation?" Charlie asked, prepared to hang up.

The man laughed. "Oh, Christ, no," he said and then cleared his throat. "I mean, *no*." There was a pause. Then, "Actually, it's an opportunity. I'm calling on behalf of National Testing Center."

National Testing Center. Anyone who'd ever attended school had taken a standardized test that had been either created or evaluated by National Testing Center. Iowa City was their headquarters.

"And?" Charlie said.

"I see here that you're graduating."

"That's right," Charlie said coldly.

"Well then," the man said, "as you probably know, we do a lot of hiring this time of year. It looks here like you'd be a perfect fit for us. We could use someone with your educational background to help us score tests this season."

"What are you looking at?" Charlie asked.

"What?"

"You said, 'It looks here . . . ' "

"Ah-ha, you caught me. Nothing gets past you, does it?" He coughed into the mouthpiece—an explosion of phlegm and technology. "I'm not looking at anything, really. Just a list of graduates. Fresh meat," he added and laughed again.

Charlie politely explained to the man that while he had other plans for the summer, he appreciated the call.

"Do you mind if I ask you just one more thing, Charlie Wolf?" the man said.

Charlie hung up. He walked over to the bay window in his living room. The streets were lined with everything the departing students didn't want anymore—frayed couches, useless computer parts, curling irons, answering machines. Someone had stabbed a beanbag chair with a kitchen knife. The knife was still in it, pushed all the way to the hilt. The beanbag chair was concave at the point of impact, the way a man's stomach might give in under similar circumstances.

Charlie decided to go for a walk. He loved this time of year. There was no telling what he might see when he rounded a corner. For a few days, the city would be full of surprises, shopping bags begging to be dug through, boxes demanding to be searched. It was as though Christmas had arrived over seven months early. It was that much fun.

On the day after the graduation ceremony that neither of them attended, Petra Petrovich walked into Charlie Wolf's apartment with the gusto of a protagonist. It was May, but the temperature had dropped significantly, and the wind, clipping powerfully through town, rattled the Victorian's old bones. Petra, out of breath from battling the elements, shut the door behind her. She smiled and said, "Now what?"

"Now what *what?*"

"Our lives," Petra said. "Now what?"

"Do you want a pot pie?" Charlie asked.

Pot pie was code: it took about as long for a pot pie to cook as it did for them, on average, to have sex. Like most things, they had discovered this by accident, and so now, whenever Charlie asked if she wanted a pot pie, he meant it both literally and figuratively.

He took two Banquet turkey pot pies from his freezer, and while he moved through the motions of preparing them—sawing a slit across the frozen crust, locating a clean cookie sheet to place them upon—Petra unbuttoned her blouse, then reached behind her to unclasp her bra. It was this precise image (hands behind back, elbows pointing away from the body) that always succeeded in getting Charlie worked up, more so than the final revelation of flesh. For Charlie—and he couldn't say why—the anticipation of flesh, especially that split second before the actual revelation, did something profound to his inner chemistry. Such moments took him straight to the boiling point. The same held true when Petra stripped down to nothing but her panties with her thumbs hooked into the elastic and beginning to push down, but only after she'd pushed them down an inch, two inches at the most, and then Charlie's heart would start to thump, his lungs suddenly a poor organ for holding air. Sometimes he yelled, "Wait! Hold that!" and Petra would stand there impatiently. Once, she simply mooned him.

Today, by the time he'd slid the pot pies into the oven, Petra was already naked, everything off and piled on the floor, except for her socks. She liked keeping her socks on. This was about as decadent a life as Charlie could have hoped for, and he was grateful for it. He knew that his parents would never have spent their early afternoons doing anything like this, and so Charlie felt a degree of satisfaction that, in the long history of his own genealogy, the general trajectory of his sex life was heading in the right direction.

"Where do you want to go?" he asked, using his right foot to remove his left shoe.

Petra patted the kitchen table.

"Here?" Charlie asked. "Really?"

Petra nodded.

"Okay," Charlie said. "The table it is! But let me move the salt and pepper. And these bills," he said. "Let me get them out of the way. Oh, and the napkins . . ."

"Charlie," Petra said. "Stop it." She hoisted herself up onto the table. "Come here," she said. "Come here, and stop worrying." She was a lovely sight wearing only socks. How could Charlie possibly disobey?

After sex, Petra always did the same thing. She paced in front of Charlie's bookcases, head tilted sideways, silently reading the books' titles. Charlie could never decide if she read the titles critically, as if his selection of books, his *taste,* indicated the likelihood of their staying together, or if she was simply passing the time. Occasionally, Petra pulled a book from the shelf, turned it over, read the back cover, then returned it, pressing the spine flush with the others. Usually, she wore one of Charlie's button-downs and nothing else while doing this, but today she had put her clothes back on.

"Those pot pies aren't burning, are they?" she asked.

"Two more minutes," Charlie said.

Pot pies. Charlie had numerous eating idiosyncrasies, and when it came to pot pies, he had a ritual from which he never strayed. First, using a butter knife, he lopped off the entire top crust and then broke it into four equal sections. Next, he dipped each section into the pie's broth and ate the crust down to its burnt edges, which he set aside. Then came the innards, the broth and chicken and carrots, all of which he ate with a tablespoon, but only after fishing out the peas, setting each one next to the pile of burnt edges. The best part was the soft bottom crust, the crust that was shaped like the aluminum pie pan itself, and this he rolled up into a ball and, holding it as he would a sandwich, devoured it in three quick bites.

He knew that Petra watched him while he ate, the way an anthropologist, attempting to learn about an aboriginal culture, kept a watchful eye on her subject in order to write down the subject's behaviors later. Petra herself had no rituals when she ate. She dug in with a fork or spoon—it didn't matter which—and she ate until it was gone. For Petra, food was food.

"Okay," Charlie said after he'd collected the burnt edges and the peas, put them back into the empty aluminum bowl, and crumpled it closed. "Here's what I'm thinking." Charlie shook open a copy of the local newspaper and held it toward her, clasping it at the top with his index fingers and thumbs, like a magician about to perform a trick.

"What's this?" Petra asked, squinting.

"The classifieds," Charlie said. "Look!" He reached around, pointing to an advertisement.

SCORERS WANTED !!!

National Testing Center

Seeks college graduates
To score standardized tests
For national project.

Employment Fair: May 5

Across the street
From the Hy-Vee on Hawthorne

"Scoring?" Petra sounded unimpressed. This was precisely what Charlie loved about her: the ice-blue Siberian blood flowing through her veins. "What about your big summer plans?"

"What plans?"

Petra said, "Running for city council? Doing something *big?*"

"Oh. That," Charlie said and snorted. "I was just talking."

"Talking?" Petra asked. "You didn't mean any of it?"

Charlie set the paper aside. For a good year, presidential candidates had flown in and out of Iowa, sharpening their stump speeches, either rising or falling in the polls. Iowa was the first place they had to prove themselves in the primaries, and so every week Charlie and Petra met up somewhere on campus to watch presidential hopefuls deliver their messages. The rallies were infectious. For a brief period, Charlie and Petra had thrown all their energies into grassroots campaigns for the Democrats. Charlie had even started feeling the itch to get involved in a more serious way on the local level, to participate in that noblest of community services—politics.

One night, Charlie and Petra attended a meeting in the basement of what had once been a lodge. Moose? Elk? The lights were so dim, Charlie couldn't identify the animal on the wall.

"What *is* that?" Charlie whispered to Petra.

"Looks like a rat," she whispered in return. She squinted at it. "With horns," she added.

"Maybe this isn't the right place," Charlie said, but he had no sooner spoken when a man wearing a "Save Democracy" T-shirt approached them. He was in his fifties and looked like a former drug-addled veteran who'd long since cleaned up his act. He was holding a bottle of Evian in his left hand, a clipboard in his right.

"Bosco," he said by way of introduction. "Welcome to the Soldiers of Democracy. Local Chapter 4141. I'm Chapter President." After tucking the clipboard under his arm and pumping their respective hands, he led Charlie and Petra to another room—an antechamber—full of people engaged in passionate conversations. In the center of the room there hung a piñata in the image of George W. Bush. A blindfolded man with a small bat swung wildly at it. Every time he missed, he yelled, "Fuck! Fuck! Where are you, you son of a bitch?"

A woman with dark, intense eyes appeared from behind Charlie and Petra, draping her arms over their shoulders and saying, "Welcome! Welcome!" Her name was Lola—"Like the song," she said—and she introduced them around. Soon, Charlie and Petra had fallen into one of the many discussions, and Charlie surprised himself at how much he had to say, how articulate he was, how each and every political scenario he presented to the group came to him in perfect clarity. He made hammering motions with the side of his fist when he spoke; he used his splayed fingers to good effect when expressing concern over the current political situation.

"Wow," he overheard Lola saying. "Look at him. He's a natural."

"And such a nice ass," the woman next to her said.

Petra, who must have overheard the women, nudged Charlie with her elbow.

Later that night, Charlie, blindfolded, hit the George W. Bush piñata with enough force to split him open. He lifted his blindfold in time to watch Bush's innards come tumbling out: hundreds of photos, each one of a U.S. soldier. They were fresh-faced and serious, and most of them were young. On the backs of the photos were the dates they were killed. *K.I.A. June 6, 2003. K.I.A. January 17, 2004.* Charlie's heart literally ached at the sight of the fallen soldiers surrounding his feet.

On their way out, Petra paused in front of a mirror to fix her hair. Charlie, suspecting that it was a two-way mirror, leaned toward the glass. Sure enough, a man on the other side was leaning toward him, peering into Charlie's eyes.

"*Ah!*" Charlie said and jumped back.

"What?"

"Nothing. Let's go."

It was daylight when he and Petra finally emerged from the building. A few people were already heading to work. Petra, grinning, rested her palm on Charlie's back. Charlie didn't say a word on the way to his apartment. Something magical had taken place in the basement of the lodge, and he didn't want to spoil it.

For a while, it had seemed that Charlie and Petra were going to abandon their studies altogether. Something had to be done to stop George W. Bush from winning, and it was their duty as Americans who loved their country to participate in the political process. They talked about driving to small towns nearby—Solon or Hills—and going door to door, outlining Bush's disastrous policies and ill-chosen war. They rehearsed what they would say. But then a man named Howard Dean, the Democratic front-runner, squealed like a stuck pig during one of the Iowa rallies, and that was the beginning of the end: the image of Dean squealing was replayed a few million times, and by the next day, no one took him seriously anymore. It was as though a man with a big cigar had walked up to a child with a balloon and popped it with the cigar's red-hot tip. The circus was over. And that's what it all had been, hadn't it? One big circus. Charlie and Petra returned to their studies, shifting their energies toward finishing their master's theses. Neither brought up Charlie's summer political plans until today. But who had Charlie been fooling? He wasn't a politician. He barely cut it as a film major.

Charlie decided not to tell Petra about the phone call from NTC. He wanted her to think this had been solely his idea—a calculated plan, an adventure. "Don't you see the beauty of scoring standardized tests? It's a stupid job. That's what we want for the year, isn't it? Something stupid? Something we really won't need to think about? Something we won't bring home with us at night?"

"Petra Petrovich. Professional Scorer."

"Exactly!" Charlie said. "And we won't be alone. It's what everyone in this town does when they stick around after graduation."

"*That,*" Petra said, "is what I'm afraid of."

THURSDAY NIGHT, while on her way to Mrs. Grant's, Jainey stopped off for gas. The signs in the gas station's windows were mostly in Arabic, and Jainey, bored at the pump, stared at the funny squiggles and wondered what they could possibly mean. *Cheap cigarettes? Lottery tickets? This country is for the dogs?* The neighborhood was changing. Jainey herself had a Palestinian friend at school named Hani. Hani's parents had welcomed Jainey into their home as if she were their own daughter, and they fed her more food than she'd ever eaten in one sitting. Jainey wished she could reciprocate the invitation, but she knew her mother would slap together a couple of ham sandwiches and then casually bring up 9/11, as if to say, *I know what you're capable of, young man.* It didn't help that the FBI had recently swooped into town and arrested several suspected terrorists. One day last fall Hani quit coming to school, and when Jainey finally walked over to his house for a visit, she found it empty. No one at school knew what had happened. Was it possible to simply disappear like that? One day you're here; the next—*poof*—you're gone?

The building Mrs. Grant lived in was three stories tall and squat. DE-LUXE CONDOMINIUMS, the sign outside announced, but it looked like every other housing complex on the southwest side: a brick cube with windows, out of which no one ever looked.

Jainey pushed the buzzer.

Mrs. Grant, her voice augmented by the tiny speaker, spoke Jainey's name, as if from another planet: "*Jainey?*" The speaker made her sound slightly desperate, the way Auntie Em had said, "*Dorothy?*" while Dorothy peered into the Wicked Witch's ever-fading crystal ball.

"Yes! It's me!" Jainey yelled. "It's Jainey! Can you hear me?" The door buzzed, and Jainey climbed the two dark flights up to Mrs. Grant's. The door was already open, waiting for her.

"Hello?" Jainey called out.

She walked inside but didn't see Mrs. Grant. The rooms were surprisingly barren. No artwork. No sculptures-in-progress. Jainey stepped over piles of unwashed clothes. She was starting to think she'd walked into the wrong apartment when she found Mrs. Grant standing in front of the sink in her kitchen. She was a plump woman who always wore silver jewelry with gigantic turquoise stones. She had on a tentlike dress and fuzzy pink slippers today instead of her usual paint- and glue-stained smock. She was washing two cups from a pile of dishes so high that she could barely use the faucet to rinse.

When Mrs. Grant finally looked up, she yelled, "Jainey! It's you!" It was as if Jainey's sudden appearance had been a total surprise. "Would you like some tea?" she asked.

"Sure."

Jainey hated tea—it tasted like water mixed with a spoonful of dirt—but she'd never have told Mrs. Grant that. The fact that Mrs. Grant liked tea probably hinted at a deficiency on Jainey's part, a lack of refinement. From now on, Jainey resolved, she would drink tea. She'd drink it, and she'd like it.

"I wanted you to come over," Mrs. Grant said, "so that I could tell you something."

Jainey sipped the tea. It tasted awful, but she smiled, tight-lipped, and remained silent.

"I'm not going to be a teacher anymore," Mrs. Grant said. "I'm leaving the profession. They're making it too hard on us."

"Who?"

"The government." And then Mrs. Grant, who never complained about anything, not even the time Mike Tatlinger put Joanne Messina's baloney and cheese sandwich into the kiln, launched into a diatribe about the No Child Left Behind Act, and how politicians were a bunch of hypocrites when it came to education, how they set new standards, in some cases *impossible* standards, even as they cut schools' budgets.

"And because of the budget cuts," Mrs. Grant said, "I'm spending over a thousand dollars each year out of my own pocket on school supplies for my students." She met Jainey's eyes and said, "He's trying to kill me. He's trying to put me in an early grave."

"Who?"

"George W. Bush." Mrs. Grant sighed. "I can't talk about it. It's too upsetting. Oh but listen. I have something for you." She handed Jainey a key. "It's a spare."

"For what?"

"For the condo. I wanted you to have a place to go if you need to get away while I'm gone. I plan on taking a long trip soon." She said this almost dreamily, as if her new destination were materializing even as she spoke. She smiled and said, "Do you want to see what all I'm getting rid of?"

Jainey rubbed the key's teeth with a forefinger and then pressed it hard into her skin, imagining it biting her and thinking, *Ouch!* She followed Mrs. Grant to a small bedroom, which, unlike the rest of the apartment, was full-to-bursting. Antique lamps. Old sheet music. A Victrola. *This,* Jainey thought, *is more like it.* "Look at these!" she said, picking up the smallest book she'd ever seen, a book the size of her thumbnail. It was so tiny she could have placed it on her tongue and swallowed it like a pill.

"I have a whole collection of miniature books," Mrs. Grant said. "You have to use tweezers to open some of them, and a magnifying glass to read them."

Jainey failed to imagine a scenario in which she would be inspired to read a book so small she'd need tweezers and a magnifying glass.

"Do you want to see the rest?"

Jainey didn't, not really, but she nodded and said, "Sure." She loved Mrs. Grant. She'd have set herself on fire or walked in front of a train to prove it, too. If looking at a few stupid books would make the woman happy, then so be it.

CHARLIE LOVED LIVING in a university town, and he loved eking out a meager existence, but as a student he had never been particularly crazy about the actual coursework that was required of him. Now that he'd graduated, however, he realized how much he missed it. He missed looming deadlines for critical essays. He missed time spent in the library, pulling old bound copies of *Cahiers du Cinéma* off the dusty top shelf. He missed sitting through grainy sixteen-millimeter prints of European movies he'd never have watched on his own. He missed dozing off during lectures on semiology, Russian formalism, and phenomenology. He missed it all!

Even so, he had to admit that graduate school was a peculiar way to spend one's time. There wasn't a single practical use for anything he'd done. He'd written essays on film theorists, film genres, and film *auteurs.* If he hadn't written any of those essays, the world would have been absolutely no different than it was today, no one's life would have been altered, and the same people who'd killed or been killed would still be living or dead. For two years he'd indulged himself in the life of the mind—*his* mind—and now, if he felt the urge, he could talk at length about the importance of Hugo Munsterberg, the first film theorist; he could deconstruct the elements of film noir; and he could go on at length about the mise-en-scène of the climactic moment in *Free Willy,* with all its phallic imagery and full-to-bursting symbolism. But now that school was over, what could he *really* do? He couldn't build a house. He couldn't trim a tree. He wasn't even sure how to change the oil in his car. Despite these shortcomings—and they *were* shortcomings, he realized that much, at least—despite them all, his education had been well worth the time, if only because he'd met Petra in a course titled Soviet Cinema.

Petra had sat off to the side, near the fire exit, but everyone in the lecture hall knew that she was there. With her wild mane of hair, her sometimes intense, sometimes sleepy stare, and her perpetual state of dishevelment, there was no way *not* to know that she was there. She was a presence. And so it came as no surprise to Charlie that when he and Petra walked into National Testing Center's job fair, everyone watched her. Women liked Petra because she didn't have centerfold looks; she had personality, she had character. These were nearly tangible traits. As for men, they flirted with her in front of Charlie, as if he were inconsequential or not even there. It was the vibe she gave off, a purely sexual one. There was no other way to put it. Some people had it; some didn't. Petra had it. But it wasn't as though she was *trying* to send her vibe out into a room. She just did.

The job fair was populated with a healthy number of recent college graduates, but other people were there, too, some of whom looked homeless or crazy, or both. One man, who sat in the corner and talked to himself, might have been schizophrenic. Charlie and Petra had seen him around town. The man was so emaciated, so pale that his head looked more like a skull than the head of a living person. His eyes and cheeks were sunken in. His hair was sparse, patchy. A few aberrant whiskers had sprouted from his chin. Charlie and Petra had taken to calling him the Ghoul.

"I saw the Ghoul today," Charlie would say. "He was downtown, talking to himself. What's his deal?"

"I saw him driving a car yesterday," Petra said.

"No! Are they just handing out driver's licenses down at the DMV? Man oh man."

"Don't pick on the Ghoul," Petra said. And this became a playful rapport between them—Charlie would say critical things about the Ghoul while Petra defended him.

"Look," Charlie whispered now, nudging Petra. "The Ghoul."

"Stop it," Petra said, not looking.

"No, really. The Ghoul. He's here."

Petra looked. She turned back to Charlie, her brow furrowed. *It IS him.*

Charlie said, "Surely they won't hire him. Not the Ghoul."

Charlie recognized another man, a local drunk whom Charlie had seen on more than one occasion passed out cold at seven in the morning in front of the Foxhead. He saw a woman who had her own cable-access call-in show, a show Charlie and Petra had seen many times and made fun of. The woman, a burnt-out radical from the '70s, always wore some Native American getup—a leather vest, lots of beads, a headband—and offered advice on a wide array of subjects. Her name was Magda. Often, people called in simply to make fun of her. A college kid, pretending to work at a service station, called to tell her that her spaceship had been repaired and that she could pick it up whenever she wanted.

"Ha-ha," Magda said dryly—and it was this image that pierced Charlie's heart: Magda all alone in her apartment, operating her own video camera and answering calls on an old speakerphone—all alone and replying, "Ha-ha," to disembodied insults. Why *do* that to yourself? Why host your own cable-access show? Why wear the same faux Indian costume every day?

"Jesus," Charlie said, pointing out Magda to Petra. "They're coming out of the woodwork, aren't they?"

"Are you sure we're in the right place?" Petra asked. "This isn't the soup kitchen, is it?"

"I bet these characters show up at *every* job fair," Charlie said.

Charlie and Petra filled out employment applications. Next, they were herded as a group into a large room to listen to National Testing Center's mission statement. Afterward, each prospective employee met with a supervisor. Charlie's supervisor was a slight man, totally bald, with thin wire-frame glasses. Charlie himself wasn't violent, but for the sake of perspective, he often put people and objects into a violent context, and the supervisor, in Charlie's humble opinion, could probably be killed by a single blow to the head.

"What would you do," the supervisor asked Charlie, "if your group leader tells you to score a particular answer *one* point when you think it deserves *six* points?"

"Would we be able to discuss our rationale with the group leader?"

"Sometimes, yes," the supervisor said, "but not in this instance. Discussions are over. The criteria have been established."

Charlie nodded. "I guess I'd give it one point then." He smiled.

"And you wouldn't have a problem with that?"

"No. I don't think so."

"Some people," the supervisor said, "get caught up in their own *personal* criteria. They forget that the project as a whole is more important than any single individual test answer. They forget that we have a well thought out rationale for our own criteria. It's best if our scorers remembered that."

When it was time to go, Charlie shook the supervisor's hand. It was like shaking a damp sponge with a spring inside, if such a thing existed. If Charlie squeezed any harder, he'd have brought the man to his knees, no problem.

Back at Charlie's apartment, after a round of early-afternoon sex, Petra, wearing nothing but a necklace of tiny seashells, rolled onto her belly and said, "The supervisor I met with, he kept talking about their *group leader.* I felt like I was talking to someone from Outer Space. I was about to say, 'Take me to your leader. Let me meet this Supreme Being.'"

"*My* supervisor," Charlie said and rolled his eyes. "He must have gotten beat up a lot when he was a kid. You know the kind—the high school dork who's suddenly in a position of power. There's nothing more dangerous."

"George Bush was a cheerleader in college," Petra said.

"*Exactly.*"

"Do you think your supervisor ever does anything like this?"

"Like what?"

Petra humped the bed twice, then waggled her eyebrows. "Hm?"

"Uh . . . *no,* I don't think so."

"Poor guy," Petra said. "Do you want to get drunk?"

"It's only two o'clock."

"We don't have anything to do, do we? I think we should get drunk and screw some more."

Charlie, trying not to smile, said, "What happened to the little Russian intellectual I used to know? What happened to the brainiac who used to bash certain well-regarded translators for their—what did you call it?—their unconscionable syntax?"

Petra said, "She's thirsty. And horny."

"Okay then," Charlie said. "So what'll it be? Absolut Citron?"

Petra sat up and, eyes narrowed, rubbed her palms quickly together—a devious plan about to be embarked upon. "Now you're talking," she said. "Bring a lemon and some sugar."

"Chips? Salsa?"

"Nope. Just liquor. Liquor and sex."

JAINEY EXPECTED a truant officer to eventually pull her over, but when it became clear that this wasn't going to happen, she began to conjure one up. He would be a man not much older than herself—just a boy, really—and he would be wearing a dark suit with a starched white shirt. Victor, she named him. Victor Benedetti. Lying in bed on those fourth, fifth, and sixth nights of her truancy, Jainey whispered Victor's name over and over while visualizing her own imminent capture. She liked picturing the hunt through Victor's eyes: *driving, driving, driving, and then: Jainey! Seventeen years old. Streaks of purple and green in her hair. Pierced lip, pierced nose, but what else? What were her clothes hiding? What was underneath?*

What Jainey was really doing, she realized, was simply imagining her own self naked, and it crossed her mind that this might be an odd way to go about getting herself off, and yet it was always at this point—when Victor the truant officer actually conjures up the naked Jainey—when the *real* Jainey, touching herself, swirled into that dark sinkhole of orgasm, followed shortly thereafter by sleep more intense than any she'd previously experienced. The next morning, Jainey never remembered to wonder whether what aroused her was normal or not. The only thing that mattered was that Victor had done his job. The rest was moot.

THE SUPERVISOR phoned Charlie the next day to tell him that he had the job.

"Congratulations," he said. "We'd like for you to start next Monday. Eight o'clock."

Hungover, Charlie had to cluck his tongue a few times to get it to work. It had been stuck to the roof of his mouth. "Thanks," he finally croaked.

Later in the day, after she'd managed to choke down a piece of toast and a cup of black coffee, Petra checked her voice mail. She, too, was offered the job.

"This calls for a drink," she said. Charlie groaned, but Petra was already pouring herself a vodka tonic.

For eight dollars and seventy-five cents an hour, no benefits, and no guarantee of employment from week to week, Charlie and Petra would be scoring America's Report Card, the government's most important assessment of primary and secondary education.

"Just think of all the people we beat out," Petra said. "Drunks! Crazy people who have their own TV shows!"

"The Ghoul," Charlie reminded her.

"The Ghoul," Petra said. An uncharacteristic sadness crept into her voice. "The poor Ghoul," she said. "That poor, poor man."

Charlie nodded. "What's he going to do now?" Even Charlie was momentarily moved. "Poor Ghoul," he agreed.

ON THE SEVENTH DAY of her truancy, feeling antsy, which was how she felt most of the time, Jainey drove the Turd downtown and parked at a meter in the south Loop. *The beast,* her father called the Loop. Jainey's palms were sweating and the back of her neck itched, this being the first time she had actually entered the beast's belly. Was she excited? Was she nervous? Both, she decided. She walked up Wabash Avenue, where train tracks ran above her head. Pigeons scattered when she approached them. A homeless guy repeated, "Quarter," over and over. He met her eyes and said, "Quarter, quarter, quarter." A man wearing a nice suit jumped over a puddle to reach the sidewalk. A cab driver honked his horn, and someone behind Jainey yelled, "Fuck *yoooooooooou!*" When a train came roaring overhead, Jainey looked up and yelled "Holy *shit*" as loud as she could. The train's deafening screech was such that no one heard her. But even if they had heard her, no one would have cared. Welcome to Chicago!

It was beautiful, all of it. Jainey had never seen anything like this, except on TV. But on TV you couldn't get the full flavor of it, the rotted-fruit smell, the sparks shooting from the train's rails, the mysterious swamps of shape-shifting oil. Jainey had always thought of Burbank as the center of her universe, a kind of mother ship upon which she sailed through life, but what Jainey saw now was that the real mother ship was Chicago and that Burbank was nothing more than a tiny moss-covered barnacle desperately clinging to the ship's hull.

Jainey walked past pizza places, shoe stores, coffee shops. And then she came upon a store that sold only wigs. Wigs! How strange was that? Jainey didn't know anyone who wore a wig. And to think, here was an entire store that sold nothing *but* wigs. Jainey peered inside: a thousand fake heads stared dead-eyed back at her, each one wearing its own wig.

When Jainey opened the door, a buzzer announced her arrival. The buzzer stopped only after the door had shut. An Al Green song was playing on the boom box next to the cash register. Jainey knew the song because it was on the *Pulp Fiction* soundtrack, and she'd lost her virginity to a bizarre part of the CD where Samuel Jackson is telling John Travolta that in France they call a Quarter Pounder with Cheese a "*Royale* with Cheese." Jainey, naked and kissing a boy named Ron Zurvo, had thought, *Why's there a scene from the movie on the CD?* and then Ron Zurvo entered her. It was like some dream-version of getting stabbed: the penetration was both sharp and soft at the same time, and it made her really sleepy. "Ouch," she had said without much conviction. It burned worse each time he thrust into her, but she knew she wasn't going to die. When it was finally over, she drifted to sleep to the sound of Al Green's silky voice.

A black woman, who was maybe ten years older than Jainey's mother, stood behind the counter, talking on a cell phone. She wore a wig that looked from some angles purple, from other angles black. When she saw Jainey, she said, "Gotta go, honey," and when the person she was talking to wouldn't shut up, the woman said, "Didn't you hear what I just said?" and she clicked off before the person could start talking again. She looked at Jainey, then up at Jainey's hair.

"Girl," she said. "It's not a *wig* you need."

Jainey was ready to take offense but then the woman smiled. She had a gold tooth. She held out her hand. "Mariah," she said. Her hand was rough, like sandpaper, and strong. Below their joined hands was a newspaper with the headline "U.S. RIDS ITSELF OF MINORITIES! *The Real Reason George W. Bush Invaded Iraq*." It was a newspaper Jainey'd never seen before, *The Afro-American Advocate.*

"My name's Jainey," Jainey said.

"Jainey," the woman said. "Like the Tarzan movies." She winked. "You too young to know about Tarzan, I imagine. Tarzan? King of the Apes? Hell, I'd give a hundred dollars to see my man Johnny Weissmuller walk through that door right now wearing nothing but that skimpy-ass loincloth of his!" She shook her head. Her wig was so tall, Jainey expected it to topple off, but amazingly it didn't budge. "Make that *two* hundred." She laughed and said, "You don't know *what* I'm talking about, do you? Well, now, if you saw Johnny Weissmuller, you'd know then. Puts that pretty boy Brad Pitt to shame."

"Is that true?" Jainey asked. She motioned to the newspaper's headline.

"Course it's true," Mariah said. "Why wouldn't it be? You don't see no rich white boys fighting Arabs, now do you? You should see how hard they recruit over where I live. Can't send black boys over there fast enough."

"I didn't know," Jainey said.

"Lotta things you don't know," Mariah said but with more sadness than anger.

Not quite sure what to say next, Jainey ducked her head and wandered the store—up one aisle, down the next. Every so often, she reached out and patted the top of one of the wigs, as she would a dog. *Good wig,* she thought. *Sit! Sit!* And then Jainey saw one she liked. A sign under the wig read, "Real Hair." Jainey removed it from its head. It didn't *feel* real. Or did it? Her own hair, after it had been cut, felt different somehow, the way the stem of a flower feels different once it's been snipped from its life source.

"You like it?" Mariah said. "Try it on. Give it a whirl."

The wig was red and long. She put it on top of her head.

"It's not a top hat, girl. Here. Let Mariah help." Mariah slipped her fingers between the wig and Jainey's head, then pulled until it was snug. She leaned back for a quick appraisal before adjusting it some more—a little to the left, a little more to the left, then down. "There!"

Jainey walked to a full-length mirror. She couldn't believe how different the wig made her look. She could have been twenty-four or five. Instead of looking punk, she looked sexy. Her normal expression—brooding and suspicious—now appeared mysterious, less angry. She could have been the *femme fatale* of Burbank, the South Side's woman of danger. She could swoop into a man's life, promise to stay with him forever, and kiss his face until her own puckered lips felt bruised. After telling him how much she loved him, she would whisper what he wanted to hear, she would burrow into his heart—*Let's run away to Dublin! . . . Let's run away to Morocco!*—and only after he was hooked would she leave without a trace, flipping a still-smoldering cigarette onto his lawn, and never to be seen again. She would hurt them deeply, man after man. She would be the ruin of many respectable men, and all because of what, a *wig?* The wig store now made perfect sense. Of course. Buy a wig! Change your life!

"How much?"

"You have champagne taste, I'll give you that, honey. That one there's four twelve."

Jainey turned her purse upside-down on the glass countertop and watched the flotsam of her life come pouring out. Her purse was beaded and delicate but bursting at the seams. It was like carrying around a small concrete block with a strap. She shook it a few more times for good measure, and out came its final three inhabitants: a tampon; a wallet-sized photo of her ex-boyfriend, a wad of chewed gum strategically covering his face; the key to Mrs. Grant's condo.

"You got more shit in that purse than I keep in my closet," Mariah said.

Jainey fanned her junk across the counter, the way a magician would fan a deck of cards, and—*voila!*—the change purse appeared. She opened it, pulled out a five-dollar bill, and handed it to Mariah.

Mariah took the money, looked at it. "What's this?"

"For the wig," Jainey said. "I'll take it."

Mariah laughed. "You'll take *nothing.* Not for no *five damned dollars.* The wig is four *hundred* and twelve dollars." She laughed louder, handed back the money, and said, "You're crazy! You know that? Crazy! But Mariah likes you. You got spunk. I used to have spunk, but it's gone. *Long* gone."

Jainey, trying not to show her disappointment, swept everything back into her purse. After cleaning up her mess, she reached up and gently patted the wig on her head. "Whose hair is it?"

"Don't know. Ain't mine. But this ain't mine, neither." She tipped her tall wig toward Jainey. "I got cheaper ones. You want one that's thirty-nine ninety-five? They're over there. But I ain't got no *five-dollar* wigs, I can tell you that much."

Jainey removed the red wig. She watched herself in the mirror, and was startled to find that she looked like a boy without it. After returning the wig to its head, Jainey walked toward the exit. "It was nice to meet you, Mariah."

"Pretty girl like you," Mariah said, "you don't need a wig. But maybe you want to look into a new hair color. Purple and green." She frowned and shook her head.

Pinned between the Turd's wiper and its windshield was a ticket for an expired meter. "Goddamn it!" Jainey yelled. "Goddamn son of a freaking bitch!" People walking by could hear her, but no one looked. She ripped up the ticket and tossed it into the air. It rained down on her like New Year's Eve confetti.

All the way back to Burbank, Jainey couldn't shake the image of her old boyfriend, even with that wad of hardened gum covering his face. She had promised never to have anything to do with him again, but seeing his shoulders and the top of his head—the only parts not covered by gum—had made her heart thump faster. Disappointed with her lack of willpower, she groaned loudly but turned anyway onto the road that led to the apartment complex where he lived with his grandfather.

His name was Alex, but when they were still boyfriend and girlfriend, she called him "Al Licks." "Dear Al Licks," she'd write. "Thanks for the sick pornography you sick mental case." Or, "When am I going to see you again, Mr. Licks?" Or she'd draw a heart and write inside, "Al Licks Jainey."

The main door to Alex's building was already open, so Jainey walked up to his apartment, but when she noticed that this door was also open, she hesitated. "Alex?" she asked. She tapped on it. When no one answered, she pushed it open.

Alex, peering into the freezer, looked like he'd grown a foot since she'd last seen him. He was always tall and gangly, but he was even taller and ganglier now. And there was something odd about what he was wearing today: a clean black T-shirt tucked into blue jeans. Dress shoes, too. He never wore dress shoes. "Oh. It's you," he said. He shut the freezer door.

"Yep," Jainey said. "It's me!" Alex walked to the stove; Jainey followed. An empty can of soup sat next to a pan on a burner. "Dinner?" Jainey asked.

"It's for him," he said, tipping his head toward the back bedroom, where his grandfather spent his days and nights.

Jainey was starting to feel the first tingles of arousal—a tickle across her spine, a chill, followed by a distinct sensation between her legs that reminded her of a dry sponge slowly absorbing warm water, causing her to shift and breathe more deeply.

"Al *Licks,*" she said and smiled. She walked up behind him. "Al," she said, slipping a finger through a belt-loop, "*Licks.*"

"Don't," he said. "Now's not the time." He carried the bowl of soup into his grandfather's bedroom, then returned with a few crusty plates from an earlier meal. Alex glared at Jainey. "Is that what you're wearing?" he snapped.

Jainey took stock of her own clothes. What she had on wasn't any different from what she normally wore—clothes with lots of holes, lots of loose threads, lots of cryptic phrases written on her jeans with a Sharpie, like, "Give me that TUBA!"

"I thought you liked her, that's all," Alex said. "I thought you'd give her a little more, I don't know, *respect.*"

"Who?"

"Who? Mrs. Grant. That's who." He stared at Jainey a moment. "Are you stoned?"

"No, I'm not stoned. What do you mean *Mrs. Grant?* I don't know what the hell you're talking about. What the hell are you talking about?"

"Where've you been? Huh?"

"Nowhere," Jainey said.

"You really don't know, do you?" He sighed. "Oh, boy." He combed his long, bony fingers through his hair so that it stood on end, a kind of sight gag, and then he said, "Mrs. Grant killed herself."

"No, she didn't. I just saw her. Last week. She gave me a bunch of her stuff. She gave me these little books and . . ."

"This was four days ago, Jainey."

"Four days ago? I don't believe you." She shook her head. She snorted. She put her hands on her hips. "Okay then. How'd she kill herself?"

"She blew out all the pilot lights on her gas stove."

Mrs. Grant dead? It wasn't true. "You're lying," Jainey said.

"Whatever. But I need to go."

"Where?"

"Her funeral."

Even though she wasn't buying his story, she was starting to breathe faster, and she grew more lightheaded each time she inhaled. "And where's this supposed funeral taking place?" she asked.

"79th and State Road. I forget the name of the place. *You* know it."

Jainey nodded. It wasn't far from McDonald's. A few months ago, in fact, she had stood on the sidewalk outside the funeral home, sucking down a shamrock shake, and wondered how many dead bodies rested inside the place. It was one of those weird things to think about: dead bodies only a few yards away from where she stood. She had wondered if one day someone would be standing outside wherever her own dead body was stored, chugging down a shamrock shake and trying to picture who might be inside.

Jainey was about to tell Alex again that he was lying when Beth Ann Winkel stepped into the apartment, dressed as if for a prom. Beth Ann Winkel was Jainey's arch nemesis, the girl who had spearheaded a smear campaign against Jainey.

"Oh," Beth Ann said when she saw Jainey. "What's this?"

Alex shrugged. "She hadn't heard about Mrs. Grant."

Beth Ann said, "Of course she hasn't." She clearly wanted to say more but was restraining herself for Alex's benefit. "Well!" Beth Ann said, too cheerily. "We better go, hon."

Alex said to Jainey, "I need to lock up." Outside, before going their separate ways, Alex turned and said, "I'm sorry, Jainey. I know you really liked her."

The Turd bounced like Mr. Toad's Wild Ride each time she hit the slightest bump. The springs, Jainey figured, were probably shot. On her way to the funeral home she hit a deep pothole, and the rearview mirror broke free, bouncing off the dash and onto the floor between her feet.

"Shit!"

She looked down, and from the dark floorboard she saw her own eyes staring back at her and nothing else—just eyes. It was one of the creepiest things she'd ever seen.

Jainey wheeled into the funeral home's parking lot, and sure enough, the place was hopping. *It's a setup,* she thought. *Alex, Beth Ann, and their stupid friends are going to jump out from behind the shrubs and scare the piss right out of me.* But no one jumped out from the shrubs, even when Jainey kicked one.

The funeral home was freezing cold inside. No one looked familiar. Then Jainey realized why no one looked familiar: the boys were wearing suits, the girls skirts or dresses. These were the same boys who normally wore hand-me-down Pink Floyd T-shirts or White Sox ball caps, girls who wore hip huggers and too-tight tops, exposing here and there all that baby fat they wanted boys to stare at but not touch, or touch but not lick, or lick but not bite, or bite but not draw blood: it was always *this* but not *that* with them, go *here* but not *there,* which was why the boys liked Jainey better once they got to know her, because there was no *stop,* it was all *go, go, go.*

Jainey, dizzy from the too-bright lights and the trapezoidal patterns on the carpet, followed a group of well-groomed classmates into a viewing room, and then she followed them up to a casket, and then she saw for herself: Mrs. Grant. Mrs. Grant's face was sunken in, like a latex mask without a skull behind it, and she was wearing eye shadow, which she never wore when she was alive. Her hands, which were shriveled and deflated, lay one on top of the other. She wasn't wearing any of her turquoise, either. One thing Jainey knew for sure. She was going to be sick.

Back home later that night, lying in a chaise lounge in her yard, Jainey tried snuffing out the image of Mrs. Grant in her coffin, and so she thought about Victor, the imaginary truant officer, but even Victor, who'd brought her so much pleasure these past few days, couldn't provide distraction. Looking up, she hoped to recognize a constellation, but the air was gritty from nearby factory smokestacks, and she couldn't see any stars. She could, however, hear an airplane. Her house lay under the flight path for Midway Airport, four miles north. Even when she couldn't see one, as she couldn't now, she could hear the approaching purr of the plane's engines.

When Jainey was a little girl, she didn't know that there was an airport nearby—her parents never drove that far—and she assumed that the planes, one by one, were crashing. She'd watch them go down, a dozen planes an hour, disappearing somewhere behind a horizon of distant chimneys and roofs. She'd wait for an explosion, a puff of smoke, but nothing ever happened. What she finally surmised was that the planes were too far away for her to see or hear any of the actual devastation.

The summer she turned five, Jainey marched inside the house, several times each day, and made an announcement. This was five years before the police came to take her father away; ten years before her brother, Ned, had taken up permanent residence in the attic.

Jainey, out of breath, would yell, "Another plane just crashed! Another plane just crashed!"

Her mother always said, "That's fine, Jainey," but her father was the real reason she kept returning. He would meet her eyes and smile, and then he would raise his beer, as if to toast her, and say, "Bombs away, sweetheart! Bombs away!" And then he'd wink at her. The wink was what she waited for. It told Jainey that she was special. It told her that she and her father shared something that she and her mother didn't. The wink made each burning plane worthwhile.

THE GHOUL was in Charlie's group of eight scorers. Magda, the wannabe Indian, was in Petra's. The town drunk wasn't in either Charlie's or Petra's group, but he too had secured employment with NTC; his group scored nothing but logic problems.

"Is there anyone they *didn't* hire?" Petra asked Charlie during break.

Charlie looked around. "I don't think so," he said.

Charlie had driven past NTC's building many times before, but since there was no sign advertising the company's name, no hint as to what they did, Charlie had assumed it was a warehouse or a small factory, possibly even a gathering place for AA meetings. The men and women standing around the parking lot, drinking from Styrofoam cups and smoking, looked haggard. Charlie had always glanced over because it was such a grim-looking building, constructed primarily out of corrugated sheet metal, and now, close up, Charlie could see where the screws had been powered through the thin metal, sometimes at an angle, or where one had been unsuccessfully screwed in, taken out, and then screwed in next to the now-jagged hole. Charlie could also see where hail had left dents, where lawn mowers or skateboards had smashed into its base. If need be, the entire building could be broken down overnight and hauled away on a flatbed trailer. The illusion that the building was only temporary was, in fact, not an illusion at all. Charlie was quickly learning that *everything* having to do with National Testing Center was temporary. Charlie and his co-workers were temporary; the people who hired Charlie were temporary; even the group leader, who had traveled all the way from Virginia to train Charlie's group of eight scorers, was a temporary government employee. He'd overheard someone call it *migrant work for the overeducated underemployed,* and this was true: some of his co-workers had Ph.D.s in fields where there was no gainful opportunity. Music, for instance. Or English. That was the odd thing about this job. Some of the groups had scorers with daunting credentials, while other groups were comprised of whatever riff-raff had shown up at the job fair.

"Shhh," Charlie said. "Listen. What's that sound?"

It was a terrible noise, an ominous chomping and moaning, like a rat caught in a garbage disposal. When Charlie and Petra turned slowly around, they saw that it was coming from the Ghoul. He was eating an apple with the single-minded conviction of a starving dog. He bit and swallowed without pause, *bite-bite-bite swallow, bite-bite-bite swallow,* all the while holding the apple with both hands and turning it counterclockwise, grunting and groaning. His eyes darted from person to person, group to group, as if making sure that his territory was secure, the apple all his.

"Weird," Petra said.

Charlie, unable to turn away from the Ghoul, said, "*Weird* is generous. *Weird* would be a compliment."

Charlie's group leader was a temporary employee of that sub-sub-government agency, the National Evaluation of Educational Achievement. Her name was Rachel, and when she spoke, she held both hands in front of her and moved her fingers as if gently tickling a crystal ball.

"The important thing," Rachel said after break, wiggling her fingers, "is that we score this project consistent with how the last group scored this *same* project three years ago. Consistency is the thing. Remember: nothing is more important than consistency."

Charlie took notes. He wrote, "Why is the Ghoul here?" He wrote, "If a tornado ripped through town, we'd be the first to go." He wrote, "Nothing is more important than consistency."

Charlie had been assigned "Reading Tests," and his group was to score short answers for a single question based on a short passage. This particular batch represented every second-grader in Pennsylvania. The answers had been scanned, and now they were about to pop up, one by one, on their computer screens.

It wasn't until Charlie began scoring the project that he fully understood what Rachel meant about consistency. The perfect answer for this particular question was "alligator." *Alligator,* Charlie was told, was the only answer that could earn a student the full six points. In order to monitor consistency, one answer in every fifteen that appeared on Charlie's screen was actually an answer that had been scored three years earlier. Charlie, however, would have no idea which answers were the old ones and which were the new ones. Rachel, like Scotty monitoring the progress of the USS *Enterprise,* kept an eye on her computer to see how everyone was doing in regard to consistency.

"Stop! Stop!" she yelled after the first hour. "Everyone stop! We have a problem."

From the best Rachel could tell, based on her own analysis of the answers and scores, the team three years ago had accepted "reptile" for the full six points.

A burly musicologist named Rex raised his hand. "But reptile is too vague. That should be worth only five points. Or four."

"Doesn't make a difference," Rachel said. "That's what they took three years ago for six points, so that's what we're taking this year."

"What about the ones we already scored?" Rex asked.

"Doesn't make a difference," Rachel said again. "We've scored only a few hundred. We have *thousands* more to go. It'll have no effect so long as we get back on the right track."

"*Thousands,*" Rex whispered to himself. "Oh, Christ, no."

Everyone in the group, except for the Ghoul, looked bemused at the change in scoring policy, but it was an easy enough adjustment to make. Charlie, however, had a more difficult time with what Rex had said: *Oh, Christ, no.* The words echoed inside Charlie's head long after Rex had spoken them. Had he met Rex somewhere else? He must have, but where? Where? he wondered. Charlie scored a few dozen more answers when it finally came to him: the man who'd called Charlie the day before graduation to ask if he was interested in working for NTC had also said, "Oh, Christ, no." It was the same voice, the same timbre and cadence.

Charlie leaned toward Rex. "Hey, Rex. How long have you been working here?"

"As long as you," Rex said.

Charlie said, "Did you ever do anything else for NTC?"

"No. Why?" Rex stared hard into Charlie's eyes, and Charlie shivered.

"Just wondering," Charlie said. "No reason."

Rachel cleared her throat. "Let's not fall behind, folks," she said. An hour later, however, she stopped them again.

"Whoa! Halt!" she yelled. "We've got a *big-big* problem." Now it appeared that the scorers three years ago were accepting 'green' for the full six points.

Rex said, "Green? That's crazy. We're not accepting *green,* are we?"

"We are *indeed* accepting green," Rachel said.

"But then the test doesn't mean anything," Rex said.

"It means we're being consistent with how the test was scored three years ago," Rachel said, "and if we're consistent, then the test evaluators can determine how that state—in this case Pennsylvania—has improved or not improved."

Rex took a deep breath. He said, "But if the answer is the *wrong* answer, then the whole test is meaningless."

"The answers are irrelevant," Rachel said. "And now we need to keep scoring before we fall behind." She smiled and said, "Remember everyone: *green* is now worth six points."

A little later, a man named J.P., who sat on the other side of Charlie, leaned over and said, "You *realize* why they want everything consistent, don't you?"

"For accuracy, right?"

J.P. wagged his head. "Guess again."

Charlie shrugged. He could barely decipher these kids' pathetic chicken scratches as it was; he certainly couldn't do it with someone yapping in his ear. J.P. was causing him to fall behind.

"The *only* thing those education bureaucrats in Washington look at is the printout for accuracy, you see. And if things *aren't* accurate from year to year, it looks like we don't know what the fuck we're doing. Are you following me?"

Rex, who had been listening, leaned toward them. "And then what—the bureaucrats yank the contract and give it to another company waiting in the wings?"

"Bingo!" J.P. said. "It's about money, Chief. Big, fat government contracts. It's not like anyone really gives a crap if some first-grader in Big Dong, North Carolina, knows the difference between an alligator and a duck."

Charlie loudly cleared his throat, and the men swiveled back to their computers.

An hour later, Rachel stopped them again: "Okay, folks. It appears that the group three years ago was also accepting *yellow* for the full six points."

"What?" Rex yelled. "Oh, this is bullshit." He stood up, gathered his belongings, and said, "One hundred percent, grade-A *bullshit.*" He removed his nametag and tossed it at Rachel.

Charlie felt the urge to yell, "Yeah, *bullshit,*" and storm out of the room right behind Rex. It *was* bullshit. But Charlie wasn't sure how he'd explain it to Petra, who was probably diligently at work this very minute scoring her own test answers, and so Charlie said nothing. At first Charlie worried how Rex's absence would affect the group dynamic. Rex, after all, had been the voice of reason. But it soon became apparent that without Rex, the group shifted into complacent servitude. And once Charlie gave up the notion that the purpose of the test was to accurately evaluate answers and accepted the fact that he was merely a tooth in a much larger, far more mysterious gear, then he could accept whatever Rachel *told* him to accept without question.

By the end of the day, Rex's protest seemed foolish. After all, why should Rex have cared? It was a summer job. A paycheck. Charlie sure as hell didn't feel compelled to overhaul the way the country tested itself. He just needed a few extra bucks.

When his group took their last break of the day, Charlie wandered over to find Petra, but her group had already dispersed, save for their leader, a plump woman who drank orange soda straight from a two-liter bottle. According to Petra, the woman had a cache of two-liter bottles, all orange soda, stored under her work area. Although she was tipping the bottle up when Charlie walked over, she managed to raise a single finger indicating for Charlie to hold on.

"Yes?" she said, catching her breath while capping the bottle.

"I'm looking for Petra."

"I think she went somewhere with her boyfriend."

"*I'm* her boyfriend," Charlie said. He smiled.

"Oh." The woman shrugged. "Can't help you then." She uncapped her bottle and took another swig.

Outside, Charlie joined two men huddled around a large oil drum that served as the communal garbage can. He felt conspicuously like some kind of homeless person waiting for a fire to take root inside the drum's belly. One of the two men was Jacob Bartuka, a short, odd-looking fellow who had worked as a temp at NTC longer than anyone else. Fifteen years. The other man, Hastings, was new, like Charlie.

Hastings said, "My hand is frickin' killing me from filling in all those little circles."

Charlie said, "I thought all the tests were scanned for the computer."

Hastings snorted.

Jacob said, "Not first-grade science. It's all Scan-Tron sheets. We have to work from their booklets."

"Jesus Christ," Charlie said. "That's awful." And then Charlie told them what had happened in his group today—Rex calling the job bullshit and then quitting on the spot.

"The job *is* bullshit," Jacob said. "But not for the reason your buddy Rex thinks."

"What do you mean?" Hastings asked.

"Rumor has it," Jacob said, "that the tests are really psychological profiles."

"Profiles?" Charlie asked. "I'm not following you."

"The questions are written with the intent of analyzing the person *taking* the test. Just imagine what you can find out about a person after testing him every year for twelve straight years."

"You're joking," Charlie said.

"You work here long enough," Jacob says, "you hear a lot of funny things."

"But you don't *believe* it, do you?"

Jacob shrugged.

"So what you're saying is that this whole thing is a front?" Charlie asked. He smiled and shook his head. He said, "Scoring tests—it's all a front to compile psychological profiles?"

"No, no, no!" Jacob said, looking frustrated. He scratched his head—too hard. Lowering his voice, he said, "Scoring tests is legit. There's just a shadow operation *within* the company. The government's trying to get more bang for its buck. I mean, if you're going to have access to every kid in the country, why not take advantage of the opportunity?"

"So," Charlie said, "what else have you heard?"

"Supposedly, NTC stores every test ever taken at an undisclosed location, some kind of massive, fireproof, underground bunker with armed guards. I hear they call it Deep Storage."

Hastings snorted. "Wasn't that the name of a Star Trek movie?"

"Hey," Jacob said defensively. "I'm just saying what I've heard." He gave all of his attention to Charlie now, but Charlie had a difficult time following the rest of Jacob's theories: that the scorers themselves were being watched, that every group of scorers had a mole who watched everyone else, that the scorers were sometimes hand-picked for reasons Jacob had yet to figure out, that it was possible the government had bigger plans for some of them.

Hastings pivoted toward Charlie and surreptitiously rolled his eyes. Jacob must have seen the gesture, however, because the mood around the oil drum palpably shifted, and all three men fell silent.

A few minutes later, a forklift wobbled up to the side entrance. It was carrying a box the size of a compact car. The forklift lowered the box, retracted its forks, then wheeled around and sped away. The three men, still not talking, sauntered over to the box. It was overflowing with hundreds of thousands of papers bound by rubber bands.

"What the hell's that?" Charlie asked.

Jacob lifted one of the bound batches. "Looks like they found more first-grade science booklets."

Hastings looked like he might cry. "How many booklets do you think are in there?"

Jacob stood back to take it all in. "I don't know. Fifty thousand? Sixty thousand?"

Hastings groaned. He wiggled his fingers, then pumped his fist a few times to get the blood circulating. A whistle blew, and all three men headed back to the building. Charlie surveyed the grounds, hoping to catch sight of Petra, but everyone was clumped together, funneling toward the double doors, and Petra was nowhere to be seen.

That night, Petra lay in bed with a copy of *The Brothers Karamazov.*

Charlie, lying next to her, asked, "How do people get so weird?"

"What do you mean?"

"The Ghoul," Charlie said. "Or that fake Indian with her cable show."

"Magda?"

"Yeah. Magda. And then there's this guy Jacob. A total whack job. He has all of these conspiracy theories about NTC. You should hear this guy talk. I think he thinks he's working for the CIA. What *happens* to people?"

"They're the walking wounded," she said.

"What do you mean?"

Petra said, "When they first come to town, they're full of hope, but then something happens to them, something terribly, terribly sad, and they never lose their sadness."

"And then what happens?"

"They turn into ghosts. Walking, talking ghosts."

"That's awful."

Petra shrugged. She rolled onto her back and started to read the book, but after a few pages she tossed it aside. "My eye. It's twitching."

"It's from reading test answers for eight straight hours," Charlie said.

Petra rolled towards Charlie and pressed her eyebrows against Charlie's eyebrows, and said, "My EYE. Do you SEE it?"

"That's *all* I see, Petra."

"It has a case of the twitch." She leaned back and said, "What a crazy job. Do you want to know a secret?"

"Sure."

"It makes me horny."

"Horny? You're joking."

"No, listen. We're *told* not to think too much about the answers, right? We should be able to just look at an answer and score it without really thinking about it. What do they call it? *Holistic* scoring? And so what I do is start thinking about all the times we've screwed and *where,* and then I start thinking about all the places we *haven't* screwed."

"Like?"

"Like the women's restroom next to the Film Studies office."

"The women's restroom?"

"Absolutely. We could've sneaked in there during the semester when it was really busy and gone into one of the stalls."

"Someone would've heard us."

"Not if we were really quiet."

Charlie laughed, but he couldn't deny that Petra's plans were getting him worked up. "Where else?" he asked.

"The beer garden at Gabe's."

"The beer garden? Okay, smarty pants, how would we pull *that* one off?"

"It gets cold out there some nights," Petra said, "and we could put a blanket over our laps. And then, well, you know . . ."

"Holy shit! Where else?"

"At work."

"At work? Where?"

"I haven't figured it out yet," Petra said. "I've been thinking, though."

"Well, let me know when you figure it out, okay?"

"I most definitely will."

MRS. GRANT'S CONDO looked as it did the last time—the *only* time—Jainey was there. Dishes in the sink. Credit card bills in the napkin holder. The same postcards on the fridge. The same magnets holding them in place. A leopard-spotted banana reclining in the fruit bowl. But at the sight of Mrs. Grant's fuzzy pink slippers, Jainey faltered. This was the first time since the wake that she felt like weeping. There was something crushingly sad about the obliviousness of inanimate objects. It was as if the two old slippers, always faithful, were patiently awaiting their owner's arrival. What they didn't realize was that someone would eventually take one look at them and toss them in the trash.

Jainey draped her coat over the slippers before walking to the far end of the hallway. She was about to enter the room where Mrs. Grant had shown her the collection of miniature books—books that now lay in a box in Jainey's trunk next to a tire iron, a can of WD-40, and an ice-pick—but when she reached for the knob, she noticed another door she hadn't seen on her first visit. This door was white, same as the wall, and therefore hidden. It looked hidden on purpose, though.

Jainey walked over. She hesitated a beat, then jerked it open.

An old man stood just inside the doorway with his arms wide open, as if he'd been waiting for her, but he said nothing. Jainey clutched her chest. She backed up and stumbled over her own feet before noticing that the man's legs, arms, and torso were weirdly puffy. And then she noticed straw poking out of his clothes. The old man wasn't a man at all. He was a scarecrow.

Jainey, catching her breath, returned to the room and turned on the light. "Fuck-a-duck," she said. The scarecrow's head belonged to Osama bin Laden. It was a bizarre, creepily realistic likeness of him, except for his eyes, which were too small. Even so, the eyes followed her, watching her every move.

Jainey stepped closer. She poked its chest. It *was* straw. Up close, she saw that Osama's beard was a cheap one with a rubber band holding it in place, the kind of beard you'd buy at Kmart when you wanted to be a pirate for Halloween. And his nose: it was fake, too. Why would Mrs. Grant go through all the trouble of sculpting a head only to put a fake nose on it?

Gently, Jainey removed Osama's turban. He was wearing a long, scraggly witch's wig. Jainey removed that, too. Underneath was yet another wig, a salt-and-pepper one, parted on the side. When Jainey popped off the fake nose and lifted the beard over Osama's head, she saw that the scarecrow was actually George W. Bush.

"Wow," Jainey said, standing back to take it all in. The scarecrow achieved precisely what Mrs. Grant had always said art was supposed to do: take the person looking at it by surprise. "Nothing is as it seems," Mrs. Grant used to say, "and so it's the artist's job to reveal the truth." Jainey had tried to do that with her Lloyd the Freakazoid comic strips, but she wasn't sure she had accomplished anything more than showing Lloyd for the drunken slob he was. Mrs. Grant's scarecrow, on the other hand, was so brilliant that Jainey shivered at the sight of it.

The arms and legs must have had metal rods inside to keep them straight. George W. Bush's feet were nailed to a plywood base. He was about six feet tall. Painted onto the plywood in large, looping letters was the name of the project: *The Lycanthrope.* Jainey had never seen the word before. She covered Bush's face with the beard. She capped off his nose with the larger Osama nose. She reaffixed the wig and then the turban. "You're coming with me," she said.

After tipping the scarecrow and putting her arm around its waist, she lugged it out of the apartment, snatching her coat off the fuzzy slippers on her way out. She pulled the scarecrow down two flights of stairs and across the parking lot. She shoved him into the Turd's backseat and slammed the door harder than she had intended, but once Osama was settled, he lay there peacefully, staring blankly up at the ceiling, as docile as a lamb.

Mariah gasped, dropped her cell phone, and started yelling. "Don't you go bringing his nasty ass in here, girl! You hear me?"

"It's just a scarecrow," Jainey said, dragging Osama bin Laden through the wig store's front door.

"Don't make no damned difference *what* he is," Mariah said. "That man's bad for business."

Jainey felt paralyzed. She'd driven all the way downtown for Mariah to see the scarecrow and now Mariah was sending her away. Why, Jainey wondered, had she thought Mariah could help her?

Mariah must have sensed Jainey's dilemma because she marched over to the entrance, flipped the OPEN sign to CLOSED, and locked the door. "Jainey, right? I imagine there's a story behind this. Well, I'm the sort of person who likes a story, so it better be a good one." She poked Osama in the chest and said, "But I'm putting a sheet over *your* ugly face."

Mariah drove them to a beef sandwich joint near the University of Illinois's Circle Campus. Jainey told Mariah the whole story about

Mrs. Grant giving her stuff away, how she had claimed that George W. Bush was going to be the death of her, how a week later she was dead, supposedly of suicide, how Jainey had found Osama in Mrs. Grant's apartment, only he wasn't Osama, he was really George W. Bush in disguise, and how Jainey wasn't sure *what* to think anymore. When she was done talking, she waited for Mariah to offer some advice, but Mariah, who was wearing dark sunglasses even though they were sitting inside, didn't say anything for a long time. She finally said, "Used to be Maxwell Street right outside this here window." Mariah took a big bite of her sandwich and wagged her head. She wiped her mouth and said, "Used to be you could buy a fur coat for a *third* of what you'd pay one mile thataway." She pointed toward the Loop. "Oh, sure, Maxwell Street had its problems, but who don't?" She took another big bite. After rinsing it down with a swig from her giant Coke, Mariah said, "Sounds to me like they finally got to your Mrs. Grant."

"Who?"

"You know who." She leaned close and said, "The feds. *That's* who." She picked up a french fry and pointed it at Jainey. "Remember Waco?"

Jainey shook her head. She remembered it dimly, but she was too young.

"Ruby Ridge?"

"Nuh-uh."

"You know who Leonard Peltier is?"

"Nope."

"Pentagon Papers?" Mariah asked. "Ever heard of those?"

Jainey shrugged; she hadn't.

"Know what they all have in common?" Mariah asked. "No? Well, I'll *tell* you what they have in common. Government's lying to us, girl. And each time the government lies, innocent people end up dead or thrown in jail. Might as well *be* dead." Mariah popped the french fry into her mouth. “It’s a shame,” Mariah said, shaking her head, “it really is.” And then she told Jainey all about it.

After lunch, back at the wig store, Mariah led Jainey into a dark room. Jainey’s head was swirling from everything Mariah had told her, not only about Waco and Ruby Ridge, but about the first settlers in the U.S., and how one of the British generals had ordered smallpox-infested blankets to be given to the Indians in order to wipe them out. “Honey,” Mariah said. “You want to talk about germ warfare? We *invented* it.”

The back room was musty with its exposed pipes and flaking plaster. A lonely socketed bulb hung from a long wire that reached all the way up to the twenty-foot ceiling. In one of the corners sat wobbly stacks of boxes. Each box overflowed with thick paperbacks and yellowed newspaper clippings. There were hundreds of them—books and articles about Wounded Knee, Waco, Watergate—everything Mariah had told her about.

“Mariah’s Lending Library.” Mariah dragged over an empty box. “I’ll set you up with the ones you need,” she said. “Take your time. Old Mariah’s already read everything here at least twice.”

Jainey lugged the scarecrow back to her car; Mariah, trailing, carried the box of books. Jainey popped her trunk, and Mariah set her box next to the box full of miniature books. She picked up one of the miniature books—*Treasure Island*—and said, “These for midgets?”

“I’m not sure who they’re for,” Jainey said.

“Not for me,” Mariah said, shaking her head, looking mildly disgusted. “If I tried reading one of these, I’d be blind by morning.” She shut the trunk. “You be careful now,” she said. “And remember—knowledge may be power all right, but the more you know, the less certain people like you. That’s the truth.”

America's Report Card

IT WASN'T UNTIL the end of the first week of work at National Testing Center that Charlie finally grasped the labyrinthine way in which he himself had come to be there. The chain of command, as he saw it, went like this: The U.S. Department of Education had formed a department called the Institution of Evidenced-Based Education, who, in turn, formed the National Evaluation of Educational Achievement, who, implementing America's Report Card, contracted American Testing Corporation, an independent company specializing in test development and evaluation, to do the actual scoring. This was a much-coveted, multimillion-dollar contract, but since American Testing Corporation already had their fingers in too many pies, they subcontracted the work to National Testing Center, who—because of their prime location in a city with a highly educated but vastly underemployed population—could hire college graduates for barely above minimum wage and still turn a pretty penny.

Charlie and Petra—employed by a subcontracted company to score tests for a sub-sub-department deep within the U.S. Department of Education, the verdict of the nation's children and teachers resting squarely on their shoulders—stood outside during break and shared a package of Ding Dongs from the vending machine.

"I've got it," Petra said.

"What?"

"Where we can screw."

"Shhhhhhhhh." Charlie looked around, but no one appeared to have heard her. The Ghoul was turning a pear into mulch; the town drunk was sneaking quick nips from a thermos between whistling too loudly the theme to *The Mary Tyler Moore Show;* Magda, having pushed a long stick into the ground, alternated between looking up at the sun and then down at the stick's shadow. Rex, who'd reluctantly returned to NTC after his outburst, grimly smoked a cigarette alone. "Where?" Charlie whispered.

Petra leaned toward Charlie and took a big bite of his Ding Dong. Still chewing, she said, "There's a room in the back where they run the Scan-Tron sheets."

"Someone's probably always in there," Charlie said.

"You're wrong," she said. "Once an hour Akshay pushes a cart around to all the groups to collect our scores. He's usually out of the room for twenty minutes."

"*Who* pushes the cart around?"

"Akshay Kapoor," Petra said. "But it doesn't matter *who.* The question is *when?*"

"Twenty minutes," Charlie said, thinking out loud. "That's not really enough time."

Petra said, "We'd have to work fast. And you'd have to be ready, if you know what I mean."

"We couldn't really *do it* do it, though, could we?"

"There are other ways of doing it than *doing it.* You should know that by now." She smiled. Flecks of chocolate from Charlie's Ding Dong clung to her teeth. Charlie, using his forefinger, mimed brushing. Petra ran her tongue over her teeth in response, then smiled again. "All clean?"

Charlie went back to work, hunkered down, and scored a few hundred more answers.

Alligator. Six points.

Reptile. Six points.

Alligator. Six points.

Alligator. Six points.

Green. Six points.

Yellow. Six points.

Jerk. One point—for effort.

Before long, Charlie's brain switched over to autopilot: *six points, five points, six points, one point, no points, no points, six points . . .* Charlie was free now to think about something other than the test, and what he thought about was Petra. Several times a day he thought about how lucky he was to have met her and, though he didn't normally believe in such things, how it must have been fate. When he first called his old best friend, Randy, back in Des Moines, and told him about meeting Petra in his Soviet Cinema course and how it had seemed like fate, Randy laughed. He said, "Do you ever worry that it's too easy to be fate? I mean, think about it. What are the odds that you meet the person you're meant to spend the rest of your life with in a *film class?* Of all the millions of women in all the millions of places, the two of you just happened to be taking the same class? I hate to be a nihilist, but it just seems, well, too easy."

"Maybe," Charlie said. *But not in this case,* he wanted to add. And when he caught sight of Petra today, across the length of the room, getting up from her workstation and heading for the restroom, Charlie knew for certain that Randy was wrong. Why else was his heart racing? Why did it always get more difficult to breathe when he looked at her?

Charlie mindlessly clicked the mouse, the movement of his finger no longer attached to any message from his brain. Not that it mattered. If someone were to have walked up to him right then and showed him a photo of an alligator, Charlie would have pointed at it, the way a child points at something it recognizes, and declared, "Yellow."

LYING IN BED with the scarecrow casting its shadow over her, Jainey picked up a book she had already started reading, the one about the government's siege of Ruby Ridge back in 1992, when Jainey was only five, and she turned to where she had left off.

Ruby Ridge was in Idaho, but it wasn't the name of a real town. It was what the Weaver family named their own property. The Weavers consisted of the parents, Randy and Vicki, one son, Sam, and three daughters, Sara, Rachel, and the baby, Elisheba. After the government entrapped Randy Weaver—a man who made money buying and selling guns—and after Randy Weaver, who hated the government to begin with, didn't show up to court on charges based on his entrapment, U.S. marshals began staking out his property. Eventually, they came up with a plan to capture Randy, but the plan, once set in motion, went quickly to hell.

The Weaver family had three dogs, one of whom was a big yellow Lab named Striker. One day Striker picked up a scent and started chasing it. Randy Weaver, his boy Sam, and their friend, Kevin Harris, followed with their guns, not sure what Striker was after, but hoping it was a deer. In the woods, they came face to face with the U.S. marshals. At this point, the story became tangled—who shot who first—but the version that was ultimately believed to be true was that Randy ran back toward the house, yelling for the others to follow; that one of the U.S. marshals shot and killed Striker; that Kevin, upon hearing the gunshot, turned around, and shot and killed one of the marshals; and that one of the marshals shot and killed Randy's fourteen-year-old son, Sam.

Naturally, the FBI got involved and, based on misinformation and without interviewing any of the U.S. marshals, rewrote their own rules of engagement to state that "any armed adult male can and should be neutralized"—*neutralized* meaning *killed,* of course—and so long as the sharpshooters informed the family to surrender, any armed female could and *should* be killed as well. With the new rules hastily hammered out, sharpshooters moved into place. A short time later, from his sniper position, a man named Lon Horiuchi shot Vicki Weaver through the head. She was holding her ten-month-old baby when it happened, and the men, Randy and

Kevin, had to pry the blood-soaked baby from Vicki's lifeless fingers.

When all was said and done (and there was a *lot* that happened in between) Randy Weaver was found innocent of any wrongdoing—innocent, that is, with the exception of failing to appear in court for the crime in which he had initially been entrapped. For that, he served sixteen months in prison.

Those parts of the Weaver story alone—the entrapment, the siege, the deaths—were enough to make Jainey's head swirl, but there was a twist. Randy Weaver was a white separatist, a racist of the first order, someone Jainey wouldn't have wanted to be around for a split second. Both Randy and Vicki sounded like a couple of Grade-A crackpots who believed that the world would eventually be taken over by one giant Jewish-run government, and who were always talking about Yahweh—whoever the hell *that* was—and Yahweh's laws. They had even built something called a menstruation shed. When Jainey first read about that, she turned her head, shut her eyes, and said, "Yitch!" She was convinced that these were exactly the sort of people who would have made fun of her dyed hair, told her she was going to burn in Hell, called her a lesbian (as if there was something *wrong* with being a lesbian)—and yet, in the battle between the government and the Weavers, Randy Weaver was, ironically, the good guy. And *that's* what was so hard for Jainey to come to terms with—the redneck racist as hero. The government had allowed the situation to spiral crazily out of control. The Weavers, of course, weren't much help, but even so, any idiot could see that it didn't take three hundred state and federal agents with military tanks and helicopters to make them surrender, this family who hadn't even left their mountain in over a year. What Jainey had always believed—that *good was good* and that *bad was bad*—was proving not to be the case at all. The government's actions were so wrong that they inadvertently turned an otherwise loathsome man into a poster child for America's civil liberties. Randy Weaver had a *right* to bear arms, and, strange as it was, he had a *right* to be a racist.

Instead of championing the Weavers themselves, Jainey decided to champion their dog, Striker. The dog was a true innocent, pure of heart, doing what any good dog would do—warn his owner about intruders.

After flipping to the book's glossy photos and studying the sole photo of Striker, Jainey tromped downstairs to talk to her mother, who was sitting at the kitchen table and flicking ashes into a Bundt cake pan. She was wearing a T-shirt that said, "I Bite Back." Her hair was in curlers.

"Your brother stole my ashtrays," she said, "thinking I'd quit smoking if I don't have anyplace to flick my ashes." She laughed. "What a crock!"

"Mom?"

"Yeah?"

"Can we get a dog?"

Jainey's mother coughed a ball of smoke across the room. "A dog? Are you crazy? It's hard enough putting food on the table for three people let alone three people and a dog. What kind of dog did you have in mind?"

"A yellow Lab."

"A yellow Lab? That's not even a small dog," her mother said. She smashed out her cigarette inside the Bundt cake pan. "Remember Mr. Ditka?"

Jainey nodded. Mr. Ditka was their old, senile bulldog.

"Well," her mother said. "Remember who used to pick up Mr. Ditka's shit? Remember who used to have to shampoo the rug after Mr. Ditka pissed on it?"

"We can call this one Striker," Jainey said.

"Well, well, well," her mother said, standing. "I see you've got this all figured out, haven't you?" She dumped the cigarette butts from the Bundt cake pan into the dish disposal, then filled the pan with warm water, adding a squirt of Palmolive. Jainey followed her into the hallway, hoping to tell her the whole story of Ruby Ridge, but that wasn't going to happen—not tonight, at least. Before opening the door to her bedroom, her mother turned and said, "When they invent a dog that doesn't piss or shit, talk to me then, okay? Sweet dreams, Jainey."

"Sweet dreams, Mom."

AFTER ONLY A FEW weeks at NTC, Charlie had gained ten pounds; Petra, four. Not that this should have come as any big surprise. They sat on their asses for eight straight hours each day, except for their two short breaks and half-hour lunch, during which they sprinted across the street and inhaled a pound of moo goo gai pan from the Hy-Vee International Food Market. Otherwise, they remained seated for a third of each day, hunched forward, reading their computer screens and clicking a mouse.

Weekends, Charlie did the grocery shopping while Petra cleaned up his apartment. When Charlie came home today, weighted down with heavy bags and whistling a tune from *Guys and Dolls,* he found Petra on her hands and knees in the kitchen, wearing long rubber gloves. She had on tight Lycra shorts and a half-shirt, and her bangs were heavy with sweat.

Charlie took a step back. "Holy crap! This is the sexiest thing I've ever seen."

Charlie knew Petra well. He knew her predilections, her peccadilloes. He stood stock still, waiting for her to crawl over to him, pausing only to pull off the suctioned gloves. She would look up at him with hooded eyes, eyes that said, *Hold on to your hat, this is going to get really nasty!*—and then she would rise off her heels just enough to peel down her Lycra shorts, but she would pull them down only so far, down to her thighs, before stopping. And then what? Lean toward his zipper? Lift the zipper's pull tab with her tongue, teasing it, flicking it? Eventually, she would close her mouth around the pull tab, and Charlie would feel the pressure of her teeth at work. He'd shut his eyes and wait for the zipper to open, for Petra's hot breath to warm his pulsating Fruit of the Looms.

But none of this happened. Petra put a disposable respirator over her face and then picked up a can of Easy-Off that Charlie had neglected to see. After shaking the can a few times, she sprayed its entire contents inside the oven. A fog of chemicals rolled from the oven and headed toward Charlie like a vengeful apparition. It was like the scene near the end of that famous made-for-TV movie *Trilogy of Terror.* In it, Karen Black is being chased around the house by a fetish doll that's come alive and is trying to kill her. She finally throws the doll into the oven, but when she opens up the oven door to make sure that the doll is indeed dead, a dense vapor leaves the oven—presumably, the doll's evil spirit—and Karen Black is consumed by it. Charlie was about to ask Petra if she'd ever seen the movie when his lungs started burning. A moment later, he started coughing, unable to stop. The apparition had entered him, and Charlie couldn't help thinking he was being poisoned, perhaps only moments away from death itself. At the very least he'd probably lost five years of his life. And Petra—where was she during his coughing fit? Where was the empathy? He expected her to call out, *Are you okay?* but she remained on her knees, her head and the upper half of her torso buried in the oven. It could have been a snapshot of domesticity. That, or another desperate soul calling it quits.

During one of their breaks at NTC, Charlie patted his gut and said, "Maybe I should take up smoking to speed up my metabolism."

Petra, staring beyond Charlie through eyes rimmed red from Easy-Off, said, "I'm taking up crystal meth. My metabolism *and* the number of tests I score will increase. It's a win-win situation."

"Doing okay there, Petra?"

Petra shrugged. "We better get back."

Charlie, bored, spent the better part of his workday thinking, *Thank God this isn't my life.* He'd met a number of folks who'd stuck around town after graduating, hoping to land a cushy university job, but when the cushy job never panned out, they were stuck piecemealing their work together, month after month, sometimes week to week.

Rex, the musicologist, had told Charlie a cautionary tale about his own quest for a good university job. After four years of putting in applications with the university, Rex was finally invited to interview for the sweet position of Academic Adviser—three-quarters time, full benefits, health care, retirement, vacation—the whole ball of wax. At one point during the interview, Rex said something that made everyone laugh, but when he joined them, laughing modestly through his nose, a stalactite of snot shot from one of his nostrils. Startled, he quickly inhaled and the snot retreated. It was like a party favor that unrolled when you blew it, then rolled right back up. Everyone had seen what had happened, and the director of advising quickly wrapped up the meeting. For what little time remained, Rex kept reaching up to squeeze his nose, as if to indicate that he, too, had been startled by the snot's unexpected appearance, but it was too late. The damage was done. No other job application to the university ever panned out, and Rex eventually quit applying.

"You may not think that the balance of your life can hinge on something as ridiculous as that," Rex had said, "but I'm here to tell you—you'd be wrong. Dead wrong."

One afternoon, a ruckus flared up in the cubicle next to Charlie's. Charlie didn't think much about it at first—there were always heated discussions—but then he heard the distinct sound of someone getting punched. A woman yelled, "Stop hitting him, Tony! Just get the hell out of here. *Stop it!*"

Everyone in Charlie's group, except for the Ghoul, stood up as the perpetrator made his way past their cube. Rex reached behind his back, as if to tug up his pants, but then he touched something pinned between his belt and flesh. A gun? Once the culprit had left the building, Rex's arm went slack.

Charlie peered over the partition and saw a man of forty-something lying on the floor. Blood trickled from his mouth. The skin around his eye, puffing up, was starting to discolor. The woman crouched next to him was shivering and weeping.

Supervisors rushed over to appraise the situation. When they looked up and saw everyone rubbernecking from their cubes, they marched from group to group and ordered the scorers back to work.

Charlie spotted Petra across the long room. For her benefit, he mouthed "Wow" and shook his head, then punched the air a few times, shadowboxing, before pointing down at the victim. He motioned to his own eye and then began making the face of someone in agonizing pain.

Rachel, the group leader, tapped his shoulder. "Charlie. We're not paying you to perform Kabuki. The rest of us have gone back to work. You don't want to fall behind."

Rachel walked away. *Kabuki.* Charlie had an irrational desire to walk over and strangle her. There was no call to be such a smart-ass. *No* call.

After the police arrived it was nearly impossible to concentrate, anyway, because of their hissing and squawking radios. Their heavy belts, loaded down with weapons and restraints, jingled with even the barest of moves.

"You're falling behind, folks!" Rachel yelled. "We can't fall behind! Faster, faster!"

The Ghoul began scoring with a speed unlike anything anyone at NTC had ever witnessed. Charlie, on the other hand, barely looked at the students' answers. It wasn't as though a wrong score would send some poor kid tumbling back into a lower grade level. He concentrated instead on the conversation on the other side of his partition. Apparently, the man who'd barged in and beaten up the group leader was the weeping woman's husband, and the weeping woman had been spending time with the group leader on the sly.

Jesus, Charlie thought. *It's like working in a housing project.* He didn't take any pleasure in a fellow employee getting pummeled, but he was grateful for anything that livened up an otherwise tedious day.

At break, Charlie devoured a Butterhorn Swirl from the vending machine while telling Petra everything he'd heard. He expected Petra to lean in close and whisper a litany of questions and speculations, but she finished her Big Texas Cinnamon Roll without saying a word.

"It's pretty awful," Charlie added, "losing your wife to a group leader. A group leader!" Charlie laughed, wagging his head.

"People do what they have to do," Petra said.

"I suppose," Charlie said. "But a *group leader!*" He snorted to make his point.

That night in bed, Charlie said, "I think Rex carries a gun."

Petra, distracted, nodded. She obviously wasn't listening. Charlie's words had become as inconsequential as dust motes. She said, "I had a premonition last night."

"A premonition?"

"That George Bush is going to get reelected."

"That's crazy talk," Charlie said. Petra didn't reply. Steering the conversation back on course, Charlie said, "What about that fight at work? How nutty was that?"

"I'm getting tired of it," Petra said.

"What?"

"The job."

"Yeah; well, the good thing is, it's only temporary." When Petra didn't respond, Charlie added, "You have to admit, it's not such a bad way to spend the summer."

Petra rubbed her eyes with both fists, the way children rub their eyes, and said, "I guess not, Charlie."

JAINEY SPENT a good part of the next day studying the scarecrow. She walked around it, holding her chin like an art appraiser. She examined the title of the project—*The Lycanthrope*—and found a definition for the word online. It said, "Lycanthropy derives from the Greek *lykoi,* meaning 'wolf,' and *anthropos,* meaning 'man.' Lycanthropy is a state of mind in which the man or woman is convinced that he or she is a wolf. Sometimes this person believes him- or herself to be some other type of animal. Though lycanthropy is often linked to schizophrenia, it has been found mostly in persons who believe in reincarnation or the transmigration of souls. The notion of lycanthropy originated as a superstition in which men actually transformed into some other animal."

Was Mrs. Grant claiming that George W. Bush was a lycanthrope? Maybe she was proposing that George W. Bush was a schizophrenic who *thought* he was Osama bin Laden. Was Osama bin Laden merely a product of George Bush's troubled mind? Or perhaps the point was that the modern-day lycanthrope turned not into a wolf, as the lycanthrope once did, but into a terrorist.

Jainey made another trip back to Mrs. Grant's condo. The fuzzy slippers were still there. The banana, entirely brown now, had attracted a flurry of tiny fruit flies. Inside a filing cabinet, Jainey found a thin manila folder titled "Grants." Jainey opened it, expecting the file to contain photos and papers about her teacher's family—the Grants—or perhaps a detailed family tree that opened up like a road map, but what she found were photocopied applications for various arts fellowships. "Oh," Jainey whispered. "*Those* grants."

She fingered through an Illinois Arts Council Grant and then one for the National Endowment for the Arts. There were grant applications for the years 2002, 2003, and 2004. They were all, Jainey realized, government grants, and in every instance, *The Lycanthrope* was the project for which Mrs. Grant had applied for funding.

Jainey slipped the manila file folder under her shirt. She picked up the banana, using only two fingers, and tossed it into the trash. The fruit flies hesitated a moment, hovering without purpose, then headed for the garbage can and slid under the lid's protruding lip. Jainey's hands were shaking. By the looks of the applications, the U.S. government knew a lot about Mrs. Grant. They certainly had enough information to know that Mrs. Grant wasn't happy with George W. Bush. And if George W. Bush could kill innocent Iraqis by the thousands, what could one old art teacher's life possibly matter to him?

WHEN CHARLIE woke up, he found a letter from Petra on the kitchen table. It was a quote from the very end of Chekhov's short story "The Lady with the Dog," a story Petra had read aloud to Charlie a dozen times:

> "And it seemed as though in a little while the solution would be found, and then a new and splendid life would begin; and it was clear to both of them that they still had a long, long road before them, and that the most difficult part of it was only just beginning."
>
> *My love,*
> *Petra*

Charlie read the note two more times. And then he remembered to breathe. "What the . . . ?" He turned the letter over. Nothing. He reread it, wondering what it meant. In Chekhov's story, the man and woman for whom the road was still long had decided to leave their respective spouses so that the two of them could now be together without having to sneak around. But what did any of this have to do with Charlie and Petra? They weren't married; they weren't sneaking behind other people's backs.

Charlie looked under the table, thinking maybe the first sheet of the letter had floated away, but he couldn't find another page. Apparently, this was it—the entire letter.

"Good God," Charlie said. "Is she breaking up with me? Is that what this is?"

Charlie went to work, hoping to find Petra there, but on his way inside he was stopped by a security guard. Apparently, NTC had hired a guard after yesterday's incident, but it was hard to take this man seriously. He looked like some grown-up version of Sluggo from the *Nancy* comic strip. Crew cut. Pug nose. Beady eyes. Up-to-no-good grin.

"What?" Charlie asked, more defensively than he'd intended.

Sluggo leaned in close. "Have you heard the one about the call girl and the confessional?"

"*What?*"

"The joke," Sluggo said. "Have you heard it?"

When Charlie admitted he hadn't, Sluggo proceeded to tell him. It was a lame joke, but Charlie made an effort to laugh.

"What's your name?" Sluggo asked.

"Charlie Wolf."

"Good to meet you, Charlie Wolf." He clapped Charlie on the back and said, "It's nice to meet someone around here with a sense of humor."

Charlie's heart literally clenched when he saw that Petra's chair was empty.

All morning long, Charlie couldn't concentrate on his scoring, so he gave each essay a "three." Amazingly, his reliability and speed both soared.

"Great job," Rachel said. "You're on a roll! Don't stop!"

For his break, Charlie dragged himself outside and chewed lethargically on a Hostess blueberry pie. Petra called them *lard* pies. "Eating a lard pie?" she'd ask. Charlie wanted to weep, but he was standing near two other guys—Jacob Bartuka, the man who'd worked at NTC for fifteen years, and Russ Zucker, a new employee.

Russ asked, "So what's your background, Jacob?"

"My background? I'm an artist," Jacob said.

"Oh, really," Russ said. "What kind of artist?"

"A martial artist," Jacob said.

Charlie paused eating, the lard pie half in his mouth. He pivoted toward Jacob to gauge the look on his face, but the man's expression was completely blank. Jacob was five feet tall. He was wearing a faded T-shirt with Fonzie from *Happy Days* on it. "Sit on it!" the shirt declared in a font that looked like neon tubes.

"This job," Jacob said, "it gives me the time I need to practice at the dojo. I mean, if I had to work a *real* job, I wouldn't have time for my art. You know what I'm saying? It's the flexibility that I like."

Charlie wanted to nudge Jacob and say, *Okay, pal, let's cut the bullshit,* but then Russ turned to Charlie and asked him what he did besides work at NTC. Before Charlie could answer, Jacob said, "Charlie here, he's a film scholar. He writes articles for magazines."

"Really?" Russ said. "A writer? That's great!"

Charlie nodded.

"What magazines?" Russ asked.

Mercifully, the whistle blew. It was time to go back to work.

"We'll talk about it later," Charlie said, and then he did something he'd never done to a stranger before. He winked at the guy. He *winked* at him.

Charlie understood well that the spin you put on your life affected the way people viewed you. The danger, of course, was when you yourself began to believe your own spin. And he could see how damn easily it could happen: Charlie ten years from now, a thirty-four-year-old man living in the same apartment, cobbling together his income month to month, telling people that he was an independent film scholar working outside the constraints of the academy when in reality he sat hunched on a sofa from Goodwill, ate lard pies, and watched the Weather Channel.

Oh dear God, Charlie prayed. *Don't let that be me.*

After work, Magda flagged down Charlie, who was hoping to make a swift exit. Her earrings were made of long spotted feathers, and her skin looked artificially tanned. Gently, she touched Charlie's wrist. "Carl was wondering if you'd care to join us for drinks?"

"Carl? Who's Carl?"

Magda pointed to the Ghoul. Charlie almost yelped. Apparently, Magda and the Ghoul got together once a month for drinks at TGI Fridays.

"Oh. I'd love to," Charlie said. "But not tonight. Tonight's not good. Not good at all."

Magda put her hands on her hips in mock reproach. She tilted her head to one side and said, "Now, Charlie Wolf. Name *one* thing you're going to do tonight that's more important than having a drink with us. *One* thing!"

Magda was only giving him a hard time, but her request to name one thing nearly broke Charlie down right there. She had a point: there wasn't one damned thing in his life more pressing than joining Magda and the Ghoul for drinks.

Magda must have sensed his sudden emotional fissure. She frowned and asked, "Are you okay?"

"I'm not feeling that great," Charlie said, willing the pressure behind his eyes to go away. "That's all. I think I'm coming down with something."

"Well, then, you better go home and get a good night's sleep."

Magda patted his arm. In that moment, she was the embodiment of empathy. The Ghoul, however, stared indifferently at his own shoe. "Feel better," Magda said. She motioned for the Ghoul, who trailed her out the door.

Rex, walking up behind Charlie, muttered, "Tough break, kiddo."

Charlie stopped, turned around. "What?"

"About that girl of yours."

"What about her?" His heart started pounding so hard that his windpipe contracted in time to the beat of his heart, causing an odd clicking suction noise inside his throat.

Rex said, "I heard all about it." He shook his head. "A doctor, to boot."

"What the hell are you talking about?"

"You don't know about any of this?" Rex asked.

Charlie shook his head.

Petra, according to Rex, had been seeing a co-worker on the side, a man named Akshay Kapoor. Kapoor had finished his medical residency at the university a month ago and was biding his time at NTC until a vacancy came open at a hospital in Chicago. Petra had gone with him. They left this morning. Rex assumed Charlie knew. Everyone else did.

"Petra moved to *Chicago?*" Charlie asked. "With another *man?*"

Rex nodded. "This guy—Akshay—he probably didn't even really need the money he made here. But you know how those guys have better work ethics than us."

"Doctors?"

"No. Indians."

Charlie felt pressure building behind his eyes, but he managed to stave off the tears. "And everyone knew about this?"

Rex stared at Charlie with enormous sympathy. He placed a hand on Charlie's shoulder. He cleared his throat and said, "I guess not everybody," and then patted Charlie on the back.

John McNally

WHEN JAINEY finally returned to school, no one said anything about her having been gone. Was this how school had always been, a place where no one noticed anything, not even the absence of one of their own classmates? It was like being in a zombie movie where everyone is a zombie but no one realizes it, and when you ask, "Are you feeling okay?" the zombie replies, "I'm fine. Why?"

Jainey had barely settled into her first-hour class when a man with a dark suit walked into the room. He looked like an FBI agent, and Jainey feared that he had come to take her away, but when a second man entered carrying a banker's box, they introduced themselves to the class. They were proctors, and they were here to administer America's Report Card.

Jainey sighed, partly out of relief but also in frustration. She had figured—hoped, really—that she'd missed the damned test during her truancy. Clearly, she had failed in that one simple goal.

Hour after hour, the men issued directives. Jainey didn't want to take the test seriously—it had no effect whatsoever on her life—but it was hard to break the habit of having been a good student. Even when she logically stripped away every reason for caring about the test, there lingered an almost tangible dose of guilt. It whispered into her ear, *Be a good girl.* It breathed down her neck, *Don't let everyone down.*

But Jainey grew tired of being a good girl. No one cared when she *didn't* let them down, only when she *did,* and so when it came time to write the argumentative essay, Jainey slipped her finger inside the booklet and broke the seal before the proctors gave permission. She started reading:

> Imagine that you have been voted class president after a fierce campaign with your competitor. The election results were close, and you won by a mere fraction of a percent. Now, imagine three weeks into your presidency, several uncounted ballots have been found, and the new results put your competitor in the lead. One thing is clear: If every vote had been counted fairly, you would not be president. The decision now rests with you. What do you do? If you decide to remain president, make a case for why you shouldn't hand over the office to your competitor. If you decide to hand over the office, make a case for why you should step down. You will not be judged for your decision. You will be judged by the logic of your argument leading to your decision.
>
> (Time allowed: 60 minutes.)

Jainey considered the question. She considered not answering at it all, but then she began writing:

> *I don't know who reads these things and I can't imagine what kind of sad life you must have but let me tell you a little bit about myself. My name's Jainey O'Sullivan, and when I was given an IQ test years ago I blew everyone else out of the water, but something's happened lately in that I don't care anymore. Take the question you want me to answer. I don't give a shit about school politics. I could care less. So why should I spend my time trying to answer a question on a subject that I could care less about? So*

here's what I'm going to do. I'm going to tell you about me. If you want to know more about me then read on. If not, stop here. Okay, you must be reading on. What should I tell you about me? Well, I drive my brother's shitty car around town. I write a comic strip called "Lloyd the Freakazoid" and it's kind of funny, I suppose. I'll probably write one about Lloyd taking this test and he'll be drinking a big bottle of vodka on his way into the classroom but when he opens the test booklet and reads the first test, his head will explode. Ha! Maybe you guys would want to buy that one from me to use for some kind of promotion. I don't know. Probably not. Anyway, I live in Burbank, Illinois, which is where all the terrorists seem to live these days, if you watch the news, but it's kind of bad because I go to school with a lot of Arabs who aren't terrorists but there are other kids here who want to kick their asses. Or is it just "ass"? Go ahead and dock me a few points since I don't know which one it should be. Anyway . . . Lately, my own skin feels too tight. You ever feel that way, like you're wearing an extra-small sweater? Like you want to stretch your own skin so that it's loose again. I'm trying to picture what you look like. Probably some old dude with a monocle and a long beard, right? You probably spent your life reading the classics. Plato and shit, right? Do you ever have sex? If not, you should give it a go. I can't say I've been with anyone who really knocks my socks off, but it's better than guessing how many jellybeans are in a long glass tube, if you know what I mean. Listen. Here's the thing. Someone killed my art teacher, and I'm afraid they're after me now. I can't help thinking something terrible's about to happen. But maybe worse than what's going to happen is that no one will care. I'll be dead, and that'll be that. I'm seventeen years old, and in seventeen years I haven't seen anything that would lead me to think that my life was going to end until all this stuff with my teacher began. I'm not saying any of this to get you to give me a better grade. You're probably thinking that I wrote that last sentence as some kind of reverse psychology. I'm sure that's what you're thinking because that's what you're paid to think, you being smart and wearing a monocle and in need of a good blowjob. No offense. But that's what you're getting paid for, right? And maybe now you're thinking, Ah ha! She's smarter than I first thought! She's pulling the old reverse-reverse-reverse psychology trick out of her bag, and yet I'm still smarter than her! I know what she's up to! Well, you'd be wrong. In my world there is no reverse psychology. There's only psychology. Or whatever the opposite of reverse psychology is. I have to start making a list of all the things I want to do but haven't because I thought I had my whole life to do them but now I don't. I guess this is a long way of saying that I'd hand over the presidency to the person who really won it because it doesn't make a difference since the person who won it—me—isn't going to be around to put it on my résumé. Or, now that I think about it, maybe I'd hold on to the presidency, because there's nothing more frightening than a person with power who doesn't give a shit anymore. There's no telling what a person like that might do.

Jainey ended the school day feeling something akin to a spiritual glow. Writing whatever she wanted for the essay test opened new doors inside her, doors to rooms that were full of brilliant light. This must have been what born-again Christians felt like when God spoke directly to them. How amazing! How wonderful! Jainey was seeing the world anew. Everything was beautiful! Everyone was special! The glow lasted until she got into the Turd and tried starting it a few times. The car barely made a sound. And then, after a few more cranks, it didn't make any sound at all.

"Goddamn motherfucking sonofabitch." She jumped out and kicked a tire. "Piece of cocksucking shit." She made a fist and hammered the hood a few times.

This, she feared, would be the story of her life: epiphany followed by mechanical failure. If she'd grown up rich, like kids in Winnetka or Lake Forest, things would have been different. She'd be wearing an Easter bonnet right now. Ned wouldn't be living in the attic—or, if he was still up there, he'd at least be listening to Mozart instead of

Whitesnake, Tchaikovsky instead of Ratt. Mr. Licks would be going to Northwestern in the fall instead of taking a job working with his cousin at Brookfield Zoo, shoveling up kangaroo shit all day.

Jainey was about to inflict more damage on the Turd when a tall man carrying a banker's box showed up at the car beside her. He was one of the proctors, and he looked like Victor Benedetti, her imaginary truant officer. He carried himself the way they all carried themselves—like FBI agents on their first day at work, an uneasy mix of supreme confidence and utter uncertainty. He popped his trunk, set the banker's box inside. His car was new and clean, very official-looking, like an undercover cop's.

"Having trouble?" he asked.

Victor! she wanted to say. *Don't you know who I am?* What she said instead was, "The Turd won't start."

"The Turd, huh?" Victor left his trunk open and walked over. "Hm," he said, looking at it. "It's seen better days, hasn't it?"

"Not since I've known it," Jainey said.

"May I?" he asked, nodding toward the driver's seat. He slid inside and turned the key. The Turd snorted but then made a terrible clicking noise.

"It's your battery," he said. "It's dead."

"Son of a *bitch!*" Jainey yelled. "Worthless piece of *crap!*" She slammed her hip into the rear left panel.

"Whoa!" Victor got out of the car. He reached for Jainey to stop her but pulled his hand back at the last second, as if he'd been warned not to touch the students. "It needs a jump. I've got cables in the trunk, okay? It's no biggy."

"A jump?"

"I'm sure it'll recharge. You'll want to get another battery in a few days to be on the safe side, though."

"Oh."

"Can you pop the hood?"

"How do you do that?"

"Here," he said. "I'll do it."

Jainey felt as though she were playing a role: the helpless woman who knows nothing about cars. There were women who cultivated that role, who purposely knew nothing about anything, who always relied on men to step up and take charge. The very thought of such women normally tired Jainey beyond belief, but she had to admit that she was liking it today. It didn't have to be a sign of weakness, she realized. It could just as easily be a tool of power. Why couldn't she lure men over and get what she wanted without ever lifting a finger?

Jainey turned the ignition, and as easy as that, the Turd was running again. He disconnected the cables.

"There you go," he said. He shut the Turd's hood.

Jainey wanted to ask him if he really believed in America's Report Card. She wanted to apologize for not taking it more seriously. She wanted to tell him why everyone thought it was a crock, and then she wanted to tell him how George W. Bush had killed her most favorite person in the world. Most of all, she wanted to kiss him. In the end, though, Jainey did nothing. She didn't even thank him. A paralysis took hold of her, the same paralysis that sometimes strangled her in everyday situations, making her unable to respond to even the simplest questions.

Victor was gone, and the Turd was running by itself. It coughed a few times, as if to say, *You see? I'm just a little under the weather. No need to hit me.* And Jainey felt bad now for taking out her anger on her brother's car.

"I'm sorry," Jainey said. She patted the dashboard and said, "Poor Turd."

The skyscrapers downtown reminded Jainey of a band of ragtag soldiers all standing at attention, some short, some tall, but all of them frozen stiff and stoic, as if to say, *We're here, and we're ready!* Jainey liked the city's deceptiveness. From a distance the skyscrapers gave Chicago a sense of seriousness, but once you drove deep down into its guts, you saw immediately how gnarled and treacherous it all was: the rusted train tracks, brick buildings that had settled at odd angles a hundred years ago, men curled up on flattened sheets of cardboard. It was like lifting a rock and expecting to find an ant colony but finding instead a bunch of centipedes and roly-polies. Your first reaction is to jump back, but then you start to lean in closer, much closer than if there had been only ants.

Jainey drove down Wabash, hoping to see Mariah inside the wig store, but it was already midnight and all the lights were out. She turned right, then turned again onto State Street. She decided that she would drive ever-widening loops, using Wabash as her one constant. She completed four loops, but on the outer edge of her fifth loop, the Turd died. She was too tired to yell at it.

She got out of the car and stood helplessly beside it. She wanted Victor to swoop in and rescue her, but that wasn't going to happen. She was in a seedy part of the city, far seedier now that she was standing outside without a coat, nothing but a ring of keys in her hand. She was a seventeen-year-old girl stranded in a place she didn't belong.

"Shit," she said. "Shit, shit." She decided it would be better to sit inside her car with the doors locked until she saw a police car or a tow truck.

A few minutes later, a car of the same make and model as the Turd drove slowly past Jainey in the opposite lane. Half a block away, the driver whipped a U-ey and headed back toward her. The other car wasn't in any better shape than hers. The only difference, so far as Jainey could tell, was that the other car had tinted windows.

When the car stopped alongside her, the driver's tinted window scrolled down. It was possible, since the man drove the same piece of shit, that he knew what was wrong with her car, so Jainey rolled down her window. The man was in his forties, unshaven, with bulging eyes and a tongue that was too big for his mouth. He was drinking from a flask. It soon became clear that he wasn't there to help her.

It's Lloyd, Jainey thought. *Lloyd the Freakazoid. He's come to life.*

"You working tonight, honey?" Lloyd asked.

"Huh?"

"You looking for dates?" Lloyd asked. He took a swig from his flask. He wiped his mouth with his forearm.

"Dates?" Jainey asked. It was as if English had become not just a second but a third language. "What?" She squinted at him.

Lloyd gave her the once-over and said, "Fuck it." He floored his own Turd, squealing bald tires and leaving behind a long streak of stinky rubber in his wake.

Jainey, shivering, found the hazard lights and turned them on. She had always imagined cartoon counterparts to real people, but what she hadn't anticipated were real-life counterparts to cartoons. It was almost too scary to think about. But if one such world existed, why wouldn't the inverse be true?

It was after one in the morning when a police officer approached Jainey's car and found her curled up in the front seat. He knocked several times, but Jainey was sound asleep, dreaming about the Michigan Dunes and her beautiful proctor, Victor. Victor was still wearing his starched white shirt and dark suit, but Jainey was completely naked. Everyone on the beach was staring at her. And then people started to point: *Look, look!* Jainey yelled obscenities back at them, but Victor gently shushed her—*It's okay,* he said, *everything's okay*—and then he picked her up, her arms around his neck, and carried her into the ice-cold lake. Only after she was beneath the water's surface and no longer able to breathe did she open her eyes and see the police officer looking in at her, and only after he pressed his badge and ID against her window did she finally stop screaming.

NED O'SULLIVAN didn't expect any thanks for the sacrifices he'd made on their behalves, but it would have been nice if Jainey or his mother let him know that they were at least *aware* he'd made sacrifices. What grown son in his right mind would continue living at home when he didn't have to? Ned sure as shit wouldn't have, but what was he supposed to do—abandon both women the way his father had abandoned them? Nope, no sir, he wasn't going to do that, even though Jainey and his mother sometimes looked at him with the same repulsion that people usually reserved for beggars. If they knew their Bible, which of course they didn't, they'd have realized that they, too, had an obligation to beggars. It was right there in Deuteronomy: "For the poor will never cease out of the land; therefore I command you, You shall open wide your hand to your brother, to the needy and to the poor, in the land." Not that Ned was a beggar. He wasn't.

After lighting a candle, Ned popped *The Best of Great White: 1986–1992* into his CD player. When the first song came on—"Step on You"—he cranked the volume all the way up. He lay on the futon he'd dragged up into the attic. In his ongoing attempt to toughen his body—the Lord's vessel—Ned refused to use bedsheets or blankets, no matter how cold it got. He wouldn't use a pillow, either. He would have preferred sleeping on a hard floor, but the attic wasn't finished, and it would have been difficult, though not impossible, to sleep across the two-by-fours positioned narrow side up and spaced five inches apart.

The attic wasn't such a bad place to live. Its only serious drawback was its height. The room was too low for Ned to stand upright except where the steeped roof came to a point, so he practiced keeping his balance by walking barefoot along the narrow two-by-fours that ran down the center of the attic floor while his hair, sometimes standing on end from static electricity, brushed against the roof's uppermost peak. On dry nights, his hair actually sparked, and the room would momentarily light up.

Tonight, Ned remained on his back. His goal was to lie perfectly still for the next four hours. The CD was on repeat, so there was no need to even twitch a muscle. His level of relaxation reached the point where his entire body seemed to be melting into the futon, as if body and futon were becoming one giant, shapeless entity. For a moment, he felt as though he were floating through Outer Space.

"Ned!" his mother yelled. "*Ned!* Would you shut that goddamned music off? Do you hear me? Shut that fucking music off now! Ned! Listen to me. The entire neighborhood doesn't want to listen to that shit, and I'm not going to defend you when the police arrive. Are you even *up* there? Can you *hear* me or have you gone *deaf? Ned!*"

It didn't bother Ned that she was yelling. Yelling kept her from smoking. Ned had heard somewhere that each cigarette took five to twenty minutes off a person's life. Therefore, the less she smoked, the longer she might live, and the longer she lived, the more likely it was that she would eventually come to appreciate him.

"I'm going out of my *motherfucking* mind!" she screamed up to him. "Oh my *God,* Ned. *Please* turn it down! *Please!*"

Great White's "All Over Now" came on next. Only a year ago more than a hundred people died when a fire erupted at a Great White concert at a small club in Rhode Island. The band's pyrotechnics had started the fire. By all accounts, the club, which was made of wood and didn't have a sprinkler system, was a tinderbox waiting for the right confluence of factors. Glued to CNN, Ned spent the entire day watching grainy footage of the fire: people running, smoke filling the room, flames spreading.

"Dear God!" his mother pleaded. "Why me? Huh? *Why me?*"

Ned remained frozen atop his futon—frozen but relaxed—staring up at the rafters. He'd stared up at these same rafters every day since September 12, 2001, the day he'd taken up permanent residence in the attic, but today was the first time that he saw the rafters for what they were: an upside-down ark. It was as if he were somehow hovering above an ark and looking down into it.

"Holy Christ," he said.

In moments such as this one, Ned had absolutely no doubt that God was talking to him. There were people who believed that God spoke actual words to them, but those people were dipshits. God didn't speak in *words;* he spoke in *images.* And this was precisely how it happened, when you least expected it. One minute Ned was looking at the bottom side of a plywood roof; the next, he was peering into the belly of an ark. And God wasn't going to spell out for Ned what it meant, either. That was up to Ned. The more intensely Ned stared at the rafters, the closer he felt to achieving a greater understanding.

"Ned, you bastard! You're just like your father, you know that? Always thinking about yourself and nobody else!"

Ned shut his eyes, and there it was: the fire in Rhode Island, the smoke and fire. But the band—Great White—they had continued playing their first song of the night, "Desert Moon." For the people inside the club, it must have been like being trapped on the sinking Titanic, everyone wearing life jackets and knowing their grim fates while the orchestra played "Nearer, My God, to Thee."

"I get it," Ned whispered. "I *see.*"

It was Peter who confirmed that God had created the Earth and then devastated it with water, and it was Peter who delivered the warning that God would one day burn the entire planet. Was the end of the world coming? Would Ned become a modern-day Noah? Ned doubted that the end of the world was near, but he wouldn't have minded being Noah. Noah had lived to be nine hundred and fifty years old. Nine hundred and fifty, and then he died. How fucking cool would *that* have been?

The epiphany was within Ned's reach, but then it started to fade. "Shit," he said. Whatever God was trying to tell him, it wasn't going to crystallize tonight. "Shit, shit, shit."

"If I have to come up there," his mother yelled, "you'll be sorry. Do you hear me, Ned O'Sullivan? Do you understand English?"

It was possible she had climbed to the second floor and was now standing below the hatch to the attic, but Ned wasn't worried: the hatch was locked. This was as close as she was going to get. By Ned's rough calculations, she'd already missed two cigarettes. Ned had given forty minutes of life back to her. Forty minutes might not have seemed like a whole hell of a lot, but how many sons could say that they'd given their mothers any life back at all?

Part Two

The Teeth

1997

The way Dale O'Sullivan saw it, there were two immediate tasks at hand: to concentrate on what Jainey was saying and to push the bottle of vodka behind the box of Cocoa Krispies, out of plain sight.

"Jesus Christ, Jainey," Dale said. "Calm down and tell me what happened. You're not making any sense."

Dale O'Sullivan had left work early, hoping for a quiet lunch, but then, seemingly out of thin air, his ten-year-old daughter appeared in the kitchen, still wearing her regulation gym uniform. Her two front teeth were gone, the meat of her upper gums was torn apart, and her damp, white T-shirt was covered with Rorschach blots of blood. She couldn't stop crying, her speech impeded by the new gap, and each time she tried saying a word beginning with "th," she spewed blood and then screamed at the sight of her own gore.

The carotid arteries in Dale's neck pulsed, and he could actually hear flowing blood, a muffled swish. While Jainey finished explaining it all, Dale fetched cotton balls to temporarily replace her two front teeth. After hearing her story, he knew precisely what to do next; there was never any question.

Dale dropped Jainey off at the dentist's office and then drove straight to her grade school, arriving a little before two o'clock. He had been here many times before, those late-October nights of open house, parents aimlessly wandering the halls, looking like lost and snowblind cattle among the garish drawings taped to glazed-brick walls the color of PeptoBismol. Nothing, however, was on display today. The hallway was barren; the walls, naked and old. Open house had been a ruse, a sham.

Dale walked inside the gymnasium. Class hadn't yet started. Students were still filing in. Dale nudged a janitor from behind. "Hey, bub," he said. "My daughter fell from a rope. She lost her teeth."

The janitor nodded, then grimaced. "You should have seen the blood."

Before Dale could ask what he'd come there to ask, the principal burst into the gym. "Sir!" he called out. "Yes, you! You need a pass from the main office. You can't just barge in here." A small crowd of secretaries and teachers had formed in the hall outside the gymnasium's doors. The principal escorted Dale outside, and as the two men crossed the recess blacktop, Dale explained why he was there.

"I want to know," he said, "what kind of sadistic asshole makes a ten-year-old girl crawl up a fifty-foot rope?"

The principal said, "I don't think it's fifty *feet, but I see your point. I'll have a talk with Mr. Hall."*

"Mr. Hall?"

"The gym teacher."

Dale paused on the blacktop. The principal was wearing a red blazer with gold buttons, the sort of jacket a circus clown might wear. Who were these people? How could he have entrusted his child's life to them?

"I'm sure there won't be a problem," the principal said, "with our insurance picking up the bill. I can understand your anger. Really, I can. I'd be angry, too."

They shook hands. Dale waited until the principal had gone back inside before he popped open the trunk. He pulled out an aluminum baseball bat. Dale still had a good buzz going from lunch, the kind of buzz that made his head feel as though it had been carefully packed in Styrofoam. Nobody needed to get hurt, but the bat would reinforce his point. If nothing else, the bat would scare the son of a bitch, which was all he planned to do.

When Dale pulled open the large gymnasium door for the second time, it was the top of the hour, and he saw immediately who he was looking for: Gulliver among the Lilliputians. A tan bleach-blond mustachioed beefcake. A whistle dangled from his neck like a talisman to woo and control the jailbait surrounding him. Dale tightened his grip on the baseball bat. He hated fuckers like this. Hated them.

Mr. Hall stood with his back to Dale, arms crossed, legs spread apart. Occasionally he yelled something at a fat boy who couldn't run as fast as the others.

Dale walked up and nudged Hall's spine hard with the bat.

"What the hell?" Hall said. When he spun around, Dale lifted the bat onto his shoulder, a gesture the coach would surely understand. "Hey, pal," Hall said, and he took a step back. The joggers came to a stop. "What's the problem?" Hall asked.

"I'm Jainey's father," Dale said. Hall nodded, and Dale swung once at Hall's head, stopping shy of his ear. "Don't tell me, shithead. Let me guess. This is how you get your rocks off, making these poor kids do things they can't do. Is that it?"

"She climbed a rope," Hall said. "She fell. Accidents happen. I feel bad about it, but it was an accident."

"The fuck," Dale said. "I want to see you *climb that rope. I want to see* you *have an accident."*

Hall smiled and looked down at his tennis shoes, but Dale swung again, clipping the crown of the man's head this time, causing Hall to wobble. He struck him with just enough force to show he meant business. He could still hear the rush of his own blood, all the pressure points throbbing. Together, Dale and Mr. Hall walked over to the rope. The kids followed at a respectful distance.

"You really want me to do this?" Hall asked.

"You bet your ass I do," Dale said, and then an odd thing happened: his vodka-fueled adrenaline temporarily waned, and Dale, distracted, became entranced by the strange familiarity of the gymnasium: its cafe-

teria tables, each a primary color, planted inside the walls like old-time Murphy beds; the humming fluorescent bulbs overhead; the blue floor made of thin but dense rubber. This ebb lasted only a second or two, and when Dale's adrenaline returned, it came back with the force of a heart brought miraculously back to life, a surge of power unlike anything Dale had ever felt before.

As Mr. Hall reached for the rope, Dale swung the bat and hit the man's head—hard enough to bring him to his knees. He swung again, this time leaving Hall splayed across the mat and looking like a grown man about to make a snow angel. Blood trickled from his ears and mouth. Dale was dimly aware of a noise, but he couldn't identify what it was or where it was coming from. He raised his bat again to deliver one final blow when he noticed two slits in the rubber mat. "What the . . . ? No. It can't be." He crouched to look. He pulled a Swiss Army knife from his pocket and then removed the tiny stainless-steel tweezers.

Dale sunk the tweezers into the first gash, squeezed, and retrieved a tooth from the mat. "Look," he said to no one in particular. He repeated the procedure again with the second gash, extracting the other tooth. "These are my daughter's," he said. He stood and held the teeth out on his palm for everyone to see. "These are Jainey's teeth," he said. "Look!"

Dale tucked them into his pocket, along with his knife. And then the noise he couldn't at first identify came into sharp focus: it was the sound of children screaming. It was as though Dale had been standing at the far end of a tunnel, hearing only the reverberations of noise, but now that he was getting ready to leave, it was as if he had stepped up to the tunnel's opening and heard the actual noise itself.

He was about to ask what was wrong when a blow from behind knocked him to the mat. The first pain he felt was the gritty rawness along his chin from the impact of hitting the ground. He thought, What the hell kind of kid has *that* much strength? *but then he heard a man's voice in his ear: "Don't move, you son of a bitch. You hear me?" It was the janitor.*

Before the full weight of what any of this meant began to sink in, Dale O'Sullivan experienced a moment of sober clarity, and he realized that his life from here on out would never again be the same, that the bottomless anger he'd been feeling would soon be replaced by something else. Something darker. Not only darker but sadder. Something permanent, he feared.

Summer 2004

NOT ONCE DURING THE TWO MONTHS SINCE HER DEPARture did Charlie hear a word from Petra. Two months and nothing. It was mid-July, and Charlie had begun to wander Iowa City like a man who'd seen the inside of a UFO but had been warned not to tell anyone about it. He was simultaneously focused and distracted: focused on Petra, nothing *but* Petra, but his thoughts about Petra—his memories of her and the various questions that now roared through his head—all came at once, a tsunami of Petras, so powerful and all-consuming that he couldn't separate one thought from another.

Monday, on his way to work, Charlie stepped off a curb and was almost flattened by a city bus. Someone had pulled him back at the last second. Everyone waiting to cross the street gasped, but Charlie was barely conscious of what had happened. The bus, however, was only one of many things he no longer registered as he himself passed like a ghost through the day's twenty-four seemingly endless hours.

Sluggo, the security guard, stopped Charlie on his way inside and told him a joke about a traveling salesman and a farmer's daughter, the punchline of which had something to do with a barn, a rubber chicken, and a corncob pipe. At some point during the joke, Charlie had quit paying attention, distracted by the memory of his very first day at NTC. It was the day he couldn't find Petra and ended up hanging around the oil drum with Jacob Bartuka and Hastings. Had Petra begun seeing Akshay Kapoor as early as that? It was possible, he supposed, that Petra knew Akshay Kapoor before they'd even started working at NTC. Perhaps Akshay had taken the job to be closer to Petra.

“Look, look,” Sluggo whispered. He motioned toward Fred, Charlie’s new team leader, who walked past Charlie and Sluggo without saying a word. Sluggo said, “Know what I call him? Mr. Shit-Don’t-Stink. You like that?”

Charlie snickered. Fred was a twenty-something goateed bastard who’d recently earned a master’s in Evaluation and Testing. Fred and Charlie were probably the same age, but Fred made it clear that he was pretty special—far more special than Charlie would ever be.

Sluggo said, “I knew guys like that back when I was on the force.”

The force? Charlie thought. *Who is this guy? Obi-Wan Kenobi?* “Oh-oh. The *force,*” Charlie said. “You were a *cop.*”

“A *police officer,*” Sluggo corrected.

Charlie, having been reprimanded, said, “I better get to work,” but Sluggo wasn’t done.

“Thirty years with the Sex Offender Unit,” Sluggo said. “Omaha PD. I’ve seen more sicko shit than any one person should ever have to see.”

“I can imagine,” Charlie said.

“I doubt it,” Sluggo fired back, but then he let it go. Was the guy bipolar? Did he need medication? He leaned close to Charlie and, in a conspiratorial voice, whispered, “You run into any problems in there, you let me know, hear? Us good guys, we need to stick together.”

What kind of problem? Charlie wondered. And why was Sluggo whispering? “Will do,” Charlie whispered back.

Charlie’s new group scored twelfth-grade essay tests. Some of his old fellow scorers, like the Ghoul, were also in the group, but there were new scorers, too. It was Charlie’s first all-male group, which meant more deviousness. A couple of recent law school graduates had devised a foolproof way to boost the group’s reliability. Whenever an answer lent itself to more than one possible score, the scorer rolled his chair from person to person, under the guise of consulting about the test criteria, and asked if anyone had seen this particular answer. The student answer would simply be referred to by a unique phrase that appeared somewhere in it.

"Did you see the 'shit hole' essay?"

"Shit hole?"

"Yeah. The student keeps calling his school a shit hole."

"Oh yeah. Yeah, yeah. I gave that one a four."

"Really? A *four?* I was thinking of giving it a two."

"No way. It's definitely a four. Read it again."

"Naw. I'll take your word for it."

And so it went. Reliability had never been higher. Everyone in the group, except for the Ghoul, participated. The head supervisor had even come over to congratulate them and take a group photo. "You guys are amazing," he said. "A regular Dream Team!" Charlie started feeling the swell of pride in his chest—*We ARE the Dream Team,* he thought—until he remembered that they were cheating. But what did any of it matter anyway? NTC cooked the numbers, so why couldn't the scorers cook them as well? It's either us or them, Charlie thought. And fuck them.

Charlie read a dozen essays that morning without a hitch. Some were sincere but dull attempts to answer the question. Others were only two words long: "Blow me." Charlie liked these best; they were the easiest to score.

But then came the thirteenth essay. From its first few sentences, there was something distinctly different about it.

I don't know who reads these things and I can't imagine what kind of sad life you must have but let me tell you a little bit about myself. My name's Jainey O'Sullivan, and when I was given an IQ test years ago I blew everyone else out of the water, but something's happened lately in that I don't care anymore.

Charlie's heart sped up. The pulse in his neck throbbed. *Yes, yes,* he thought. *Go on!* And on she went. She talked about driving her brother's shitty car. She talked about a comic strip she drew called Lloyd the Freakazoid. She talked about trying to escape her own skin. She speculated on what Charlie might look like, the monocle he wore, his desperate need for a blowjob. She was wrong about the monocle, but everything else was pretty much a bull's eye.

At first Charlie couldn't put his finger on what it was about this essay, in particular, that called out his name, but then it came to him: the voice. A number of essays addressed him personally but only in a general way—"You loser," "You scum bucket," "You asswipe"—but there had never been an essay like this one. The voice here was intimate, personal; she was speaking to him and him alone.

Charlie couldn't stop grinning. He knew this girl. He knew her and she knew him. But then came the lowering of the boom. She wrote,

Someone killed my art teacher, and I'm afraid they're after me now. I can't help thinking something terrible's about to happen. But maybe worse than what's going to happen is that no one will care. I'll be dead, and that'll be that.

Charlie put his forefinger to the computer screen and ran it under her words. He read them again.

NTC had a policy that required you to alert your team leader about any answer that might indicate suicidal tendencies. There did not exist, however, any official policy regarding what to do when a student suspected someone was out to kill her. Charlie'd seen tests that put forth idle threats—"This test is so boring, maybe I'll just kill myself"—and he'd let them slide, but this was the first time the threat came from someone other than the student.

Charlie printed a copy of the essay and brought it to his team leader.

"Hey, Fred," he said. "I think we've got a Code Red here. It's not your typical Code Red, though." Charlie tried handing over the essay, but Fred wouldn't look away from his computer.

"Put it in the bin," Fred said. "I'll get to it in a sec." After Charlie set it down, Fred looked up and said, "Oh, hey. Your reliability is amazing, Charlie. It's higher than anyone's. But you need to score faster. You're falling behind." He tapped the computer screen with the eraser on his pencil, indicating the statistical proof.

Charlie nodded. He said, "Okey-doke." Whatever slack Charlie had been willing to afford Fred dissolved into a nasty little puddle of resentment. *Mr. Shit-Don't-Stink,* Charlie thought. *You'd better not slip up or your days'll be numbered around here.*

Back at his workstation, he read the girl's essay again. *I can't imagine what kind of sad life you must have,* she'd written. Who was this girl? Charlie wondered. Who was she, and how did she know so much?

When Petra first left him, Charlie sent one e-mail after another to her AOL account. Since Charlie also used AOL, he could monitor when she opened his e-mails, and he could sit anxiously waiting for her replies. His first e-mails were short: "Dear Petra: Where are you? Love, Charlie." She read these promptly but did not reply. His next e-mails became longer, more involved. Some began, "It seems strange that things have come to this," or "My dearest Petra, my love, what in the world are you thinking?" or, simply, "Please!" Some went on for a thousand words. Petra deleted all of these without reading them. By the fiftieth or sixtieth e-mail, Petra had blocked Charlie from sending any mail to her at all. Each time Charlie tried sending one, a box appeared on his screen: "This member is currently not accepting e-mail from your account."

"No!" Charlie yelled. "No! No! You can't do this to me!"

Tonight, Charlie did a Google search for Petra Petrovich. There were only two entries. The first was a book review she'd written for an online film theory journal.

> *You Commie Bastard: A New Historicist Look at the Portrayal of Russians in American Cinema* by Dr. Laurence Schoenhorn. A Review by Petra Petrovich.

It was funny how her name alone, a collection of letters from the alphabet—nothing but squiggles, when you got right down to it—could alter his body's physiology. His breath became shallow; his palms were sweating. The second entry was for Petra's participation on a panel titled "The Commercialization of Russian Cinema—Or: Hey, You Just Sunk My Battleship Potemkin!"

Charlie sat in front of the computer with Petra's name entered into a search engine and hit the refresh button every few minutes, as if Google had a satellite capable of tracking her every move. Charlie searched his own name. Of the over eight billion Web sites Google checked, there were 912 hits for Charlie Wolf, but none of those Charlie Wolfs was him. For all practical purposes, Charlie was off everyone's radar.

Charlie refused to type in Akshay Kapoor's name. He feared that doing so would bring the man to life, whereas now Akshay remained an abstraction, a *name,* but nothing else. He feared that the Kapoor family was Indian royalty, that Akshay was a prince, heir to billions. Or, worse, that Akshay Kapoor was nobody special. In truth, it didn't matter who Akshay Kapoor was. Whatever Charlie learned about the man was bound to be bad news because Charlie would find a way to spin the information to his own detriment. He'd find a way to torture himself. That was the nature of heartbreak, and Charlie wasn't strong enough to rise above it.

First thing the next morning, Charlie walked over to Fred's bin and looked inside. The girl's essay was still there, untouched. Fred remained at his computer, generating charts and graphs, oblivious even to Charlie's presence.

Each test was coded and, though it would be difficult, could be traced back to a specific classroom, in the event of an emergency. At that point, a teacher could be called in to identify the handwriting. In this essay, however, the student had already identified both herself and where she lived. Jainey O'Sullivan from Burbank, Illinois. Clearly, she was asking for help, making it easy for them to find her, but now it was up to NTC to follow up.

Charlie left his cube and walked over to Human Resources.

"Mary? Do you have an atlas?"

Mary, head of Human Resources, was the only person in the entire building who wasn't a part-time or temp worker. She eyed Charlie with suspicion—*What's he doing away from his computer terminal? Why isn't he busy scoring tests?*—but finally handed over a battered road atlas.

Burbank was a southwest suburb of Chicago, bordering the city proper. Charlie'd never heard of it. Not that Charlie'd heard of many Chicago suburbs. He was from Des Moines. Chicago might as well have been a city in Paraguay.

"Mary, we have offices in Chicago, don't we?"

"Warehouses, mostly."

"Do you think they have any openings?"

"They always have openings," Mary said. "Filing jobs. Things like that. Thinking about transferring?" She smiled at Charlie, as if to say, *Of course you're not; you're a lifer; admit it.*

"Can we take care of the paperwork from here?" Charlie asked.

"Are you serious?" Mary narrowed her eyes. Her attitude shifted from mild condescension to wariness. One of the primary criteria for hiring scorers—perhaps the only criterion—was his or her predictability. If you threw a bone, the scorer would chase it. And this was Mary's talent: finding those who would do as told, those who weren't likely to stray. But now that one of her faithful dogs had turned, Charlie could see a hint of fear in Mary's eyes, the caution in her moves. There was probably nothing more unsettling to someone in Mary's position than the consistent worker who showed signs of inconsistency.

Charlie carried the paperwork for the transfer back to his cube. He removed the girl's essay from the bin, photocopied it for himself, folded it twice, and stuck it into his back pocket. NTC had a strict policy that nothing was supposed to leave the building—no tests, no test answers—but it wasn't as though anyone ever searched Charlie on his way out. Furthermore, he could count on Sluggo to watch his back. Jainey O'Sullivan's essay would leave the building, and no one would be the wiser.

THE LYCANTHROPE was a man in disguise. At first glance, you saw Osama bin Laden, but once you knew that George W. Bush was underneath, you realized that Osama's mouth was really George's. The eyes and ears belonged to George, too. The fake nose, the fake beard, the wig, the long robe, the turban: these were what made you think it was Osama.

In order to squeeze *The Lycanthrope* into her closet, Jainey had to stuff most of her clothes under her bed. Before shutting the closet door, Jainey took one last look at his plaster head, admiring Mrs. Grant's attention to the tiniest of details, like George W. Bush's misshapen eyebrows, but what really impressed her was the accuracy of his dark rodent eyes. It was a testament to Mrs. Grant's skill as an artist that she could capture not only arrogance but fear in those two ominous orbs.

"I dub thee Osama W. Bush!" Jainey said and shut the door.

From downstairs came her mother's shrill fire-in-a-movie-theater voice. "Jainey!" she yelled. "You've got company!"

"Who is it?" Jainey yelled back

"How the hell should I know *who?* Some *boy.*"

"Send him up!"

The visitor turned out to be her tall and gangly ex-boyfriend, Alex. He was wearing a brown work shirt with a Brookfield Zoo patch sewed on the chest.

"Ah! Mr. Licks," Jainey said. "And how do you do, sir?"

Alex cringed. "Why are you always so weird?"

Jainey shrugged. "Still dating Beth Ann Winkel?"

"We were never *dating,*" Alex said. "We were, you know, just *seeing* each other."

"*Screwing* each other, you mean."

"Hey! Did I say that?" Alex sighed and plopped down on the bed. Jainey had to admit that she was still attracted to him, even though he smelled like a zoo. It was a smell that was both revolting and compelling. Jainey's father used to drive her and Ned to the zoo, and on a day with only the slightest of breezes, you could smell the stink of the animals long before you reached the zoo's front gate. One whiff, and it was as if you were already sitting next to a fly-swatting ape or walking past the hippo's sludgy pond.

Jainey sat next to Alex. "So . . ." she said. "What brings you to *Chez* O'Sullivan?"

"I thought you might want to hear how my summer's going."

"Okay," Jainey said. "How's your summer going?"

Alex, looking unusually sincere, began telling Jainey about Maggie the Orangutan, how Maggie had been overweight, how her skin had been dry and cracked, and how she'd been having problems digesting her food—that is, until the zoo decided to give her an extreme makeover! Now, eighty-three pounds lighter, with cleared-up skin and revitalized hair, Maggie was a new ape with a whole new outlook on life.

"She used to be sluggish and unfocused," Alex said, "but not anymore."

When Alex moved on to the zoo's new hedgehogs, Jainey reached over and unbuttoned his shirt. This, after all, was the real reason he'd come over. Sex. And this was how it had always happened between them. Alex would show up under the guise of telling her something that Jainey couldn't give a rat's rump about, and then Jainey would start undressing him while he talked, maybe even go down on him before he'd finished telling his story.

And so, mere minutes later, Jainey lay under her grunting ex-boyfriend, unable to distract herself from his sour-sweet smell. He'd learned a few new techniques since their last time together. He pulled way out—sometimes all the way out—and then hesitated before thrusting himself back inside, hard. Had Beth Ann taught him this?

For the last few minutes of sex, during which Alex frantically pumped away on top of her, Jainey stared up at the ceiling fan. The bed springs creaked, a kind of *Psycho* getting-stabbed-in-the-shower squeak. Between the flickering fan blades, she noticed what appeared to be a hole in the spackled ceiling and then, inside the hole, what appeared to be an eye staring down at her. An *eye.* Was Ned, her brother, watching her?

Jainey was about to nudge Alex, ask him to hold on a sec, but then he came and rolled off her. It had happened so fast, his rolling off, that Jainey was left spread-eagled on the bed, naked and open for anyone to see, especially her brother, if it was indeed his eye she saw inside the hole. Quickly, she swaddled herself in a thin cotton bedsheet.

"You should go," Jainey said to Alex.

"You sure?"

"I need to take a shower," Jainey said.

"Oh." He slipped back into his underwear, pants, work shirt. He tucked the shirt in. "If you ever want to come visit me at the zoo," he said, "Thursdays are free." He thought about this. "I *think* Thursdays are free. Maybe it's Wednesdays."

"I'll keep that in mind," Jainey said.

After Alex let himself out, Jainey looked up at the flickering fan blades again, but the eye was gone. In its place was plaster, thick goopy swirls of it.

Jainey tiptoed into the hall and removed a broom from the closet. Back in her bedroom, she turned off the fan, barely breathing while the blades came to a stop. She took the broom handle, lifted it above her head, and poked the part of the ceiling where she had seen the eye. The ceiling, at the exact point, easily gave in. A funnel of plaster served as a plug. Since it was wider at the top than the bottom, Jainey herself could not remove it, but Ned could. It rested comfortably inside the hole. "Oh my God," Jainey whispered. It was true then: her brother had been watching her. "Freak," Jainey said. For a moment, she thought she was going to be sick, but she managed to stave it off by thinking about something else. She raised her broom and, picturing Maggie the Orangutan, began poking the rest of the ceiling.

Downstairs, Jainey grabbed a cold Pop-Tart. She wasn't hungry, but she ate it. Her mother was sitting in the living room, wearing only a terry-cloth robe and blue fuzzy slippers. The TV was on but so was the MUTE button. It was two in the afternoon.

"Who was that boy?" she asked.

"Alex."

"Why did he smell so bad?"

"He works at Brookfield Zoo."

"Oh really?" Her mother perked up.

Jainey instantly regretted having mentioned the zoo. Jainey's mother loved talking about the past, how much better and more interesting the South Side *used* to be, and this was all the woman needed, the mere mention of a local landmark. Jainey could see it coming, too, the way her mother leaned back in her recliner, feet propped up, and lit a cigarette. After the first puff, she barked out a derisive half-laugh: *Heh!* And then the endless litany of places and memories would begin: "Did I ever tell you about Korvette's? It was a department store at the corner of 87th and Cicero? I saw Tiny Tim there when I was four years old. He pulled out this little ukulele and played 'Tiptoe Through the Tulips.' Did I ever tell you about Burbank Records? It was on the corner of 79th and Austin? An album would set you back only three dollars and ninety-nine cents. Imagine!" It was always the corner of *something* and *something*, and the old place was always better than the new place.

She sucked for a good long while on her cigarette. "When I was your age," she said, filling the entire room with smoke, "we used to take trips to the zoo and then at night we'd all go to the Sheridan Drive-In for a movie. Imagine! A drive-in movie theater in Burbank! It was right there on the corner of 79th and Harlem. And what's there now? A strip mall! Good God." She snorted in disgust. "I saw *Easy Rider* there. First movie I ever saw. I saw *The Poseidon Adventure* there, too. Gene Hackman, Shelley Winters." She sighed, shook her head. It was like listening to an aging actress talk about the golden era of Hollywood. Whenever her mother slipped into one of these moods, Jainey'd grit her teeth and think about other things. Explosions. Natural disasters. How the universe might have begun. Anything loud enough to drown out her mother.

"Did I ever tell you about Old Chicago?" she asked. "It was this indoor amusement park in Bolingbrook. Or was it Romeoville? That's funny, I can't remember now."

"I need to go," Jainey said.

Her mother snuffed out her cigarette. She shot Jainey a look that said, *You disrespectful little brat,* but then she nodded. *Go,* the nod said. *Scat.*

Jainey lay in bed, trying to listen to a David Gray CD, but her brother's stereo pounded an endless stream of Megadeth, drowning out Gray's Irish lilt. The battle between Megadeth and David Gray reminded Jainey of the time Matt Tatlinger, the school bully, tripped Thomas Carrier and then pinned him down for a good pummeling. Thomas Carrier was the most sensitive boy Jainey had ever met, a sweet boy who wanted to be a movie star but was too shy to try out for the school plays. Megadeth's insistent thrumming over David Gray was not unlike Matt's bony fist repeatedly hitting Thomas's soft, pink face. Ka-POW, Ka-POW, Ka-POW.

Jainey'd had enough. No one wanted to listen to Megadeth. No one! She walked into the hallway, grabbed the rope for the ceiling hatch that opened up into a rickety ladder, and gave it a good tug. Music poured out with such force, Jainey wouldn't have been surprised to find the actual members of Megadeth upstairs performing a private concert for Ned. For dramatic effect, she stomped up each step, prepared to read her brother the riot act.

The attic was pitch black and the heat was unbearable, but what nearly stopped Jainey from entering at all was the smell. For a few seconds it smelled like stinky cheese, but then another smell came rolling toward her. Jainey couldn't even begin to imagine what it was. A dead horse? A dozen pairs of sour shoes? A pile of poop cooking on a charcoal grill? Jainey's eyes watered. How could her brother *live* up here? She reached around until she found the string for the overhead bulb. When she pulled it, the room lit up.

Ned O'Sullivan, wearing his father's camouflage army uniform, stood in the far corner of the attic. He was pointing a loaded crossbow at Jainey. His face was painted green and black to match his clothes. The music—suffocating, brain-damaging—continued to throb.

"Jainey?" he yelled over Megadeth. "Is that you?"

"Jesus Christ, Ned, what're you doing?" She wasn't sure whether to raise her hands in surrender or scold him. What she did was fall to her knees. She couldn't catch her breath. It was as though she were trying to breathe through the world's narrowest straw.

Ned put down the crossbow and walked over to her. "You shouldn't be up here," he said, lifting Jainey into a sitting position. "This is where I pray."

"You don't even believe in God," Jainey said.

"Things change. Besides, I'm closer to God up here than you are down there." Ned pressed his mouth up against her ear and said, "Listen. From now on, the attic is off limits. Understood?"

Jainey nodded. With that, she began her shaky descent down the ladder. Shortly after Ned pulled the hatch shut, the music stopped. It was an unreal moment, the entire house deathly quiet after so much noise, and for a short time afterward, Jainey wasn't so sure that her own heart, which had fallen in sync with the pounding bass drum, hadn't stopped as well.

ONLY A FEW DAYS after his formal request, Charlie's transfer to Chicago was approved. He didn't want to lose his apartment in Iowa City, in case things in Chicago didn't go well, so he paid several months' rent in advance, using leftover money from his student loan, and he asked the woman who lived across the hall to keep an eye on things.

The night before his final day at NTC, Charlie drove to an adult bookstore near the railroad tracks. Once Charlie realized he was moving to Chicago, he began to think of ways to settle his score with Fred the team leader. The solution eventually came to him, but it would require Sluggo's unwitting help, and though Charlie knew that Sluggo wouldn't have minded watching Mr. Shit-Don't-Stink go down in flames, Charlie felt bad that he couldn't let Sluggo in on the plan itself.

Charlie'd never been inside such a store before, and he was stunned, upon entering, by the pegboard wall display of latex penises. What was he expecting? Barnes & Noble? A Parisian café with people like Henry Miller and Anaïs Nin lounging about, sipping cappuccinos and admiring Picasso nudes? Some of the penises were so large that Charlie initially mistook them for flesh-colored nightsticks. There were battery-operated vaginas, too. Did people actually use these for pleasure, or were they gag gifts meant to scare friends?

Charlie held up a box with a rubber-molded vagina inside and asked the clerk, "Batteries come with this?"

He was trying to be funny, but the clerk didn't crack a smile. Apparently, it wasn't the first time he'd been asked. "Batteries sold separate," he said. "The Quick Stop across the street sells batteries. They'll ream you, though."

Charlie felt himself clench. He was sorry he asked. He brought up to the counter a hardcore gay pornographic magazine with glossy photos of nearly every imaginable sexual position. It was exactly what he needed to bring his plan to fruition.

Charlie stayed awake all night, cutting off the heads and arms of guys in a *Soldiers of Fortune* magazine he'd bought earlier that day. He then pasted those heads and arms onto the various bodies inside the skin mag. The result was an unnerving collage of burly machine gun–toting men doing it every which way with other burly machine gun–toting men.

The next morning, Charlie felt energized in a way he hadn't felt since Petra's departure, this despite not getting any sleep. At work, he scored the essay tests accurately for the first time, using his own criteria rather than NTC's. It was the first time he felt the kids were getting a fair shake. Not surprisingly, his reliability plummeted.

"I realize this is your last day here," Fred warned, "but it's not in your best interest to screw up our statistics. It's clear you're not even reading them."

Charlie didn't argue. He waited until Fred and everyone else had gone on break before slipping the now-altered porn magazine inside Fred's desk drawer.

At the end of the day, after telling everyone goodbye, Charlie pulled Sluggo aside.

"You know Mr. Shit-Don't-Stink?" Charlie asked.

Sluggo's grin vanished. He nodded. It was as if he'd known this moment would come sooner or later, and now that it was here, it was time to get serious.

Charlie lowered his voice: "Rumor has it, he keeps a Ziploc baggie of marijuana in his desk drawer. Now, I don't know if that's true or not, but he looks like a pothead to me."

The wheels inside Sluggo's big, bald head were starting to turn. "Mm hm," he said. "Mm hm, mm hm."

Charlie said, "Do me a favor, though. Don't tell anyone I told you. If it turns out not to be true, I don't want to be the one who, you know, made problems for some innocent guy." Charlie feigned inner turmoil. "You know, maybe I shouldn't have even said anything. Tell you what. Forget I mentioned it, okay?"

"You're a stand-up guy," Sluggo said. "You have a safe trip now, you hear?"

The two men shook hands.

Sitting in his car, Charlie watched Sluggo pull Mary of Human Resources aside. After chatting, the two walked briskly back into the sheet-metal building. When Charlie noticed that Fred was getting into the car next to his, he felt a moment's remorse. Fred owned a new VW Beetle; the complimentary flower arrangement still bloomed from its cupholder. "Ah, shit," Charlie said. Maybe he'd just wait until Fred drove away and then go confess to Sluggo. Putting the magazine inside Fred's drawer was a terrible thing to do, and Charlie, who wasn't at heart a malevolent person, could see that now.

Charlie honked his horn and waved at Fred, but when Fred saw who was honking, he wagged his head sadly and then gave Charlie the finger.

"Are you giving *me* the finger?" Charlie yelled. "*Me?*" Though everyone's windows were rolled up, Fred understood the question and nodded. Fred shrugged, then put his car in reverse, backed up, and zoomed away.

Charlie laughed. "Why, that little prick," he said. Well, well, well. So that's how it's gonna be! Maybe Fred's outburst was for the best, after all. Charlie could now wipe his hands clean of whatever remorse he was starting to feel. And as for Fred, well, perhaps the time had finally come for him to learn that his shit stunk just as much as, if not more than, everyone else's.

Nights alone in his apartment were the worst. This was when Charlie missed Petra the most. It was also when he realized how few people he knew in this world. It was strange, really, given all the billions of people on the planet, that he could count on one hand the people he cared enough to call friends. But even in the darkest hours of night, he didn't want to talk to any of them. It was Petra and Petra alone he wanted to talk to.

On his last night in Iowa City, Charlie finally broke down and plugged Akshay Kapoor's name into Google. He cringed, turning away from the computer screen during the 0.47 seconds it took for the results to appear, but then he slowly pivoted toward the screen to see what Google had yielded. It didn't take long for Google to suck Charlie into its evil whirlpool. Within seconds, Charlie was clicking link after link, learning everything he possibly could about the man. It was like a new form of interrogation, only without pliers or a blowtorch.

Akshay Kapoor was born in a small village in India. His father was a fisherman. His mother stayed home, raising eight children. Some of the information about his life came from biographical notes that were attached to essays he'd published; others were embedded in the essays themselves, like his essay about the connection between illness and poverty. Akshay wrote eloquently about the cause and effect of the two, seamlessly weaving anecdotes from his own life as a sickly child in India into the study.

Charlie had expected to taste the burning bile of rage, but the more he read, the more he had to admit that Akshay sounded like a decent man. He could see how Petra could fall for him. And how had he failed to make the obvious connection? Anton Chekhov had been a doctor, too. A writer *and* a doctor. Of course! It made perfect sense. Ironically, this realization gave Charlie hope. Petra was in love with the *idea* of Akshay, but once she spent serious time with him, living with his bad breath and bald spot, she would realize the truth: Akshay Kapoor was *not* Anton Chekhov. And since Charlie wasn't a substitute for anyone—Charlie was Charlie—Petra would realize her grave error and return to him.

Charlie, who'd never before tried his hand at creative writing, not even a silly love poem, walked to his closet and pulled out his dead father's old Smith-Corona typewriter. He plugged it in, turned it on, and rolled in the first sheet of paper. He had used the typewriter only a few times in the past, mostly to fill out job applications when he was in high school, but this was how he imagined real writers wrote: sitting at a typewriter, not a computer. He thought if he wrote something about Akshay Kapoor, maybe he'd better understand the man. What were the man's motives? What was his character? And so with only the barest of details to go on, Charlie started typing a short story. It wasn't a very good short story—Charlie recognized that almost immediately—but this didn't stop him from finishing it. He was, after all, a man possessed.

Akshay Kapoor and the Russian Beauty:
A Childhood in India
By Charlie Wolf

When Akshay Kapoor was a little boy of seven, he dreamed of meeting a Russian beauty, but in India, in the tiny village of K___, the chances of meeting a Russian beauty were as slim as finding an oyster with a pearl inside, and not just any pearl, either, but one the size of his tiny fist. Nonetheless, little Akshay could dream, and dream he did.

LABRADORS, according to a book about dogs that Jainey had stolen from Prairie Trails Library, were highly intelligent, loyal, and high-spirited. They craved human attention and needed to feel like they were part of the family, too.

Jainey ripped those pages from the book, stapled them together, and drove to the local pound to see if they had any yellow Labs. She showed the receptionist the photos, as if they were Wanted posters, but the pound had only a sweet-faced cockapoo, a ratty little terrier mix, and about a million scraggly cats.

Jainey drove all over the southwest side of Chicago, but she barely paid attention to the road. Ever since Mrs. Grant's mysterious death, she assumed that she herself was being followed, and there were nights when the same car would stay on her bumper for miles, or when an older man at a stoplight would look over at her and nod, as if to say, *We're on to you.* But lately her thoughts, always spiraling outward, kept returning to Labradors in general and, more specifically, to Striker.

Since reading the book Mariah had loaned her, Jainey hadn't been able to shake the grim fate of Striker at Ruby Ridge. The U.S. marshal had killed the poor dog when all it had done was warn the family of intruders. On March 1, 1996, the U.S. Marshals Service gave its highest award for valor to five U.S. marshals who participated in the Ruby Ridge seige. The man who shot Randy Weaver's son in the back and killed him received a medal. Arthur Roderick, dog murderer, received a medal, too. According to U.S. Marshals Service Director Eduardo Gonzalez, these five men were heroes, and the award was given for "their exceptional courage, their sound judgment in the face of attack, and their high degree of professional competence during this incident."

"Motherfuckers!" Jainey yelled. The very idea of Arthur Roderick, that son of a bitch, getting a valor medal made her blood boil.

Rounding the drive-thru at McDonald's, Jainey floored it, as if Mr. Arthur Roderick himself were in the parking lot, but instead of turning the wheel sharply to avoid the lamp pole in front of her, Jainey hit it dead-on.

You bastard, she thought. *Look what you've done to my car.* The front headlight was shattered, the fender accordion-shaped. Jainey prayed for Arthur Roderick to end up in Hell and spend his eternal afterlife getting chewed apart by pitbulls. Only then would poor Striker have his day in court.

THE DRIVE from Iowa City to Chicago took less than four hours, and Charlie arrived just as the sun was starting to set. It was hard to believe that only one day ago he'd been embroiled in the lives of Mr. Shit-Don't-Stink, Sluggo, and the Ghoul. Already his life in Iowa seemed like some bizarre and distant dream about a subterranean world full of modern-day scriveners sitting in front of endless rows of computer screens.

In the suburb of Burbank, where Jainey O'Sullivan presumably lived, Charlie pulled into Pompeii Inn's parking lot. Was this the right place? He examined the printout of the photo, then studied the hotel itself. The discrepancies were difficult to ignore. The photo showed a fountain outside, multicolored spotlights illuminating the building's façade, and a man wearing white gloves and a top hat greeting happy customers at the door. In truth, the fountain was cracked in half and inoperable, the outside lights were dim, and the only man greeting anyone was drunk.

Charlie eased himself from his car and carried his suitcase to the entrance.

"Bitch *took* it," the drunk man yelled at Charlie. "She *took* it."

Charlie nodded; he picked up his pace. He wondered what the woman had taken from the man. His wallet? His car? His dignity? Would this be Charlie in a few months, drunk and standing outside, shouting about Petra?

"Charlie Wolf," he told the night clerk, but the girl, who looked too young to be working legally, was watching a miniature TV behind the counter and hypnotized by whatever reality TV show was on. "*Wolf,*" Charlie repeated. "*Wolf.*"

The girl looked up, as if Charlie had barked at her, but then she gave him a magnetic key and told him his room number.

"Thank you." Charlie turned around, sizing up the lobby. Why Pompeii Inn was named Pompeii Inn was a mystery. The fact that the place lacked even cheesy Roman-themed wallpaper spoke to the management's absence of imagination. The interior's décor was from the early '80s. The place clearly hadn't been renovated since the photo had been taken. The bar's carpet had pink-and-blue swirls that may have once glowed in the dark but no longer did. Video games filled the bar's dark recesses. Squinting, Charlie recognized Tron, Ms. Pac Man, and Galaga, plus one dedicated to the rock band Journey. Charlie didn't enter the bar, but when he walked by, the machines let loose a series of electronic farts and belches, as if offering their low opinion of him.

Inside his room, Charlie collapsed across the bed. For two nights now, he'd barely slept at all. He was resolved to getting some serious sleep tonight, but after turning out the light and shutting his eyes, he lay awake for over an hour, listening to his heart thump. “Shit,” he said and turned the light back on. He was sleepy, so why couldn’t he sleep? He tried watching TV; he tried reading; he tried masturbating. Nothing worked. He was tired—he *wanted* to sleep—but whatever was supposed to make sleep possible refused to kick in. He found the bottle of Tylenol PM in his suitcase, and he washed down three pills, but two hours later he found himself hanging precariously between sleep and wide-awake panic.

“Son of a bitch,” Charlie said, sitting up. He turned on the light. He opened the Burbank phone book and found addresses for three O’Sullivans. He wrote them down and then ripped the city map from the book. This was why he’d come here, wasn’t it? To save some poor girl’s life? To come to her aid? What, he wondered, was he waiting for?

ALEX LAY ON TOP of Jainey, pumping and grunting, pumping and grunting. Jainey wanted to let herself go. Sex, after all, was one of the few times she could truly escape her persistently darkened thoughts. She could float outside her own body, the way the spirit, detaching after death, hovers above and thinks, *Hey, this is better than being alive.* Sex was life’s one and only truly magical experience: Houdini actually escaping his own skin. During the height of those transcendent moments, Jainey could even forgive Alex for the time he had spent with the rotten Beth Ann Winkel, but today Jainey couldn’t even relax. Alex might as well have been screwing a sheet of plywood, moving in and out of a knothole. Not that Alex noticed. He was blissfully unaware. But Jainey couldn’t stop staring at the point in the ceiling where Ned had been watching her, the hole that was now plugged up. She expected it to come unplugged at any moment. She expected to see plaster replaced by a watery eye.

On Jainey's bedside table was a can of Raid. This particular can had the capacity to kill hornets several yards away. Jainey was prepared to take care of the Peeping Tom problem; she was going to blind her brother. It would be his own damned fault, too.

The pumping slowed. Alex said, "What's that?" He motioned with his head to Jainey's hand. Her hand was clasped around the can.

"Raid," she said.

The pumping halted. "Raid? The bug killer?" he asked.

Jainey nodded.

"Why are you holding it?"

Jainey shrugged. Her fingers loosened their grip on the can. When she touched Alex's cheek, he smiled at her. The pumping resumed. Jainey pressed her fingertips into Alex's back, as if responding to his moves, but there was still the issue of her brother, his eye, the can of Raid, and how it would all finally come down to a split-second decision.

CHARLIE FOUND JAINEY at the first O'Sullivan address. He'd seen her peering out the window. Purple-and-green streaked hair. An old button-down shirt from the last rack of the Salvation Army. Worried eyes. He knew it was her the second he saw her. That was four hours ago. A boy had arrived in the meantime, but now he was leaving, standing in front of her house and tucking in the tail of his brown work shirt. He looked up one last time at Jainey's room before getting into his car and driving away. After he was gone, Jainey peered out her window again. Charlie slid down in his seat; he didn't want to scare her. "Who's following you?" he whispered. Somewhere, a dog started barking. Jainey squinted at the dark night. She lived in a two-story shotgun house with a dirt yard and a storage shed that looked about to implode. She walked away from the window. A few moments later, her bedroom light blinked off.

Charlie wasn't sure how best to approach her. What could he possibly say? *Hello! I was reading the essay you wrote for America's Report Card, and when I realized that your life was being threatened, I broke all company rules, found out where you lived, and decided to follow your every move!*

Charlie decided he would simply be the girl's protector from afar. He would make sure she didn't come to any harm. Any conscientious person would do the same.

Charlie was about to start his car when the attic light blinked on. There were no windows up there, only a vent the size of a small window, and the light, sliced into four slats, shone through. Was Jainey up in the attic now? The house was so small, Charlie couldn't imagine how anyone could actually fit up there. Charlie squinted. Was he seeing what he thought he was seeing? The vent appeared to be moving, not attached to the house anymore, just hovering in space. Then Charlie saw a hand on either side of it. Someone was removing the vent from the inside. The vent finally lowered, revealing a man wearing a camouflage T-shirt. Holding the vent as though it were a cafeteria tray, the man leaned further out the window, sucking in the air. Did Jainey know that a man was up there? Was this the same person who had killed Jainey's teacher?

Charlie's heart was thumping. He waited until the man reinserted the vent before driving back to Pompeii Inn and calling the police. He explained some of what he knew—that a girl might be in danger, that a man was hiding in the attic above her—but when the dispatch woman asked how he knew all of this, Charlie refused to answer.

"You have to trust me," he said.

"Would you like to leave your name?" she asked.

"No," Charlie said. "I'd really prefer not to."

The woman sighed; she'd heard it all before. The phone conversation was making one thing clear: Charlie was a piss-poor protector. Why hadn't he simply walked up to her house, knocked on her door, and asked her if she knew that someone was up in her attic? But what if she *did* know? What if someone lived up there? Then what?

"All right," the woman said. "We'll send a squad over there. But if we don't see anything unusual, we're probably not going to wake those poor people up. Understood?" There was a pause. "If we need to talk to you, you're staying at the Pompeii Inn, is that right?"

"How do you know that?" Charlie asked. He parted his curtains, looked outside for a police car.

"Caller ID," the woman said. "We'll be in touch."

The next morning, Charlie began his new job at NTC's Chicago branch. Charlie spent his first hour at work sorting a pile of test scores by the first digit of the student's ten-digit identification number. Ten neat piles, from zero to nine. Once completed, he was joined by nine more workers, each of whom took a pile and began sorting the *second* identification digit into ten more piles. And so on. It was a mindless, laborious task, and by the time he was sorting the fifth digit, his vision started to fade in and out.

The second half of Charlie's day was spent filing. He wandered endless rows of aluminum shelving units with a heavy stack of tests cradled in the crook of his arm. The job looked a lot easier than it actually was. His knees ached from repeatedly squatting for the bottom two shelves, his lower back hurt from bending over for the third and fourth shelves, and his arms were sore from reaching up to the top shelves. The hundreds of fluorescent lights buzzing overhead contributed to a nagging headache, and after eight long hours, the pain had turned into a full-blown atomic blast inside his skull, his eyes two red-hot fireballs swirling in their sockets.

At the very end of the day, Charlie was required to fill out a "Productivity Report," which calculated, based on how many files you *separated* (measured by the inch) and then how many files you *filed* (also measured by the inch), how productive you had been. No one ever reached or exceeded one hundred percent productivity. What was expected, however, was ninety percent or better.

Charlie, after working as fast as he possibly could, calculated only a fifty-two percent productivity percentage.

"Is this right?" he asked the calculator. "Is this *possible?*"

Charlie couldn't fathom why, in the year 2004, this sort of work was being done manually, anyway. Weren't all of these scores already stored in some computer bank, and couldn't the computer files be backed up? He felt like Bartleby the Scrivener. All he needed was a quill pen with a foot-long goose feather to complete the picture.

At the end of the day, his supervisor summoned him over for a little talk. Her name was Maggie Waushinski, and she spent the first part of the conversation telling vapid anecdotes about people she knew personally, perhaps even intimately, referring to them by their nicknames, as if she and Charlie traveled in the same social circle and their identities would be obvious. She quoted someone named Jair-Bear often and with reverence, as if he were Abraham Lincoln or Confucius, this despite the fact that what Jair-Bear had to say was never interesting or original.

"I see here," she finally said, "that you're barely above the fifty percent productivity range. Now, I don't expect you to hit ninety percent your first day, but this is pretty bad even for your first day."

"I know, I know," Charlie said, "but I honestly don't think I can work any faster."

Maggie narrowed her eyes. Her eyebrows had been plucked entirely off, replaced by two thick arches. From a distance, it looked as though someone had painted the letter "M" across her forehead. She looked down at a file—Charlie's file. She drummed her nails and then looked back up. "It's like Jair-Bear always says: 'Those who can, *do.* Those who can't, *teach.*'"

Charlie had no idea what the hell she was talking about.

Maggie says, "You have a master's degree, right?"

"Right."

"You plan on being, what, a *professor* or something?" She said *professor* the way a Nazi might say *Jew,* the way George Bush talked about *liberals:* it was that distasteful in her mouth.

"Actually, no," Charlie said. "I wasn't planning on it."

Maggie looked confused, as though she might have been holding the wrong file. She shrugged, took a deep breath, and said, "I'll give you another day or two to get your productivity percentage up, but if things haven't changed, we'll have to look at our other options. *Comprendez?*"

"Sure," Charlie said, nodding.

"No, no," Maggie Waushinski said. "*Com*-pren-*dez?*"

Did she think he was Hispanic? Charlie shrugged. "*Comprendez,*" he said.

WHEN I'M OLDER, Jainey thought, *I'll look back on this summer and think, oh, that was the summer everyone was beheaded.*

Every time Jainey walked past a TV, someone was either being beheaded or about to be beheaded. And if they weren't being beheaded, they were being blown up. Instead of the world stretching itself back into the shape it was in before 9/11, it had begun to balloon out to the point of nearly bursting.

Jainey sat in front of the TV all day long watching CNN. She wanted to turn it off—she could tell that the damage being done to her brain was irreversible—but the longer she watched, the less power she had to get off the couch. She even sat through interviews conducted by Larry King, a man who reminded her of a corpse that had been exhumed from a long-forgotten cemetery and then brought back to life with a billion watts of electricity. Every time

Larry King laughed, a shiver ran through Jainey, as if she were witnessing the cackle of some unholy being from the netherworld, and yet she couldn't muster the energy to turn him off.

When she finally fell asleep on the couch, CNN's pulse still beating like a living, breathing thing in the darkened room, Jainey dreamed that Burbank was under siege. Another country—she wasn't sure which—was attacking. Bombs fell from planes, leaving fountains of fire after each hit. And then her own house was hit, killing her mother and brother, leaving their bodies in bits and pieces. The house was totally leveled. Stripped of her loved ones and with no place to live, Jainey took to the streets with a machete, wanting revenge. Angry and crying, she searched for the enemy, ready to chop off his head. Any civilized person would do the same, she reasoned. After all, the enemy had come to her—not, as people might later prefer to believe, the other way around.

Two days later, rattled by all the gory dreams she'd been having, Jainey refused to watch any TV at all. That evening, she left the house and took stock of the Turd.

"What you need," she said, "is a little TLC."

She hosed down its rust. She drove to a gas station and filled the bald tires with fresh air. She reattached the rearview mirror to the window with Krazy Glue and then hung a deodorizer the shape of a pine tree around its neck.

"Look at you!" she said. "Now don't you feel better?"

She decided to pay Alex a surprise visit at Brookfield Zoo, but she got lost on her way. On Harlem Avenue, a few feet from the Eisenhower Expressway, the Turd overheated.

"Piece of shit!" Jainey yelled. "Ungrateful son of a whore!"

She leaned against the Turd, its hood popped open as if it were a giant hand greeting passersby: *Hi there!* Across the street loomed the Ferrara Pan Candy factory, the place where Lemon Drops, Red Hots, and Boston Baked Beans were made by the ton. Jainey loved the candy, but the building itself, with its old bricks and smokestack, was as ominous as the blacking factory she'd read about her sophomore year in a Dickens novel. This was one of the things Jainey liked to do: focus on an image, a wisp of fog, say, or a church spire, and then imagine that she was living in a different time and place altogether. Leaning against the Turd, she transported herself to Victorian London, and when she heard footsteps approaching, she braced herself for something awful to happen. *It's him!* she thought. *It's the Ripper!* She turned to look, and with the headlights of a dozen cars lighting him up from behind—headlights that just as easily could have been flickering gas lamps—the man walked toward her like some shadowy figure out of *Oliver Twist*.

"Who are you?" she called to him in a faintly British accent. "Do you mean to harm me, good sir?"

"What?" the man asked. When he came into view, she saw that he was wearing a plaid short-sleeved shirt tucked into khaki shorts. He was only a little older than her imaginary Victor. He said, "Hurt you? No, I thought maybe you needed a jump."

His car, she noticed, was parked behind hers, its hazard lights blinking. "Oh," she said, dropping the British act. "I don't know what's wrong with it. A light started blinking and then a bunch of green junk shot out of it. I can't get the smell out of my nose."

"Radiator fluid," the man said. "Your car's overheated. You'll need to get it towed."

Jainey turned and kicked one of the tires. "Piece of shit," she said.

"I can drive you to a gas station," the man said.

"I don't have money to get it towed," Jainey said. "I guess we can just leave it here for the next sucker who wants it." Given the look on the man's face, Jainey might as well have walked down the plank of a flying saucer and announced, "We come in peace!" His look made her so uneasy that she pointed at the factory across the street and, hoping to defuse the tension, said, "That's where they make Red Hots."

The man nodded; he didn't even turn to look. "Tell you what. I'll drive you to a gas station," he said, "and then I'll pay to have your car towed. We'll see what's wrong with it. Maybe it's just a hose that needs replacing. I can pay for that, too. You can pay me back when you get some money. Or not. But we can't just leave it here."

Jainey hated to admit it, but the idea of abandoning the Turd had turned her stomach. She loved the Turd. She did. Truly. She hadn't really realized it until this very moment. It was like adopting a crack baby. What's the new mother to do—give up the baby because it won't stop crying? Of course not. You nurture it. In the Turd's case, you bought it a new hose, if that's what it needed.

"Okay," Jainey said. "Let's go then."

The stranger's car had Iowa plates, but the import of this information didn't register until the car was moving with her buckled into the seat beside him. Didn't serial killers travel to other states to abduct their victims? Wasn't that what Jeffrey Dahmer did, drive down to Illinois from his ghoulish lair in Wisconsin to lure back young boys? Was the man next to her a *cannibal?*

At the next stop light, he held out his hand and said, "I'm Charlie, by the way. Charlie Wolf."

"Jainey," Jainey said. "So! You're from Iowa." She wanted him to know that *she* knew that he wasn't from around here.

"Home of Herbert Hoover!" Charlie pitched in.

"He was one of the fat presidents, wasn't he?"

"Pretty fat, I guess. Sure."

When the light turned green, Jainey asked, "So what're you doing here? All the way from Iowa?"

"Work. I scored standardized tests back in Iowa, but they have an office here, too. This is where they store everyone's test scores."

Jainey sat up. "America's Report Card?"

"Exactly."

"Wow. So you must be like a genius or something."

Charlie laughed. "A monkey could do what I do," he said. "I'm not kidding."

"Don't insult the monkey." Jainey waited a beat before adding, "It's a joke."

"Oh." Charlie wheeled into a BP station that had a garage. "Here we are," he said.

"Well, it's about time!" Jainey said. She said this as a joke, too—it was a pitch-perfect imitation of her impatient mother—but Charlie didn't laugh. He opened the door to get out. Jainey, studying him under the car's dome light, realized that he was the saddest man she'd ever seen. She wanted to reach over and hug him. She wanted to tell him everything was going to be okay, but he had already gotten out and shut the door. And besides, *would* everything be okay? Would it really?

Three hours later, the Turd was fixed. The problem turned out to be only a broken hose, as Charlie had predicted, but the mechanic gave them a checklist of other necessary repairs that would have required rebuilding the car from scratch.

The mechanic had streaks of grease across his face, like war paint. He said, "You want my opinion? Junk it."

In the parking lot, walking to their respective cars, Jainey said, "Opinions are like assholes."

Charlie nodded. "Everyone's got one," he said.

"And they all stink," Jainey added.

Before they reached their cars, Charlie turned to Jainey and said, "You don't have to pay me anything, okay?"

"Okay," Jainey said.

"But listen. The mechanic's probably right. Something else is going to happen to it, so let me give you my number. That way, if something *does* happen and I'm around, I can come help. Or I can *send* help. You shouldn't be standing at the side of a busy road without a plan." Charlie pulled a pen and a business card from his shirt pocket. On the back of the card he scribbled a number.

"Pompeii Inn," Jainey said, reading the front of the card. "That's right by *my* house." She looked up and said, "It's kind of a dump, though, isn't it?"

"I booked it online," he said. "Paid for a month in advance. I didn't realize how far it was from my job."

"Holy crap, you're staying there for a *month?*"

Charlie nodded.

"I hope you don't get robbed," Jainey said. She tucked the card into her back pocket. "Maybe we'll bump into each other again, especially now that we're neighbors."

"I hope so," Charlie said.

AFTER HELPING Jainey with her car, Charlie drove back to Pompeii Inn and, sitting on the edge of his bed, called directory assistance.

"Do you have a number for a Petra Petrovich?" he asked. "Or a *P.* Petrovich?"

"I'm sorry, sir," the operator said. Before she could hang up, Charlie asked for an Akshay or an A. Kapoor, but again he had no luck.

Charlie shut his eyes. He still couldn't sleep. He'd driven past a hypnotist's office last night during one of his wanderlust bouts of insomnia, and though he'd initially thought of going as a joke, the idea was actually starting to appeal to him. He opened his eyes and sat bolt upright. "Fuck," he said.

Charlie found the hypnotist's number in the phone book. He called, expecting a recording letting him know the hours of operation, but a woman answered. Grateful for someone to talk to, Charlie explained his situation—that he was new in town, that he couldn't sleep, that he had never been to a hypnotist.

"Can you come over now?" the woman asked.

"Now?" Charlie looked at the bedside clock. It was eleven p.m.

"Are you busy?" she wanted to know. "Is now a bad time?"

The office was on Cicero Avenue, right around the corner from Pompeii Inn—walking distance, really, but Charlie drove. It was dark, and Charlie was a stranger to the area. Besides, this was Al Capone territory. No telling what might happen to him.

The building that housed the hypnotist's office was brick with no windows—*a fire hazard*—information Charlie committed to memory in case the hypnotist fired up a cigarette or lit candles before putting him under. A bell jingled when he walked inside. The office was dimly lit, giving everything the fuzzy quality of a bad film-to-video transfer. He heard his name before he saw the woman who spoke it: "Charlie? Is that you?"

Charlie turned. A side door had opened, and there she stood—the hypnotist. He wasn't sure what to expect, for the only hypnotists he'd ever seen were on TV shows, and they were always older men with intense eyes who wore dark suits and had mustaches and trim pointed beards called Vandykes. Charlie rubbed his chin, as if he himself were sporting such a beard. "Yes, I'm Charlie."

The hypnotist smiled. Her name was Jill. She was in her mid-thirties. Five feet tall. She looked sleepy herself, as if she'd just woken from her own deep trance. She led Charlie to a room with even weaker lights. She motioned for him to sit in one of the overstuffed chairs. The only sound in the room was the ticking second hand of a battery-operated clock on the wall. A musty, water-soaked smell rose from the carpet. When he yawned, Jill said, "Good! Makes my job easier if you're already tired."

"Actually, that's the problem. I can't sleep anymore. I'm tired, but I can't fall asleep. I want to sleep—I'm sleepy—but I just can't seem to get there." Was he so sleepy that he was repeating himself? Was he already going under?

"Other problems?"

It hadn't occurred to him that they could work on more than one thing at a time. "I don't like public restrooms," he said without giving her question much thought.

"Meaning?"

"Meaning . . . I can't pee if someone else is in the same room." When he sat back, the cushion hissed, as if trying to get his attention: *pssssst.* Every object in the room—the clock, the carpet, his chair—seemed eerily alive. "I guess that's all," he said.

Jill nodded. She smiled. Her posture was semi-serious, especially the way one hand draped itself over the knotted fist of her other hand. "Good," she said. "I think we can do something about this. Are you afraid of germs?"

Charlie shook his head. "No. Nope. I can, you know, *go* if I'm the only one in there. But if someone else is in the restroom, forget it. Or if it's one of those one-person restrooms and someone's waiting outside the door for me, I can't do it." Why, he wondered, was he talking so much about peeing? He cleared his throat. "The real problem, though, is that I can't sleep."

Jill had dark, inviting eyes, and Charlie now saw the power of suggestion in them—the hallmark of any good hypnotist, he figured. He leaned forward slightly, staring deeper and deeper into those two pools of swirling tar. He hadn't really thought about it before, but the relationship between a hypnotist and a client was an intimate one. If this had been a date, he might have reached over and put a hand on her knee right about now.

Jill said, "I think what we need to do is find out *why* you can't sleep. As for your issues with public restrooms, it's possible you're repressing a memory. Something traumatic may have happened to you in a restroom when you were a child."

"I don't think so," Charlie said.

"But if you're repressing it," Jill said, "how would you know? Am I right?"

"Yeah, but . . ." Charlie began, and he wanted to tell her that he didn't believe in repressed memories, that it all seemed like fodder for talk shows and wannabe victims. He was about to say as much, but when he took in the whole of Jill and the sad, musty carpet smell that filled the air between them, he didn't want to disappoint her. "Well, maybe. Okay, I suppose it's possible."

"Good, good. What do you say? Shall we begin?"

After explaining to Charlie the nature of hypnotism and what was about to transpire, she leaned forward, so close that Charlie could feel the heat that she was generating and could smell her faint but distinct body odor, sweet and sour, not at all unpleasant. Human, he thought. There was nothing artificial about her. He liked that.

That was the last thing he remembered.

"It'll take more than one session," she said after he'd given the check to her. "I think this one was productive, but don't expect miracles. These things take time."

Charlie agreed. He shook her hand. He drove home, confident that he'd done the right thing.

Back in his room at Pompeii Inn, Charlie lay in bed about to doze off when he jumped awake with the irrational fear that he was being videotaped. There was a huge vent in the ceiling, unlike anything he'd ever seen before in a hotel room. Mounting a camera up there and then controlling it via some remote device would be a cinch. Charlie knew it was ridiculous, but he'd long harbored the unreasonable fear of ending up on someone's Web site, the victim of a voyeur cam. He wasn't sure why they would be interested in him, especially tonight. There was no market for streaming videos of tired men lounging in bed and eating potato chips. Even so, he stood on a chair and peered inside. He couldn't see anything, but that meant nothing in this day of microchips and cell-phone cameras.

Charlie, knocking dust from clothes, looked down and saw that his shirt was off by one button. "What the hell?" he muttered. The shirt had been buttoned correctly before he'd stepped into the hypnotist's office. He distinctly remembered straightening the shirt when he'd stepped out of his car. He had even looked down at the bottommost button when she asked him why he had come to see her. And he remembered touching it once with his forefinger, as if it were a talisman, before she put him under. There was only one logical conclusion: the hypnotist had seduced him.

AROUND MIDNIGHT, and with the Turd back in working order, Jainey drove to Mrs. Grant's condo. Jainey hadn't been there in a month, since she was afraid of getting caught. Fortunately, she'd managed to sneak out most of Mrs. Grant's important documents—tax returns, credit card invoices, grant applications—but she hadn't yet started the serious work of ripping up carpet, prying off paneling, and removing tile. She was certain that she would find hidden under surfaces the evidence she needed to implicate the government in Mrs. Grant's death. Jainey tried putting herself in Mrs. Grant's shoes—What would *she* do if she knew the government was out to kill her?—and it always came back to her writing a document and then hiding it in a secure location.

Jainey carried a crowbar up to the apartment. She unlocked the door and, stepping into total darkness, felt around for a light switch. It was darker than normal, and Jainey's fumbling took longer than usual, but she finally found the switch plate.

The furniture wasn't Mrs. Grant's furniture. The previously barren walls were now covered with photos. The apartment even smelled odd, too, like some unholy union of kielbasa and air freshener.

At first Jainey thought she was in the wrong apartment, and her palms began to sweat, but then she looked down and recognized a large plum-colored stain on the carpet, the exact same stain that was in Mrs. Grant's condo. It *was* her place.

The bedroom door opened slowly, and an elderly woman stepped into the hallway. When her eyes focused on Jainey, she opened her mouth to scream. Jainey, in response, raised the crowbar. She wasn't sure *why* she raised it, but instinct told her that this was how to respond.

"Don't," Jainey said. "Don't make a sound!"

"You're going to kill me," the woman said. She was wearing a nightgown with tiny rosebuds all over it. Her trembling hands, bumpy from thick veins, reached out for Jainey, as if with a mind of their own. "Please," the woman begged.

"Listen," Jainey said. "No one's killing anyone, okay? When did you move in?"

"Last week," the woman said.

"What happened to the other woman's stuff?"

"What woman?"

"The woman George Bush killed," Jainey said.

The old woman brought her scary hands up to her mouth. "Oh dear God," she said and stared at Jainey, and Jainey knew what she was thinking.

"Look," Jainey said. "I'm not crazy, okay? Mrs. Grant—the other woman—made this statue of Osama bin Laden, only it wasn't really Osama, it was George W. Bush, and . . ." The old woman was weeping now. "Okay, forget it. I'm going now."

"Thank you," the woman said. "I won't tell anyone. I promise."

"It doesn't matter," Jainey said. "I'm already being followed. In fact, I bet they know I'm here right now."

WHEN CHARLIE showed up to work on Friday, the end of his first week in Chicago, Maggie, Charlie's supervisor, called him over. "Look," she began, "I decided to transfer you. Your productivity percentage isn't budging. I already called Jair-Bear and got approval."

"Jair-Bear works here?"

"Of *course* he works here." Maggie sighed, shook her head. "Corporate is moving you to Deep Storage. I'll call HR and tell them it's a done deal."

"Deep Storage?"

"It's where we store every test ever taken. Someone else will do the filing. What we need is a security guard."

"Who's HR?"

Maggie put her hands on her hips and stared at Charlie. The look said, *Are you fucking with me?* "Human Resources," she said. She wrote down an address and handed it to Charlie. "Here's where you'll need to report. But you won't have to report there until later tonight. We're switching you to the graveyard shift. It's a short drive from here. Do you know where Hickory Hills is?"

"I've got a map in the car. A security guard?" he asked. "Isn't there some scoring that needs to be done? Something requiring a little more, I don't know, *thinking?*"

"Thinking is overrated," Maggie said. "You'll have plenty of time to *think* when you're a security guard. Besides, it's not easy getting a security guard position. They don't just hand these out to anyone, you know. You must know someone pretty big around here. Well, that's neither here nor there. You should count yourself lucky. Especially for someone with your background." She opened up a file folder and looked down at Charlie's job application. "A master's degree in, what, *film studies?*" She snorted. She pursed her lips to hold back a smirk. She shut the folder, then looked back up and met Charlie's eyes. "It's like Jair-Bear once told me: this day and age, you should be thankful to *have* a job. And like I told Jair-Bear: you just said a mouthful, my friend."

That night, Charlie wheeled onto a road that led into a forest preserve. A quarter mile in, he found a security checkpoint manned by some mustached dude wearing a gun holster holding what appeared to be a real gun. *Deep Storage.* Why did it sound so familiar? Was it the name of a bad science-fiction movie? The good news was that Hickory Hills wasn't far from Burbank—only a short commute from Pompeii Inn, in fact.

"Hi there," Charlie said. "I just got transferred here from—"

"ID," the guard said, cutting him off. After looking at Charlie's ID, the security guard sauntered around the car with a mirror attached to a long metal handle, making sure the car wasn't rigged with explosives. The device looked like a dentist's mirror, the kind used for reaching deep inside the mouth and checking for plaque behind teeth, except that his was four feet long. This was the problem, of course, with not sleeping: the world became one surreal episode after another, and commonplace objects were easily transformed into something absurd.

When the guy passed Charlie's window, Charlie smiled and asked, "Any cavities?"

The security guard glared at Charlie a moment before looking down at the tool he was holding. "Okay, funny guy," the guard said. "Move along."

He wasn't trying to be a smart-ass, but after the security guard took offense, Charlie couldn't help feeling superior to him. Charlie, after all, had a master's degree under his belt. In his Film Theory seminar, he had led the class discussion on Brian Henderson's essay "Toward a Non-Bourgeois Camera Style." He'd read what Susan Sontag, James Agee, and Pauline Kael all had to say about the movies, not to mention Pudovkin, Metz, Bazin. And thanks to Petra, he knew more about Soviet cinema than any other student in his program, save for Petra herself.

Of course, he could see the guard's point. The poor guy was just trying to get through his day and then here comes some jackass poking fun at the accoutrements of his job. Maybe the guy's wife was terminally ill. Maybe he himself had prostate cancer. Why couldn't Charlie just keep his mouth shut and let the man do his job?

Shit, Charlie thought. Why can't I *sleep?* Everything would be fine if I could just *sleep.*

Charlie parked in front of an underground bunker. From outside, the only visible part of the building was its entrance. The rest of the building disappeared sharply into the ground, giving the illusion that the entire building was simply a pair of double doors and nothing more. After barely stepping inside, you had to take an escalator down into the bowels of the building, a long and steep descent that made Charlie think he was heading toward the Earth's inner core. It grew increasingly colder, and Charlie was pretty certain he was seeing his own wispy breath. When the ride down the escalator finally ended, Charlie stepped onto a marble floor—the lobby. A guard stood up from behind his station and said, "Charlie Wolf! Charlie *fucking* Wolf!"

Charlie nodded. He shook the man's hands. And then Charlie recognized him. It was Rex, the musicologist, from Iowa.

"Rex? What the hell are *you* doing here?"

"You inspired me, buddy," Rex said.

"How so?"

"You had the balls—the *cojones*—to leave Iowa. When I saw you do that, I thought, why the hell don't *I* do that? And so I filed for a transfer."

"Really?" Charlie asked. "You did?" Rex must have left Iowa City the same day Charlie left Iowa City. Charlie, after all, had been in

Chicago less than a week. Was his lack of sleep screwing with his sense of time? The math wasn't adding up. "Huh!" Charlie added. "Hey, listen. Someone down here's supposed to show me the ropes. Do you know who?"

"That would be me," Rex said.

"You? But you just started working here."

"I know," Rex said. "But I'm the only one down here. And you gotta trust me on this, pal. There's not a hell of a lot to show you. If you know how to sit on your ass, you pretty much have the job mastered." Rex smiled, slapped Charlie's shoulder. "Jesus Christ, it's good to see you. Listen. We should get a drink tonight. What do you say?"

"I don't get off until, what, eight in the morning?" Charlie said. "I don't think any place will be open."

"Oh yeah; shit; that's right," Rex said. "I'm on frickin' moon time. What about this weekend?"

Charlie wasn't sure he wanted to socialize with the old Iowa contingent. For starters, it was Rex who'd informed Charlie that Petra had moved to Chicago. It would seem pathetic to admit after a few drinks that he was trying to track her down, especially when his real motive for moving here was to help Jainey O'Sullivan. But how could he explain any of this to Rex? And now that he thought about it, was Jainey O'Sullivan his real reason for coming here? What had he done to help the girl—to *really* help her? Nothing.

"Sure," Charlie said. "Okay. Tomorrow."

"It's a deal then," Rex said.

ALEX STOPPED off at Jainey's when his shift at Brookfield Zoo was over. He smelled especially bad tonight. Like a donkey, Jainey imagined. Or a llama. She wasn't sure. All zoo animals smelled more or less alike. Despite the stink, she was glad that they were a couple again, even though neither of them had ever put it in quite those terms. It was true, Jainey wasn't as fond of Alex as she'd once been—his short romance with Beth Ann Winkel had deflated a good deal of her enthusiasm for him—but she still liked sex, and it was hard to turn down screwing Alex when the opportunity presented itself.

"Do you want to take a shower first, Mr. Licks?" she asked.

"Would you *please* quit calling me that?"

"What?"

"Mr. Licks!"

"Why?"

"It's . . . I don't know . . . it's kind of juvenile."

"Whatever," she said. "Alex. Al Licks. Either way, you still stink."

Alex sniffed under his arms. "I don't smell any worse than normal." He looked as though he were waiting for Jainey to say something, but when she didn't respond, he relented. "Okay, okay, I'll take a damned shower." He stood up and headed for the closet. "I just need a towel." Jainey started to warn Alex about *The Lycanthrope,* but it was too late: the door was open, and Osama bin Laden greeted Alex from the semi-dark.

"*Holy son of a . . .*"

Alex, cowering, froze in a half-crouch. With his head tucked into his shoulder and one leg up in the air, he looked like a flamingo. Jainey had read about something called *imprinting* in her biology class—the baby animal learning behavior from its mother or mother substitute—and birds, according to her textbook, sometimes imprinted with humans. Jainey, however, had never heard of it happening the other way around—humans imprinting with birds—but given all the time Alex spent at the zoo, Jainey supposed anything was possible.

"What the hell is that?" Alex asked.

"*That,*" Jainey said, "is the president of the United States. But you wouldn't know it by looking at him."

Alex lowered his leg in an attempt to regain some of his dignity. He shut the closet door. "I'm going," he said.

"Really?"

"This is just too weird." He met Jainey's eyes. "*You're* too weird." He opened her bedroom door and headed for the stairs.

"Yeah; well!" Jainey called out after him. "At least I don't smell like ape shit! At least I've got *that* going for me!"

SUNDAY, CHARLIE walked from his motel to the Castle. It looked like it might rain, so he carried an umbrella, but every day since he'd arrived in Burbank it looked like it was going to rain but never did. He was still fearful of walking around at night, but his fear of getting arrested for drinking and driving overshadowed his fear of assault. He might survive getting beaten up, but how would he survive in Chicago without a car?

The Castle was a local bar that half-heartedly attempted to look like a castle, but other than the series of fake-looking parapets surrounding the top of the wall, or the series of gaps between the raised portions—gaps from which, if it had been a real castle, defenders would shoot flaming arrows at the enemy—the building was more likely to be confused for a small penitentiary than anything remotely medieval. Rex was already sitting near the jukebox when Charlie walked inside.

"Didn't think you were going to show," Rex said. "Thought you were going to stand me up."

"Long day," Charlie said.

"No shit. They moved me to another shift, so my sense of time is all fucked up. I never thought I'd say this, but I actually prefer scoring those stupid goddamned tests. It beats sitting on your ass for eight straight hours with nothing to do."

"I need another job," Charlie said.

"You and me both, buddy." Rex flagged down a waitress, ordering two shots and two beers for them. "Hey, isn't your ex-honey out here? What was her name? Petrol?"

"I don't want to talk about her."

"Ah, the wound is still raw. I can respect that. But listen. Don't let it sidetrack you, you hear? Only a few people are destined for greatness. And *you*"—he poked Charlie with his forefinger—"you're one of them, Charlie Wolf."

Charlie laughed. "Get the fuck out of here."

"No, no," Rex said. "I mean it. You gotta trust me on this one. I know. You may think I'm full of shit, but you gotta believe me. I know what I'm talking about." He stared at Charlie, as if he were dead serious, but then his eyes went out of focus and became moist. When he snapped back from whatever reverie he was having, he said, "Whoa, Nelly. I shouldn't have had that Jägermeister before you got here. That shit takes its toll on me every time."

The two men drank another round without saying a word. Normally, Charlie hated these encounters, two people sitting around with nothing to say, but it didn't particularly bother him today. He was so tired from not being able to sleep that he was starting to see traces of colored lights off to the side, and this alone was enough to keep him entertained. Was there actually something colorful blurring off to his side, or was he imagining it? No, no, something was there, and if he didn't look at it head-on, he could see what it was: a woman holding a tiny dog in her lap. "Chekhov," Charlie muttered.

Rex perked up. "What?"

"Did I say something?"

"I'm not sure, but it sounded like you said *Jagoff.*"

Charlie feigned confusion. He shook his head: *no, I didn't say anything, you must have misheard.* More and more Charlie was talking out loud when he shouldn't have said anything, muttering words that were supposed to remain inside his head. There were times when he wondered if the hypnotist had failed to fully bring him back to the surface of consciousness, but deep down he knew the truth: the side effects of sleep deprivation were finally starting to reveal themselves. He was seeing things; it wasn't the first time he'd seen the woman with the lapdog, either.

"I need to hit the restroom," Charlie said, his voice surprisingly heavy.

While standing at the urinal and starting to piss, he noticed that he was standing next to another man who was also pissing. Charlie wasn't just pissing, either, but pissing copiously. The hypnotist may not have done anything for his sleep problem, but his peeing-in-public problem appeared to be solved. It was a miracle, really, and Charlie almost turned to the urinating man and hugged him but then thought better of it.

Another round of drinks, and Charlie yelled, "So!"

Rex, startled, sloshed his beer. "Huh?"

"You're a musicologist, right?" Charlie asked, breaking the silence. "What the hell does that mean exactly?"

"Not much," Rex said. "I have a Ph.D. in music."

"What kind of music are you into?"

"Tough question," Rex said. "I like almost everything. Okay, maybe I don't like *everything*, but I have an appreciation for *most* kinds of music. My area of specialty, if that's what you're asking, would be the composers who also did movie soundtracks. And if you want to get more specific, we're looking at the 1940s, '50s, and '60s."

"Such as?"

"Such as Bernard Herrmann," Rex said.

Charlie perked up. "Really? Bernard Herrmann? He did a bunch of Hitchcock movies."

"Exactly," Rex said. "Interesting guy. Pretty experimental, too, if you ask me."

"I can see that," Charlie said. His interest was piqued, but Rex didn't want to talk about it.

"Enough shop talk," he said. "Let's hear about you. Where are you from? Where are your parents? Any brothers? Sisters? Who *is* Charlie Wolf?"

Charlie indifferently offered up a thumbnail sketch of his life, that he was born in Omaha but grew up in a suburb of Des Moines, a place called Clive, where he spent his youth obsessively watching *The Floppy Show* on Channel 13, a local kids' show that featured a wooden-headed puppet dog named Floppy and the man who operated the puppet, Duane Elliot. Duane, God rest his soul, didn't give a rat's ass if kids bought into the reality of Floppy or not, and so he barely made an effort to conceal his moving lips. And it was precisely *this*—the show's unabashed lack of slickness—that fascinated little Charlie. As for Charlie's parents, his mother died of a heart attack when he was five and his father passed on a few years ago of cancer. There were no brothers, no sisters. For all practical purposes, Charlie Wolf was alone in the world.

Rex ordered another round. And then another. Drunk, Charlie began to imagine his own head as a large, bobbing helium balloon with two eyes, a nose, and a stupid grin painted on it.

At closing time, while on their way out, Rex abruptly turned around, and Charlie almost plowed him down. Rex put his hands on Charlie's shoulders, partly out of camaraderie but mostly to keep his balance. He said, "The story of your life? The one you told me? Jesus Christ, man, that's the saddest fucking story I've heard in years. Especially the part about that damned wooden-headed dog." Rex turned too fast and slammed his shoulder into a wall. "*That's* gonna hurt tomorrow," he said, laughing at his own pain, but then his expression changed into that of a baby on the brink of a meltdown. "*Ow,*" he said.

Outside, Rex and Charlie shook hands before Rex dropped himself, rear end first, into his car. He saluted Charlie, then cranked the engine. Backing up, he nearly hit two drunken patrons.

"Whoa," Charlie said. He watched until the car was far, far away and all that he could see were the dim taillights—and then, finally, nothing. A pellet of rain hit Charlie's nose.

My umbrella, Charlie thought. Without meaning to, he yelled it the same time he thought it: "MY UMBRELLA!"

The bouncer didn't want to let Charlie back in, but Charlie convinced him that he needed the umbrella. "I'm on *foot,*" Charlie slurred. "I should be *rewarded* for not *drinking-driving.*" Did what he just said make sense? He wasn't sure.

"Hurry it up," the bouncer said.

Charlie found his umbrella on the seat of a chair. He was about to leave when he spotted a thin briefcase under the table. He picked it up, studied it. Embossed on it were the initials "R.T." Was the briefcase Rex's?

"R.T.," Charlie said, rubbing his fingers over the letters. "R.T., the Rextra Terrestrial." He laughed and then decided to try out his Elmer Fudd impersonation. "The Wextwa Tewwestwial." This was something Petra would have laughed at. She would have offered other movie titles, egging him on to do more Elmer Fudd. *Mista Wahbutts. The Gods ah Cwazy. Mean Stweets.*

The bartender, swabbing the counter, said, "Hey, buddy, you okay?"

Charlie nodded. He carried the briefcase and umbrella toward the exit. He raised the briefcase in a friendly so-long-see-you-later gesture, and for an instant Charlie could have been a London bank teller pleasantly leaving the pub after a long day at work rather than what he really was—a disillusioned cuckold heading back to the ridiculous Pompeii Inn, a shit-hole hotel where the sheets were probably infested and where, despite being too drunk to see straight, Charlie still wouldn't be able to sleep.

Charlie laughed maniacally all the way across the four lanes of 79th Street. A pickup truck almost hit him. Fortunately, the rest of the drivers saw him in time and stopped to let him pass.

Charlie, drunker than he'd been in years, waved at the last driver, a woman smoking a cigarette and glaring at him. "Good night," Charlie yelled. "Good night, my beautiful princess!"

At the curb, Charlie reached over to knock on her window, but the woman floored it, leaving him alone and temporarily confused until he saw the beacon of Pompeii Inn's shining light in the distance, and he remembered where he needed to go.

A RINGING PHONE woke Jainey from a sound sleep. It was two a.m. "Jesus!" When it became clear that no one else in the house was going to pick up, Jainey rolled over and answered. "Hello?"

Silence.

"Hello?" Jainey asked, scooting up in bed. "Is this a pervert?"

A man cleared his voice.

"C'mon, pervert, you can do better than that."

"It's Alex."

"Alex?" She caught her breath. "Alex! You scared the crap out of me, dude. Well, I guess it's only fair. I mean, I didn't warn you about my closet. I should have said something, I *tried* to say something, but . . ."

"I'm in the hospital."

"You're *where?*"

Slowly, with many pauses due to the apparent difficulty it took to breathe, Alex told her what had happened. A few hours after he left Jainey's, a man wearing camouflage clothes and makeup dragged Alex into an alley and nearly killed him. He didn't say why, and he didn't steal anything; he just beat the living hell out of him.

Jainey turned on her light. She looked up at the ceiling. She was certain that she saw her brother's eye in the dark recess of plaster. She looked for the can of Raid, but it was gone. Her brother must have sneaked into her room and taken it. Jainey turned the light back off.

"Which hospital?" she whispered.

"I'm at Christ," he said.

For a beat, Jainey thought Alex meant that he was dying, that Christ himself was draping his cloaked arm over Alex's bruised shoulder, but then she realized that he meant Christ Hospital.

"I'll be there as soon as I can," she said.

Alex, wheezing into the phone, said, "Be careful."

Jainey was afraid that her brother was going to descend from the attic as soon as she walked out of her room, so she lay perfectly still for a good hour before moving at all. Barely breathing, she slipped on shoes and put a coat over her pajamas, then eased open her door.

Outside, she shifted the car into neutral and let it roll backward down the slope of their driveway. Only then did she risk starting the Turd and pumping the gas pedal.

Alex's face was almost unrecognizable: puffy, discolored, stitches across his forehead, stitches across his chin. He looked like the featured monster from some stupid 1970s horror movie. He was sitting in the emergency room's waiting area when Jainey walked inside.

"Oh my God," she said. She sat down and tried hugging him, but he asked her not to touch him.

"I hurt everywhere," he said.

"And the guy who did it, he didn't say anything?"

"Nothing."

"And you don't know who did it?"

Alex shook his head. "He broke a few ribs, too. The doctor thought at first maybe my lung was collapsed, but I guess it's okay."

"You poor thing," Jainey said. "You look like a monster."

"Thanks."

"No, seriously. You do. You look awful."

A nurse arrived with a wheelchair. Jainey and the nurse eased Alex up and into the chair, then Jainey pushed him outside. The Turd, still running, was illegally parked at the curb. Blue-gray exhaust rolled toward the electric doors with the determination of a spirit looking for a body to possess. The nurse took one look at the Turd and asked, "Is that thing road-legal?"

"It runs," Jainey said, "if that's what you're asking."

They helped Alex stand up. When they tried maneuvering him into the car, Alex started to complain. "Ow-ow-ow, easy, ow-ow-ow." Jainey, losing her patience, slammed the door shut as soon as Alex's foot cleared the gap.

Alex dozed on their way back to Burbank, but when he woke up two blocks from his apartment building, he begged Jainey to let him stay at her house.

"I'm afraid this guy knows where I live," he said.

"You can't stay at my house," Jainey said.

"Why not? Your mother'll never know."

"You're staying here, Alex," Jainey said, pulling up to Alex's building. "And that's that."

Alex stared at her in disbelief. He opened the door to go. Under the dome light's dim bulb and crazy shadows, Alex's brow protruded. Jainey told herself not to be repulsed at the sight of him, but she couldn't help it. He was repulsive.

"I'm sorry," Jainey said. "I wish I could let you stay at my place, but I can't."

"Fine," Alex said. "But I hope you can sleep well if you find out tomorrow I've been killed."

"I don't sleep well anyway," Jainey said.

Alex snorted, slid out, moaned, and shut the door. As soon as he reached the front entrance, Jainey sped away.

She didn't want to go back home—what if Ned was sitting in her room waiting for her?—so she drove to the cemetery where Mrs.

Grant was buried. The main gate was locked for the night, but she knew of a weak spot in the fence where her classmates sneaked inside to get stoned. The cemetery was darker than she anticipated, so she used the tiny penlight on her keychain to guide her from grave to grave. She recognized at least a dozen last names—probably the grandparents of her classmates. There was a Jesinowski, an O'Brien, even a Ruth Winkel, who was no doubt related to the evil Beth Ann Winkel. Jainey paused. She took a deep breath.

"Your granddaughter is a bitch," Jainey said. "I'm sorry to be the one bringing such bad news from the world of the living, but there you have it."

Mrs. Grant's grave was located conveniently at the end of an aisle, next to the fence that ran alongside 79th Street. There it was, a flat stone with her name and dates: 1950–2004. Jainey knelt. She ran her fingers across the dates. Her kneecaps grew cold from the wet ground. She would have to spend the rest of the night with two damp spots on her jeans.

"I'm so sorry," she said. "I haven't found out who killed you, but I will. I promise."

The first thing Jainey ever made of any significance in Mrs. Grant's class was a coffee cup for her father. She was in the second grade. She had spent so much time getting the coffee cup just right: narrow at the bottom, wider in the middle, narrow again at the top. For the handle, she twisted clay over and over so that it looked like a piece of rope, and when she attached it to the cup itself, she made it look as though the ends of the rope—the parts attached to the cup—were frayed. It was the first time Mrs. Grant had put her palm on the top of Jainey's head, a gesture Jainey would eventually grow used to, even come to expect, but that first time, with the damp heat of Mrs. Grant's palm touching the top of her warm head, Jainey wanted to cry. It was a simple thing, really, that touch, but it gave Jainey a feeling that she belonged in the world.

"Goodbye, Mrs. Grant," Jainey whispered.

Still on her knees, she bowed all the way forward to kiss the grave marker. She realized, once she'd assumed the position, that this was the way her Muslim friend Hani prayed—arms stretched all the way forward, head to the ground, Allah praised.

Jainey wanted to drive downtown and talk to Mariah, but it was way too late and Jainey was too tired to wait up all night for Mariah to open the wig store. She drove to Pompeii Inn instead. This was where the man who helped her with the Turd was staying. She couldn't remember what kind of car he drove, but she remembered the Iowa license plates. She pulled in next to him and curled up in her front seat. She dreamed about Ned's eye. Wherever she went, there it was, watching her—just the eye. Occasionally, it blinked, the lid appearing out of nowhere, swiping over the large black pupil. When Jainey woke up, it was already morning. She looked around. She didn't know what time it was, but Charlie Wolf's car was already gone.

"Shit," she said.

SO THIS IS WHERE *Petra is living with Akshay Kapoor, where she walks around nude, where she showers, where she's having sex with someone else—her worn panties tossed aside during the throes of whatever intense banging occurs after Akshay arrives home from his own long, adrenaline-saturated day of saving some lives while letting others slip recklessly through his bony fingers.*

Fuck, Charlie thought, standing across the street from the brownstone in Lincoln Park. *Fuck, fuck, fuck.* Only that morning he had called Gerry West, an old friend from his master's program who now worked in the Alumni Office at the university. Charlie made up some cockamamie story about being friends with Akshay. Before Charlie could even finish the lie, Gerry was reading the information off his computer screen. And now Charlie regretted it. *Fuck, fuck!*

Maybe he should have brought a sign to hold up, something that would have made Petra laugh: "Remember the Ghoul?" The trip to her house should have been lighthearted, casual. As it was, the tone was all off. He felt like a stalker.

"Look at this house," Charlie said, talking out loud again. "*Look* at it!" It was the sort of house Charlie and Petra used to talk about living in one day, but who was Charlie fooling? They could never have afforded such a house. Not on a professor's salary. Not even *two* professors' salaries, for that matter.

Stupid, stupid, Charlie thought, berating himself for even heading in that direction. He was starting to sound like Jacob Bartuka, a man who told strangers that his job allowed him time to study his art, his art being the *martial* arts, when in truth the poor fool probably had to squeeze in karate classes on days when he wasn't brain dead from his shitty, low-paying job. Charlie didn't want to delude himself that he might have been a professor, *could* have been a professor, if only he and Petra had stayed together. After all, how many film majors were out there bagging groceries and, like him, unable to remember the vast majority of what he'd spent the past two years studying?

One thing was clear: Akshay Kapoor was rolling in dough. The bastard was probably a dentist—or, worse, a plastic surgeon who spent his days filling women's breasts with silicone, one after the other, like a carnie filling balloons with helium. *Pssssssssssssssssht. Next!*

Charlie was snorting and shaking his head when someone tapped his shoulder. He turned around. "Petra!"

Petra narrowed her eyes. She couldn't have looked any more beautiful, though. My angry Russian, Charlie thought.

"What the hell are you doing here, Charlie?" she asked.

"What am I doing here? I got *transferred* here."

"Transferred where?" Petra asked. "This *street?*"

"No, no," Charlie said. "Chicago. And since I was here, I figured I'd look you up."

"Why?"

A pulse was beating in Charlie's throat, and the longer Petra acted as though nothing had ever passed between them, the harder the pulse beat. How could she pretend that all their intimate moments together had now been eclipsed? What about all those times, naked and covered in sweat, they had collapsed in postcoital bliss, laughing at the madness of whatever sexual gymnastics they'd just put themselves through?

"*Why?*" Charlie repeated. "For starters, I think you owe me an explanation."

"I don't owe anyone anything," Petra said. "Nothing." She turned her head and made a fake spitting gesture for finality: *thpuhhhhhhh.* In that moment, she looked quintessentially Russian.

"Okay, okay," Charlie said. "How about a cup of coffee? I'll even pay for it."

An offer was on the table, and Petra considered it. "All right," she said. "One cup, and then we're even."

What struck Charlie most was how awkward they were together. Charlie had to keep reminding himself, *I've seen this woman NAKED, I've seen her PEEING. I've been INSIDE this woman.* Not that it was all about sex or nudity. It wasn't. But here they were clunking elbows on their way inside Clark's. They bumped into each other when the tattooed waitress tried seating them. They spoke out of sync, sometimes starting to talk at the same time, then stopping abruptly to let the other one go on, followed by long, excruciating pauses.

"So," Charlie finally managed to spit out without interruption. "Tell me about Akshay."

"You *are* stalking me," Petra said. "You know his name."

"Everyone at NTC knew his name," Charlie said, trying not to yell. "Everyone knew about the two of you. They told *me.* It wasn't much of a secret. In fact, I'm the only one who *didn't* know."

"Oh." Petra blew on her coffee. She couldn't argue with him. "He was born in India," she said, as if reciting facts from a history book. "He's an obstetrician. He's renting office space from another ob-gyn. He works the emergency room at Northwestern, and he's started working at Planned Parenthood on Thursdays. A grim neighborhood on the South Side." She wagged her head, as if to say that Akshay had taken on too much. She sighed and said, "He keeps busy."

"Why did you leave me?" Charlie asked. Until now, Charlie had remained stoic, but hearing himself ask the question was in and of itself an acknowledgment of failure, and he had to force himself not to cry in front of her. Anything but that.

"Poor Charlie," Petra said. She said it the exact same way she used to say *Poor Ghoul.* She reached for Charlie's hand, but he jerked it away.

"No, no, I'm okay," he said.

"Oh, baby," Petra said. She handed him some napkins.

"I'm fine," Charlie said. "I need to go, though."

Petra tried reaching for him. "Hold on," she said, but Charlie was already heading for the exit. Outside, he started to run. He wasn't sure why he was being so melodramatic—it wasn't really his nature—but sitting there and listening to Petra talk about the man she was with now, the man who had replaced Charlie, was too much. Charlie must have secretly hoped that Petra, upon seeing him again, would realize the mistake she'd made, but it was clear—*more* than clear—that she didn't see her decision as a mistake. If anything, *Charlie* had been the mistake. And though Charlie knew deep down that this was one possible outcome of such a meeting, he hadn't really thought it through. It had been a huge failure of imagination.

JAINEY DROVE HOME and, sneaking back into her house, carried all of her precious belongings out to the Turd. Any second her brother might drop down from the attic's hatch and ask her what the hell she thought she was doing. Her heart pounded the entire time. Fortunately, no one stopped her. It took only three trips up and down the stairs. *That's it?* she wondered when she was finished. *This is my life?*

Pompeii Inn at night was much worse than Pompeii Inn in the daytime. There appeared to be a tailgate party at one end of the parking lot, with loud rap music and a keg. The rest of the parking lot was empty save for Charlie's car with the Iowa plates. When Charlie finally came outside, Jainey almost didn't recognize him. He was dressed like a cop, but when he got closer, she saw that he wasn't a *real* cop. The badge was dull instead of shiny, and the uniform didn't fit very well. Instead of a gun, he wore a holster for pepper spray.

Jainey rolled down her window. "It's me! It's Jainey!"

"Jainey?"

"Yeah. The girl with the piece-of-shit car." She banged on the door with her fist for emphasis. "Remember? You told me to call you if I needed anything."

"Sure, I remember. Is something wrong? You need something?"

"Okay, here's the deal. I need a place to live. For a little while. I got kicked out of my house, and I need a place to stay until I get a job and find a new place. No biggy." Charlie didn't say anything, so Jainey added, "Look at you!"

Charlie looked down at his uniform. "Oh, yeah, I got transferred," he said. "Same company, different job."

Jainey rolled up her window, stepped out of her car, and locked the doors. "Why're you working so late?" she asked.

"They gave me the graveyard shift," he said. "The pay's better. I can't sleep, anyway. It's a win-win situation." His smile looked forced.

Jainey followed Charlie to his car, slid into his passenger seat.

Actually, he looked pretty handsome in his stupid uniform. She'd have to draw a cartoon of Lloyd the Freakazoid as a security guard, a bottle of vodka in his holster instead of a gun. His fly would be open, and his tongue would be hanging out of his mouth when the supervisor finds him asleep on the job. *You're fired!* the supervisor could yell, and Lloyd, startled awake by the voice, would quickly pull the vodka bottle out of his holster and hit the supervisor over the head, all in one swift move. In the cartoon's last panel, Lloyd would be pulling the supervisor into a room full of other dead employees, all of whom had startled Lloyd while on the job.

Charlie handed Jainey his motel key. "It's room 122. It's kind of a mess, but—."

"Look," Jainey said, cutting him off. "I don't want to turn this into anything weirder than it already is, but I don't think I should be alone right now. Do you think I could just hang with you at work?"

"There's one problem," Charlie said.

"What's that?"

"I can't get you past the checkpoint at work. It's a pretty secure place."

"Do they look in the trunk?" Jainey asked.

"You're not hiding in my trunk."

"Why not?"

"It's not . . . I don't know . . . it's not safe."

"It'll be fun, though!"

Charlie sighed. "We'll see. Maybe I'll have a better idea by the time we get there."

"Okey-doke," Jainey said.

In a gas station parking lot, Charlie popped the trunk and Jainey climbed inside. Charlie looked around, like a mobster doing away with a corpse, then shut the trunk. Jainey expected it to be pitch-black, but Charlie rode his brake enough that the red glow kept the trunk illuminated. If he was doing this for her benefit, it was awfully sweet of him.

The car came to a complete stop—Jainey heard muffled voices—and then the car started moving again. A few moments later, the car was turned off, the trunk hissed open, and Charlie was staring down at her.

"You okay?" he asked.

"It was a blast!" Jainey said. "*You* should ride in the trunk on the way home. I'll drive."

"I don't think so."

Jainey started climbing out of the trunk, but Charlie motioned for her to stay down. "We have to wait until the other guard leaves."

"Which guard?"

"The one I'm taking over for."

"Oh."

"As soon as he leaves, I'll come back up here and get you. Deal?"

"Do I have a choice?"

"Not really." He shut the trunk again.

A plaque in the lobby announced that the building had opened in 1970. It was a weirdly plain building, mostly concrete, with a long and steep escalator that hummed but also made another noise, like someone agreeing with you: *mmmmm, Mm-hm, mmmmm, Mm-hm, mmmmm, Mm-hm.* The building embodied what people from the past thought the future was going to look like. Stark. Wide open. Mechanical. It gave Jainey the creeps.

Jainey worked on her cartoons in silence while Charlie sat on a stool and guarded a door that led into a dark storage area, but after an hour of coming up with crazy Lloyd the Freakazoid ideas, she grew restless.

"What's in there?" she asked.

"Test scores," Charlie said.

"That's what you're guarding? Test scores? What's the big deal?"

"It's every test score ever taken by anybody, so I imagine there's a lot of personal information in there. You know, Social Security numbers, stuff like that." He rubbed a hand over the top of his head and said, "Actually, I don't know what the big deal is. I guess someone needs to guard it to make sure nothing happens. You know, arson, vandalism."

"Are my test scores in there?" Jainey asked.

"Probably," Charlie said.

"And yours?"

Charlie smiled. "I hadn't thought about that, but yeah, I guess so." He looked like he was thinking. "I suppose Charlie Manson's would be here, too."

"Who's he?"

"You don't know who Charles Manson is?"

"Sounds familiar," Jainey said, "but maybe I'm thinking of Marilyn Manson."

Charlie said, "He's a notorious mass murderer, except that he had a bunch of people do the murdering for him."

"Oh. Hey, listen. I need to pee. Is there a ladies' room around here? It doesn't have to be for ladies, though. Any toilet will do."

The bathroom was back where all the tests were stored, and Charlie had to unlock the thick bank-vault door, which opened slowly, hydraulically.

"You can shut it," Jainey said. "I'll knock when I'm done." Charlie shut the door.

The tests were filed like books, spine out, on tall aluminum shelving units. Each unit had fifteen shelves—there were ladders to reach the top shelves—but each shelf stretched on for miles. There was literally no end in sight.

Jainey found only one bathroom. All evidence suggested that it was unisex. Her mother always referred to them as bisexual bathrooms. Several times she had nudged Jainey and, in front of other customers, said, "They've got a bisexual bathroom here, if you need it." "*Mom,*" Jainey would say, cringing, but her mother misinterpreted Jainey's discomfort as a prudish aversion to discussing bodily functions in public.

Inside the dimly lit bathroom, sitting on the toilet, Jainey made a decision. She was going to steal a file. Why not? Who would notice?

On her way back to Charlie's guard post, Jainey reached over and snagged one of the thinner files. She didn't look to see whose it was; it didn't matter.

With the file tucked under her shirt, she walked casually back to the Deep Storage entrance and knocked for Charlie to let her out. He opened the door and Jainey gave him a curt nod—*Everything went A-okay,* the nod said—and then she returned to the floor. Hours later, she woke up to Charlie's hand gently nudging her, Charlie whispering, "Time to go, Jainey. Time to go."

Jainey, blinking, examined her watch. It was early morning. "What's the date today?"

Charlie consulted the calendar at his guard post. He told her the date. It was, as she suspected, her birthday. She was eighteen years old today. She considered telling Charlie, but the poor guy looked so tired. Purple lines had appeared under his eyes, and he was starting to slump. "Thanks," she said, and Charlie nodded.

DAYLIGHT CREPT into the hotel room, even with the shades drawn. Birds would periodically land on the air-conditioning unit outside the window, clank back and forth, and fly away. Someone's TV was on too loud.

"I need to be somewhere," Charlie said shortly after they returned to the motel. "I need to go alone, if that's okay."

"Sun's out," Jainey said. "I'll be fine. It's nighttime I'm worried about."

"You sure?"

Jainey nodded.

Charlie was late for his appointment with Jill the hypnotist, but Jill didn't appear to mind. She was wearing a muumuu and a necklace strung with puka shells. After hugging him, she locked the front door and flipped the "Open" sign to "Closed."

"It's dangerous for a person who's been put under to be interrupted by someone other than the hypnotist," she explained. She dimmed the lights. "To make you sleepy," she said.

Charlie sat on the sofa; Jill sunk into a leather chair across from him. She twined her fingers together and leaned forward. She cocked her head and said, "So tell me. How's your, uh, problem."

"My sleeping problem?"

"No. The other one."

"The peeing-in-public problem?"

"Yes."

"Well, I think it's solved. I mean, there was a guy standing next to me the other day and . . ."

" . . . right, right . . ."

" . . . and I didn't have a problem. I just went ahead and . . ."

" . . . mm-hm, mm-hm . . ."

" . . . and peed."

Jill crossed her legs. She was starting to look sleepy herself. "We never expect miracles overnight, but sometimes it happens. And your sleep problem?"

"No luck," Charlie said.

"Yes, well, sometimes it'll take longer to open the door of the larger problem, to climb into that dark room beyond the door, the *subconscious,* and discover the *real* issues."

Charlie nodded. It sounded reasonable. What his dark room probably needed was a new lightbulb.

Jill said, "Let's have you lie back, okay? Relax, Charlie. Why don't you kick your shoes off?"

"Really? My shoes?"

"It's better if you're relaxed. Pretend you're at home, getting ready for a nap on the couch. There," she said, her voice low. "Isn't that better?"

Charlie knew what was going on. Jill was putting him under so that she could seduce him. She had started appearing in those bizarre wide-awake daydreams he'd been having lately. She came to him like a hologram. She was there but not there. It was as if she were saying, *I'm working inside that dark room—so hang in there, buddy, be patient with me.* Most of the time she appeared to him nude. In one daydream, while Jill was on top of Charlie, she breathed into his ear, *You're not going to remember any of this later, now will you, honey? Of course you won't. Of course not.*

But he did. He always remembered.

POMPEII INN was another place whose fate Jainey's mother bemoaned. According to her, it had once been the height of elegance, the only place in town, other than the Burbank Rose, where you could actually have a nice wedding reception or eighth-grade confirmation party. Confirmation parties were all the rage in Burbank—in *all* of Chicago, for that matter. Nearly everyone Jainey knew was Catholic, and she'd been dragged kicking and screaming to dozens of baptisms, communions, and confirmations over the years.

For most of her life, Jainey had been under the delusion that Catholicism was the predominant world religion. When her friend Hani told her that Islam was the fastest-growing religion in the world, Jainey punched him in the solar plexus. "Get the fuck out of here," she said. "You *wish.*"

Even though Jainey felt no affinity to the Catholic Church, Hani's news disturbed her. Any news that turned her perception of the world inside out disturbed her. It made her realize how dangerous isolationism was, how when you socialized with a group of like-minded people your view of the world narrowed to the point where everyone in your little group looked through the same skewed prism. In the few short years since Hani broke the news to her, Burbank had undergone a radical transformation, in large part due to the ever-growing Muslim population. With more and more businesses posting signs in Arabic, Jainey could no longer deny the truth. She was starting to see the world through Hani's eyes. As for Hani, he probably saw Catholicism as some kind of fringe religion—like the Moonies or the Wiccans—and who could blame him, especially if you took one look at the pope with his crazy hat and Popemobile?

These days Pompeii Inn hosted more and more wedding receptions for the Abdallahs, the Dulaimis, and the Husams, their names appearing on the announcement sign out front, but her mother was right: Pompeii Inn's glory days were over. The entire place made you think that it had barely survived the detonation of a bomb. Jainey thought, *This is what the end of the world will look like. This is what life will be like when I'm only one of ten people left.* Lying in bed, in Room 122, she tried to imagine who the other nine survivors might be, but she could only come up with one: Charlie Wolf.

With Charlie away, Jainey reached under the bed and pulled out the file she'd stolen from Deep Storage. It was for some guy named Percival Frederick Yount, who was born in Biloxi, Mississippi, in 1968.

"Percival," Jainey said. "Dude, you need a new name."

Inside the file were all the Scan-Tron sheets Percival had ever filled out, along with essay answers, all handwritten. The paper had yellowed. Most of the dates were from the 1970s, but a few spilled over into the '80s. He was *old*—as old as her mother. She assumed that with a name like Percival Frederick Yount his scores would be through the roof, but in fact his percentiles were mediocre at best.

At the bottom of the pile was a document titled "Future Projection," a computer-generated conclusion about old Percival based on all of his test scores. There were various analyses, mostly statistical, a lot of charts and graphs. Jainey was about to toss the entire file out the window when she turned to the final document.

PROBABILITIES for Percival Frederick Yount

Political affiliation: `Moderate Conservative`

Activism: `None`

Employment: `Manual Labor`

Earnings: `Lower 10%`

Marital Status: `Married`

Sexuality: `Repressed`

Jainey parted the curtains, peeking outside. After concluding that no one was watching her, she returned to the bed. Her heart was pounding.

Religion: `Conflicted`

Threat to Self: `Minimal`

Threat to Society: `Minimal`

Most Likely Crimes to Commit: `Shoplifting; Assault`

According to the last page, the document had last been updated in July 1986—one month after his high school graduation, Jainey calculated.

"Holy shit."

Jainey slid Percival's file under the bed. On the springy mattress, she curled up into a ball and pulled the covers up to her neck. *Ruby Ridge. Waco. Mrs. Grant.* She knew from Mariah that the FBI had a file on John Lennon, too. It was all making sense now: America's Report Card was a psychological profile. It was the government's way of keeping tabs on people, their way of watching everyone. *That's* why they needed security guards where Charlie worked.

The government was watching her. Her brother was watching her. Who *wasn't* watching her?

Be careful, Jainey thought. *Be careful what you say. Be careful what you do.*

CHARLIE OPENED the door. The unexpected appearance of Osama bin Laden inside his dim room gave Charlie pause. Jainey sprung up from the bed, holding an ice pick. "I'll kill you, motherfucker!" she yelled.

"Easy, easy," Charlie said. "It's just me." He flipped on the lights.

Jainey scooted up against the headboard and crossed her legs. Her purple and green hair was flat on one side. Bed-head. "Charlie! You scared the piss right out of me," she said.

"I scared *you?*" Charlie said. "Think how *I* felt." Charlie tentatively poked Osama's chest. "He's not real," Charlie said. "That's good."

"He's not as tall as the real Osama, either," Jainey said. "The real Osama is as tall as Michael Jordan. Did you know that?"

Charlie smiled. "All he needs is his own line of sandals. Air Laden. Three hundred bucks a pop."

Jainey ignored his joke. She said, "Pull down his beard and take off his turban. Go on."

Charlie obeyed. "Hey, hey," he said. "It's Georgie Porgie."

Jainey, seemingly pleased by Charlie's revelation, grinned.

"What *is* this, anyway?" Charlie asked.

"My art teacher made it." Jainey told him the whole story, taking him up to the point of her own newfound obsession with Ruby Ridge. "The government is evil," she said. "I didn't realize that until they killed Mrs. Grant. I was stupid."

"Don't go turning into one of those conspiracy theorist whack jobs," Charlie said.

"I know other things, too, but I can't tell you." Jainey stared at him, sizing him up. "You're not ready yet."

"Oh. Okay. All right," he said. "When you're ready to tell me, I'm all ears." He circled George Bush, yawning and stretching.

"Tired?" Jainey asked.

"Actually, I am," Charlie said, "I think I might finally be able to sleep."

Jainey patted the space next to her. "It's all yours."

"Stay there," Charlie said. "I can sleep in one of those chairs."

"What? Are you crazy? If I scoot over, there's plenty of room. I was sound asleep when you came in, so I'm just gonna zonk out for a while." Jainey scooted over. "There. See how much room you have?"

"Okay. But do me a favor, would you? Put the ice pick *under* the bed?"

Jainey complied. She turned onto her side, curling up into a tight ball. A few seconds later, she was sound asleep. Charlie, envious, looked down at her. How could sleep come so easily? He wanted to smooth down a thatch of Jainey's hair that was sticking up, but he resisted. It wasn't worth getting stabbed through the neck.

Charlie sat down on his side of the bed, but the bed was harder than he remembered. He stood up, yanked back the sheets. It was Rex's briefcase. He was about to set it aside but hesitated. *Why not?* he wondered and popped it open. He wasn't sure what to expect—articles about composer Bernard Herrmann? The only thing inside was a thick file with his own name on it. Right there, in bold letters: *Charlie Wolf.*

"What the fuck is this?" Charlie opened the file and started flipping through it. His hands were shaking. Jainey moaned. Her eyelids were twitching. She was already dreaming.

The files contained data about Charlie's personal history—parents' names, birth dates, former residences, even the names and addresses of former girlfriends. Several pages were dedicated to Petra Petrovich, including a stat sheet on the small Russian village where she was born. As for Charlie, the file contained confidential information about his grammar school, high school, and college grades. There was even a blurry Photostat of a report written by Mrs. Edgar that led to his one-week suspension from the tenth grade, the result of an incident that involved money stolen from Mrs. Edgar's desk drawer, over one hundred dollars from the Drama Club candy sale. A crime Charlie'd had nothing to do with. The real criminals—a triumvirate of thugs named Jerry Pannock, Lester Newhole, and Bob Oliver—had squealed on Charlie, claiming to have seen him take it, but what it came down to in the end was the word of three boys to one. What could Charlie do but deny it? The issue of character never came up. Lester Newhole, leader of the three punks, had threatened to break Charlie's fingers, one knuckle at a time, if he ratted them out, and so Charlie opted for the less painful alternative of suspension.

Fortunately, Charlie'd had enough willpower to push this episode aside and continue on with his life as if nothing had ever happened, but this was the sort of incident that could have turned him inward in a bad way, his anger morphing into a cancerous rage at the world's injustice. Even now, reading the Photostat of the report, a report that he himself signed, an admittance of guilt, Charlie felt an irrational desire to track down all three bastards and claw their eyes out, sinking his fingers deep into their eye sockets, pushing until he felt the sponge of brain.

Charlie rifled through the rest of the file, wondering what it could all mean. There were reports on Charlie's behavior at NTC, who he talked to, who he shunned. There was documentation about his time spent with Petra, where they took their breaks and what they talked about, including a transcript of their conversation about having sex at work, a plan of Petra's that sadly never came to fruition. There were charts and graphs that didn't make any sense to him. There were even two photos of Charlie. The first one was him at work, from the point of view of the computer screen, inside of which must have been a camera. The other was one of Charlie leaving an adult bookstore the night he bought the magazine that probably resulted in Mr. Shit-Don't-Stink's termination. Charlie stuffed the files back into the portfolio. He couldn't look at them anymore. "Rex," Charlie whispered, thinking.

Charlie remembered now where he'd first heard about Deep Storage. It was Jacob Bartuka, the martial artist, who'd told him. But Jacob had said something else, something that had seemed crazy at the time, that each group of scorers had a mole, a person who spied on someone within the group, and that the government might have bigger plans for the person being spied upon. But what plans? And why Charlie? And who the hell was Rex? Was Rex the one who called him at home, asking Charlie to apply for a job at NTC? Why had he followed Charlie all the way to Chicago? It seemed imprudent, in retrospect, not to have listened to Jacob. The man had worked at NTC for fifteen years, after all. You couldn't work some place that long and *not* learn a secret or two.

"Oh, Jesus," Charlie said. "I'm going crazy."

Charlie pushed the briefcase under the bed. With Jainey's ice pick nearby and George Bush guarding the door, Charlie fell into the first deep sleep he'd had since Petra left him. It was a sleep full of dreams so dark and violent, though, that Charlie probably would have chosen to stay awake, but the choice was no longer his.

America's Report Card

DALE O'SULLIVAN studied Jainey's two front teeth. They sat on his palm, side by side, these teeth that he himself had removed from the gymnasium's rubber floor with the tweezers from his Swiss Army knife. He kept the teeth with him at all times, the way some people carried around rosaries. These teeth—these two tiny teeth—were his saving grace here at Joliet State Penitentiary.

"You and those motherfucking teeth." It was Larry Two Fingers, awake now and staring across the cell at Dale. "Let me guess," he said. "You were a dentist in a past life. Is that it, Slugger?"

Slugger. Everyone in Joliet had a nickname, and though the new name usually harkened back to some aspect of the crime he committed, rarely did it highlight a positive aspect. More often than not it illuminated how you'd fucked up, and what Dale learned was that there was no end to the ways a person could fuck up. Truth be told, Dale had never met a bigger bunch of idiots in his entire life than the men he'd met at Joliet. Larry Two Fingers, for instance, had only two remaining fingers on each hand, the result of a botched bank robbery in which the explosives went off before Larry could put them down and clear out.

Another guy tried setting his old lady on fire but made the mistake of lighting a cigarette while his own hands were still covered in gasoline. They gave this clown an Indian name. Smokes Too Much.

But the place wasn't full of just idiots. There were freaks, too. Dale knew another dude who bought black-market hormone pills so that he could grow a pair of tits. He used to be known as Handsome Tommy because he was the ugliest son of a bitch you'd ever seen, but ever since the hormone pills kicked in, the boys had begun calling him Tommy Tits. The sad thing was, Dale *liked* Tommy Tits, but he liked him a hell of a lot better back when he was Handsome Tommy. Dale had a hard time looking him square in the face without looking down at his tits. And lately, whenever Tommy caught Dale looking, he'd waggle his eyebrows and say, "See something down there you like?" prompting Dale to turn away and say, "Fuck you, man. Don't *even* say that. You're sick. You know that? Sick."

But now it was Larry Two Fingers riding his ass. "You want a coupla *my* teeth for your sad-ass collection? How many you want? Two? Three?"

Dale knew Larry meant no harm, but still . . . Jainey's teeth were the only physical reminders that he even *had* a daughter. If Dale was going to be here any longer, he might have stabbed the son of a bitch with a shiv, but his time was coming to an end. Another week, and he'd be a free man. One week after seven long years. Lucky for Dale, Mr. Hall hadn't died. His skull was cracked, but doctors were able to screw it back together . . . or *whatever* they did to repair a cracked skull.

"You know what? I'm gonna miss you," Dale said through gritted teeth.

Though Dale had said this without a hint of warmth, Larry started getting a little choked up. He sniffled and turned away from Dale. "I'm gonna miss you, too," he said.

When Dale approached a table of buddies at lunch, the men quit talking. Whenever someone's time at Joliet was coming to an end, the other guys grew distant, and it wasn't any different for Dale.

Dale, who was famous for his jokes, said, "Hey, listen. What did the doctor say to the horse?" He paused. "'*Why the long face?*'" No one laughed, so Dale added, "Well, I'm the doctor, and you guys are the horses. A sad bunch of horses, too, but there you have it."

Smokes Too Much said, "Why don't you just eat your food and shut the fuck up."

"Fine," Dale said. "Be that way. But don't expect postcards from me when I'm out of here."

"We won't," Smokes said. "So eat your goddamned food."

Dale knew that this was the way things were here—he had acted the same toward other guys who were on their way out—but he couldn't help taking it personally.

After lunch, he pulled Tommy Tits aside and said, "What gives, bro?"

"What gives *what?*"

"Why the *persona non gratis* treatment?"

Tommy smiled. He said, "Don't you know?"

Dale shook his head.

"We're making peace with you, that's all. It's like a wake," Tommy said. He patted Dale's shoulder and said, "The burial's next week."

Only Larry Two Fingers treated him the same. That night, back in their cell, Larry said, "So tell me, Slugger. What're you gonna do when you get out? If I was you, I'd go straight to a whorehouse, and then I'd go get myself a big, sloppy beef sandwich at Mr. Beef. You ever eat at Mr. Beef?"

"Nope."

"You like beef sandwiches?"

"Yeah, but we got a place near us called Duke's. That's where everyone goes."

"Really? Duke's? I'll have to keep that in mind."

"Larry," he said. "Larry, Larry, Larry. You're in for *life,* man. You won't be going to Duke's on *this* planet."

"Probably not," Larry said, "but you never know." Then Larry started talking about other good places to eat—Billy Boy's on Halsted, the Red Lion on Lincoln—but Dale quit listening. He was trying to imagine what his daughter, Jainey, looked like these days. He was trying to imagine what their first encounter would be like, those initial awkward moments followed by a bone-crushing embrace. Surely she would understand why he did what he did. What he did, after all, he did for her. To protect her. And he'd do the same goddamned thing again. No regrets.

"Old Slugger," Larry said. "It's not going to be the same with you gone. We need more guys like you in here."

Dale, suddenly interested, sat up. "Oh yeah? And what kind of guy is that?"

Larry smiled. "The quiet type," he said.

Part Three

The Hunt

1995

Ned O'Sullivan had been waiting all his life to go hunting with his father, but when the day finally came, Ned slipped off to the bathroom and threw up. He didn't want his father to know he'd thrown up, though, so he wiped off his face with a damp washrag and brushed his teeth for a good ten minutes.

"Hurry it up in there," his father yelled from the other side of the door. "The deer aren't going to wait around for us to get our pathetic asses in gear."

Ned's father, Dale, who had been in the Army before he'd met Ned's mother, got up every morning at three o'clock when it was still dark and quiet and eerie outside. At least a dozen times in his life, Ned had woken up in the middle of the night to pee and, on his way to the bathroom, found his father smoking a cigarette in the living room. It was always a startling moment: Ned would smell the smoke first, then see in the darkened room the orange tip of the cigarette glowing, growing oranger, getting hotter, followed by his father's wheeze and a fresh wave of smoke. The man never said a word to his son at that time in the morning. This was the unspoken agreement between them: you do your business, I'll do mine.

Father and son, both dressed in camouflage, drove the short distance to Palos Hills. Ned had thought that they were going to drive to Wisconsin, where most of the deer hunting took place, not the few short miles away to another Chicago suburb. And yet here they were. Dale wheeled into a narrow, closed-off entrance to the Cook County Forest Preserve. With the truck idling, Dale slid out and unlatched the chain. Ned watched, telling himself to remember this moment: his father like a ghost rattling chains as fog drifted past the headlights. After dropping the chain, his father came back to the truck and drove onto the county property.

"Hook the chain back up," Dale said. "I don't want anyone getting suspicious."

Ned worked by the red glow of the taillights, stretching the chain back across and connecting it to the thick eye-hook. A small sign flapped at the center of the chain: NO TRESPASSING.

Back in the truck, Ned waited until they'd driven deep into the forest preserve before asking if what they were doing was wrong.

*"*Wrong *is subjective," Dale said. "Let's say someone steals a ten-dollar bill from you. Well, that would be wrong to you, right? But now let's say that the man hasn't eaten in four days, that if he doesn't eat in the next few hours he'll be dead, and that your money will buy him enough food to keep him alive. You see: stealing money isn't so wrong now, is it? He's just doing it to survive. Understand?"*

Ned nodded. He wasn't sure how it applied to their present situation, but it was a compelling argument, one he would have to mull over later.

After parking, after getting their hunting gear from the truck, Ned followed close behind his father while his father told him everything there was to know about tracking and hunting whitetail deer.

"You'd be surprised by what you can learn from a deer's tracks," Dale said. "The direction it's walking, roughly what time it passed, how big it is."

"Really?"

"Absolutely. If your deer track is three inches long, we're looking at a fawn. Four inches, a yearling doe. Four and a half? Adult doe or yearling buck. Five inches, and we start looking at a two-and-a-half-year-old buck. Five-and-a-half to six inches, and we've got anywhere from a three-and-a-half to a six-and-a-half-year-old buck on our hands. A big ol' sonofabitch."

How, Ned wondered, did his father know so much? And there was more. Much more. The gun he used was a 7.62-millimeter Type 56 semiautomatic rifle, a gun that used to be popular with the Chinese People's Liberation Army.

"It's accurate for long distances," his father said, "and it's an easy gun to maintain. The Chinese put bayonets on the end of them. Can you imagine some little Chinese motherfucker running at you with a bayonet? Jesus H. Christ. I'm not ashamed to admit, I'd shit my pants. Yes sir, I'd turn into one big blubbering baby."

Ned remained silent. He didn't believe it. His father wasn't afraid of anything—not snakes, not men twice his size, nothing. One time, a man ran his father off the road, and his father followed the guy to where the man worked. Ned was sitting in the passenger seat. He was seven or eight. His heartbeat had sped up and wouldn't slow down. His father drove calmly but wouldn't look over at Ned, not even when Ned asked him what he was doing. When the man who'd cut him off pulled into a parking place, Dale shifted his car into park and told Ned to wait right there. Dale left his door wide open. When the man got out of his car, Ned saw that he was not only taller and fatter than his father but also more muscular. Dale didn't say anything to the man. He merely turned sideways and took a step back—Ned recognized the stance as his father's famous karate pose—and then, without any warning, Dale slammed the bottom half of his open hand against the man's nose. The man's knees buckled. He dropped his lunch bag and fell to the ground. Dale kicked him twice, then returned to the truck. Before he could even shut his truck's door, he floored it out of there.

"Some people," Dale said later, "need to learn how to drive. I mean, I've got a child in my car, goddamn it. I don't care what happens to me. But you . . . That's a different story, bud. My kids are my life."

Ned had witnessed a few other similar occasions. And then there were the occasions he hadn't witnessed, the ones he had only heard about over dinner, how this *man or* that *man had done something to* get his father's blood pressure up and how he'd had no choice but to act.

And so when his father told Ned that a bayonet would turn him into a big blubbering baby, Ned simply didn't believe it. Another boy's father, sure, but not his.

After an hour of walking by the dim light of an old flashlight, the day's first hint of sun finally started to show. Ned's feet were already damp from dew. He wanted to yawn but didn't. His father wasn't yawning. Ned was hungry, too, but he wasn't going to say anything until his father said something.

"Look, look," his father said, pointing to tracks on the ground.

"Is it a deer?" Ned asked.

His father nodded. He crouched to get a better look.

"How big is it?" Ned asked. "Is it a big one?"

His father said, "Take a look at this. When a doe walks, the back hooves usually land on top of her front hooves, but a buck has a bigger chest, see, and the rear tracks tend to fall *inside* the front tracks. Also—look—the tracks here are toe-out." His father looked up, laughed. "We've got a *big* one on our hands."

Ned smiled.

They followed the tracks for another hour. Ned started thinking that they were never going to find the deer, that the tracks would go on and on forever, but then his father held out his arm to stop Ned from walking. He pointed in the distance. And there it was: the biggest whitetail deer Ned had ever seen. It stood perfectly still, as if anxiously awaiting their arrival.

Dale handed Ned the rifle.

Bile burned the back of Ned's throat. He said to his father, "You can go first."

Dale shook his head. "I've shot plenty of deer. This one's yours."

Ned's hands were shaking. He'd shot only tin cans before. He wasn't sure he was ready to shoot the deer. He wasn't sure he wanted to shoot the deer—not this one, anyway. He held the gun up, positioning it the *way his father had taught him. His own breath was visible, obscuring his view each time he exhaled. He tried holding his breath, but his heart started pounding harder, causing the gun to jump ever so slightly. His nose was running. The tips of his ears, which he hadn't thought about until now, were numb from the cold.*

"Well?" his father said. "What are you waiting for?"

Ned applied a touch more pressure to the trigger, seeing how much pressure he could apply without actually firing. The deer reminded him of a man waiting at a bus stop, a man so lost in thought as to be oblivious to everything else around him. It was the kind of man that drove his father nuts, a man who lived a life of the mind without any regard for the tangible world. Fools, *his father called them.* Big wastes of breath.

Ned squeezed the trigger.

August 2, 2004

FOR A WEEK NOW, CHARLIE HAD ACTUALLY BEEN ABLE TO sleep, but each night's dreams were exponentially more graphic than the previous night's. In each dream, he's having sex with Jill the hypnotist. Candles flicker. One position melts into another. Body parts come into contact with his mouth, his tongue. She says, *You've never done this before, have you?* He shakes his head. *No, he hasn't.* He's surrounded by clothes pins, batteries, spent matches. It's like one of those dreams where you think you're able to see through your own eyelids but can't speak or move. Jill shapes Charlie into whatever position she wants, placing an arm here, a leg there. *There we go,* she says. *Fuck, yeah, there we go.*

"Oh God," Charlie said, opening his eyes. He was breathing rapidly and drenched in sweat. "Jesus Christ," he said. Jainey lay on the other side of the bed, knees pulled almost to her chest, mouth open. The girl could sleep through a tornado. Even so, Charlie had a hard-on he didn't want her seeing. It was pushing against his sweatpants, twitching like a restrained criminal trying to break free. *Easy boy. Easy.*

Charlie trudged to the bathroom. He turned on the light and, upon seeing himself in the mirror, opened his mouth to speak, but his windpipe contracted from his thumping heart, limiting his ability to make any noise at all. His hair—*all the hair on his head*—had turned white.

Charlie leaned closer to the mirror. He ran his fingers through it, searching for one remaining brown hair, but there were none. It was all white, as white as fresh snow. Just like that, Charlie looked twenty years older.

He knew the same thing had happened to his namesake Charlie

Chaplin during a particularly nasty divorce with Lita Grey. One day Chaplin's hair was black; the next, white. Stress was what did it. Sometimes shock, but in the few instances Charlie Wolf had read about, the victim, like a bug underfoot, was being crushed by life itself.

Was Charlie really that stressed out? He supposed it was possible. After all, if only a few months ago he had glimpsed his own future, he'd have witnessed a haggard Charlie Wolf driving to his security guard job in Hickory Hills with an eighteen-year-old girl hiding in his trunk, the same girl who slept platonically next to him while a six-foot-tall Osama bin Laden hovered over them, arms spread like Bela Lugosi's Dracula. And what would Charlie, after seeing such a grim vision, have done? The future would have been inexplicable. Pompeii Inn? The Castle? A hypnotist? White hair? Like Scrooge after his visit from the Ghost of Christmas Future, Charlie would have been chilled to the bone. It would have been a wake-up call, an opportunity to change course. But it was too late now. Here he was, and this was his life.

CHARLIE HAD already departed for one of his mysterious missions—missions he wouldn't tell Jainey anything about—when Jainey woke up, so she sat cross-legged on the bed and worked on a new Lloyd the Freakazoid cartoon. In this one, Lloyd was appointed Czar of George W. Bush's new education initiative, "No Child's Behind Left Untouched."

In the first panel, George Bush and Lloyd are visiting a grammar school for the public announcement of Lloyd's appointment. They are both on stage in the gymnasium: George Bush has his arm draped around Lloyd's shoulder; Lloyd is taking a swig from his vodka bottle, and his fly is unzipped.

In the second panel, a child walks by, and Lloyd touches the boy's behind. George Bush is trying not to laugh.

In the third panel, another child walks by—a girl this time—and Lloyd touches her butt, too. George is in tears now.

In the fourth and final panel, the "No Child's Behind Left Untouched" banner is falling down. Angry parents are yelling from the audience; children are crying. George Bush and Lloyd the Freakazoid are both laughing so hard, they are on their hands and knees, tears running down their cheeks. They are reaching out, grasping at any child they can reach.

Jainey liked where this comic strip was heading, but there was something missing, something she couldn't quite put her finger on. She stared and stared at the final panel, trying to concentrate. Her nerves, sizzling and jangled, had put her on edge. The very thing that she had successfully pushed from her mind these past few days now loomed over her, as if to say, *You can't escape me, so don't even try.* What she'd pushed from her mind was this one simple fact: she was pregnant.

Pregnant! *Jesus,* she thought.

She was ninety percent sure. She'd missed her period by two weeks, and she wasn't feeling quite herself—not that she was sure what her normal self was *supposed* to feel like. For her entire life she had felt unaccountably different from month to month: queasy from the sun in June, craving it in July, eating too much in the summer, barely hungry all winter long. Did other girls feel the way Jainey did, or did they feel exactly the same from hour to hour, minute to minute?

"Pregnant!" Jainey said. It felt good to say it out loud. The ominous force hovering over her eased up a little. "Jesus Christ on a cross," she said. "I'm pregnant!"

Jainey had tried ignoring her missed period. There was nothing appealing about being pregnant, not at this point in her life. What would become of her, a girl who'd finished high school but had no prospects otherwise? And what would her mother do if Jainey came home and announced that she was going to be a grandmother? Probably pick up a frying pan and hit Jainey over the head with it. *Bam!* End of story.

She sure as hell wasn't going to tell Mr. Licks. The poor kid had suffered enough. Jainey already felt responsible for his getting beaten nearly to death by her camouflaged brother. And who knew? Maybe Jainey wasn't pregnant. Maybe the missed period was a fluke, the result of a poor diet, stress, or screwed-up hormones.

Jainey barely completed the thought before running to the bathroom, bending over the toilet, and throwing up the Pop-Tart and Diet Coke she'd bought two hours ago from the hotel's vending machines. "Oh God," she said into the bowl.

JILL WAS SITTING behind the front desk when Charlie stepped inside. There was no receptionist; there were no assistants. Jill the hypnotist was a one-woman show.

Charlie had come to see what she could tell him about his hair situation. Was it reversible? Was there anything she could do? But there was another reason. Charlie was addicted to whatever it was that she was doing to him when he was under her spell. He craved her. He dreamed about her, of course, but when he wasn't dreaming, he felt a vague gnawing in his lower gut, a desire, and then that desire would attach itself to a series of images of Jill—Jill twisting her torso and unbuttoning her skirt; Jill lifting a shirt over her head; Jill rolling stockings down her legs; Jill breathing heavily through an open mouth, her eyes boring through Charlie's eyes. Lately, though, she'd begun to leave physical reminders of their time spent together. A scratch on his arm. A raw patch of skin. Last night, he found teeth marks on his leg. Despite all this evidence, Jill remained mum. After bringing Charlie back to a conscious state, she acted as though nothing untoward had transpired. She played the role of the consummate professional perfectly.

"Hello!" Jill said. She waved him in. She smiled and said, "May I help you?"

"It's me," Charlie said. "Charlie Wolf."

Jill smiled more fiercely. *Charlie Wolf, Charlie Wolf, who the hell's Charlie Wolf?* She squinted at him, then recoiled. "Charlie! Your hair! What did you do to your hair?"

"Nothing. I just fell asleep, and when I woke up—"

"You fell asleep?"

"I've been sleeping off and on, yeah."

Jill stood and walked around the desk. "Are you seeing another hypnotherapist?" she asked.

"What? No, of course not. Why would I do that?"

"You weren't really supposed to fall asleep yet, that's why. I wanted to ease you back into it."

Charlie nodded. Jill wasn't really his type. She was too short, for starters. She was probably twelve years older than him. Her face, in certain lights, resembled the face of a troll doll, with her too-big eyes and pugish nose. And yet, despite all of this, he was getting aroused with her standing so near to him. She had rewired his brain; she had that power.

Charlie walked up to Jill. Against his better judgment, he was feeling flirtatious. "I found teeth marks on my leg after our last session," he said. "What do you make of that?"

"The unconscious mind is very powerful," Jill said softly, staring into his eyes. She took a deep breath. "It's not uncommon for someone to develop physical manifestations of some past emotional trauma while in the unconscious state. For instance, I might be talking to you about your problem—your being unable to pee while other men are in the restroom—and this might bring about some memory from your childhood where your mother is yelling at you for wetting your bed, and when you wake up you see that you've wet yourself."

"But I haven't ever wet myself during a session," Charlie said.

"I know," Jill said. "I'm giving you a hypothetical situation so as to illuminate a situation where one has a physical reaction to a deeply buried psychological trauma."

"So . . ." Charlie said. "I wonder if anyone in my past ever said anything about wanting to bite me."

"Charlie, Charlie, Charlie," she said. She shook her head, as if breaking whatever trance Charlie had put *her* in. She moved away from the desk, out of Charlie's reach. "Even *I* don't always know what you're thinking when you're under. That's what all of these sessions are about. We're trying to shed some light on that dark room. The bite marks are a good sign, though. It means that you're actively battling your monsters. And that's no small feat." She cocked her head to the side, sizing him up. "Well?" she asked.

Charlie smiled. "Well what?"

"Shall we put you under today?"

Charlie wanted to say something sexual to her, something he might have said to Petra before they took off their clothes and cleared off the kitchen table, but he decided not to push it. What if she denied it and then refused to see him anymore? Charlie removed his shoes and lay on the sofa. He fluffed a pillow and tucked it behind his head. "Yes," he said. "I'd like that."

"YOUR HAIR!" Jainey yelled when Charlie returned to their room.

"I know, I know."

"It's awesome."

"It is?"

"You look like one of the guys from Green Day or something. When did you do it?"

"Do what?"

"Dye it?"

"I didn't dye it. This is what it looked like when I woke up."

"Get the fuck out of here."

"No, I'm serious."

"Well, it looks pretty sexy." She smiled. Charlie looked more relaxed than she'd ever seen him, but his shirt was all buttoned wrong, and there was a red blotch on his neck that looked like a hickey. "You okay?" she asked.

"Oh, yeah, I'm fine," he said. "You?"

"I think I'm pregnant," she said. She laughed. She gave a theatrical shrug with her arms out and palms up. She shook her head in dismay. "Don't know how it happened!"

"Have you been having sex?" Charlie asked.

Jainey nodded.

"That's probably how it happened then," Charlie said.

"You're right," Jainey said.

"But maybe you're not pregnant," Charlie said. "Are you *sure* you're pregnant?"

Jainey bit her lip, raised her eyebrows. She thought she was going to start crying. She quickly shook her head. "Nope, I'm not sure."

"Should we get one of those home pregnancy tests for you?"

Jainey's eyes began to gleam over, and yet she still staved off the full onslaught of tears. She wasn't sure why she felt like crying. It was involuntary, like blinking.

Charlie held her hand all the way to his car. He unlocked her door, waited until she was buckled in, then gently shut it. He drove her to the Osco on State Road. It was all so weird, walking into this store she'd been inside a million times before. Osco was where her mother got her prescription for Valium refilled. How many times had her mother complained to the pharmacist about the cost of drugs? And how many times had Jainey, mortified at her mother's behavior, walked over to the revolving display of reading glasses and tried on the most obnoxious pairs she could find? One time, she put on a pair of glasses with huge, square plastic frames and thick lenses and then tapped her mother on the shoulder, hoping she might laugh. Instead her mother said, "Put those back, Jainey. We can't afford them," as if the glasses were a serious purchase and not the sight gag Jainey'd intended them to be.

Jainey handed the pregnancy test to Charlie. "I can't bring this up there," she whispered.

"Why not? I'll give you the money."

"I know one of the cashiers."

"Do you?"

"Beth Ann Winkel."

"That's her name?" Charlie asked. "*Winkel?*"

"Please?" Jainey asked.

Charlie reluctantly agreed. He carried the kit in front of him as if it were a ticking bomb. Jainey waited by the automatic doors. Next to the doors was a bank of machines that sold bubble gum and plastic spiders. One machine sold tiny figurines called Homies. There was a rapper, a cop, a prostitute. Jainey put fifty cents into the machine and twisted the dial.

"Okay," Charlie said. "Let's go."

"Just a sec." Jainey opened the hatch to see which Homie she'd bought, but nothing came out. "What the hell?"

"Those things never work," Charlie said. "Let's go."

"Goddamn piece of shit," Jainey said. She kicked the machine once—hard. She started to kick it again, but Charlie put his hand over her shoulder and led her toward the exit. Before leaving, she turned around for one last look. Beth Ann Winkel was watching the two of them, hands on her hips. Jainey turned quickly back around and ducked her head, then stepped through the doors and into the muggy night.

"Impulse control," Charlie said.

"What?"

"You need to work on impulse control," Charlie said.

"Probably." She paused before getting inside the car. "Thanks for taking that up there," she said. She raised up on her toes and kissed Charlie's cheek.

Charlie, blushing, nodded. "Not a problem."

CHARLIE WAITED outside the bathroom. He sat on the edge of the bed, reading over the directions for the third time, making sure that he was clear about which color meant *pregnant* and which color meant *not pregnant.* He wanted to be prepared to deliver the news as calmly as possible. He felt like her husband, a man full of fear and hope and regret and melancholy. Never mind that Jainey wasn't his wife or that the hypothetical child wasn't his. He was a wreck; he couldn't help it.

"Are you okay in there?" Charlie asked.

"I'm trying to pee," Jainey said, "but I can't."

Charlie knew the feeling well. "Turn the faucet on. Not all the way, though. Just enough so that the water is still clear but harder than a drizzle."

"I turned the water on," Jainey said, "so you can stop yelling directions at me."

"I'm not yelling," Charlie mumbled. "I'm trying to help." He looked up at Osama, as if he were a friend of the family also awaiting the news. "I wasn't yelling, was I?" he asked. Osama stared ominously ahead.

The toilet flushed, and Jainey opened the door. "Okay, here it is."

Charlie took the stick from Jainey, checked his watch, then examined the results.

"You're pregnant," Charlie said.

"Shit." Jainey plopped down next to him on the bed. She sighed loudly, dramatically. "What am I supposed to do now?" she asked.

Charlie outlined for Jainey her various options: you could do *this* or you could do *this* or you could do *that* . . . He tried draining his voice of any judgment. His job, as he saw it, was to objectively convey information. He would answer questions; he would offer to help her through whichever decision she chose.

When Charlie was done, Jainey said, "Yeah, but what would *you* do?"

"It's not important what I would do."

"Maybe not," Jainey said. "But I want to hear your opinion."

"I'm not sure I'm prepared to offer it," Charlie said.

"You don't have any opinions?"

"I have opinions," Charlie said, "but I'd rather not make them public."

Jainey sighed. "Spill the beans, Chuck. You're my only friend left in this stinkin' world. I want your opinion."

He was her only friend? Charlie started to speak, but his voice caught, and he coughed into his hand to hide the fact that he might start weeping.

"Okay, okay," Charlie said, clearing his throat. "My opinion."

Charlie took a deep breath. He told her that, *in his opinion,* she was too young to have a baby; that having a baby right now might prove to be the end of any promise in her life, the end of any serious intellectual growth in, say, college; that she would probably end up on the government dole, given her family situation; that she'd probably have to live at home, the *last* place she wanted to be; that a child would consume everything—time, money, social life, energy. In short, he couldn't imagine anything *worse* happening to Jainey in her life right now.

Jainey looked blankly at him. "Wow. You don't hold back, do you?"

"But you have to take my opinion in context," Charlie said.

"And what context is that?"

"I'm an agnostic."

"Oh." Jainey mulled it over. "Well, I'm Catholic, but I think we're pretty much on the same page."

"Just let me know what you want to do," Charlie said, "and I'll help you with it, okay?"

Jainey reached over and patted Charlie's hand. His hand, next to Jainey's, looked obscenely old. The veins protruded too much. There were old scars from where tin-can lids had sliced through or where glass had snagged him. The creases around his knuckles were deep. He was only five or six years older than Jainey, not too old, in theory, to be her lover, but right now the only role he fulfilled was that of a concerned father, and when he looked over at her, this too-thin girl with crazy dyed hair and chipped fingernails, he couldn't fathom how anyone could fail to love her. Not loving this girl was, plain and simple, a fault of soul.

"Holy mother of Christ," Rex said upon sight of Charlie. "Your *hair.* What did you *do?*"

"Nothing," Charlie said. "I fell asleep, and when I woke up it was white."

Rex circled Charlie, as if the two of them were dogs. "I've never seen anything like this," he said. "Hey, did you happen to pick up a briefcase the other night when we left the Castle?"

"A briefcase? Nn-nn."

"You sure?"

"Positive." Charlie answered a little too fast.

"I had all my tax forms in it. Receipts. Things like that."

"A little early for taxes," Charlie said and laughed. "Isn't it?"

"Not if you're making quarterly payments," Rex said.

"Oh." Charlie wasn't sure yet what to do about NTC and Rex's file on him. He knew he should just quit the job—that would be the smart thing—but then what? He'd be stuck in Chicago without an income, and at least his NTC work paid a wage, paltry though it was.

Rex handed Charlie a CD. "I burned this the other night for you. It's got some great soundtrack compositions by Frank Waxman on it. Do you know who he is? No? Well, he was one of the great movie composers. Great stuff. I figured you might want something to listen to. Do you have a laptop? You could bring your laptop down to work and pop it in."

The CD was probably designed to download everything from Charlie's computer. Rex probably wanted Charlie to hand it back to him, telling him it didn't work, and then he'd possess whatever secrets Charlie stored on his hard drive. There *were* no secrets, but Rex didn't know that. The only secrets, from Charlie's perspective, were who Rex was and why he was investigating Charlie.

"How's the city treating you? Been to Kingston Mines yet? Great blues. Do you like blues?"

Charlie fell reluctantly into a conversation with Rex, but the whole time he worried about Jainey. Was there a finite amount of oxygen in the trunk? What about the pregnancy? Would that compromise her ability to breathe? Would the pregnancy make her more susceptible to claustrophobia? He tried communicating with Jainey telepathically. *Hold on. I'm coming, okay? Sit tight. I'll be there in a sec!*

"You all right?" Rex asked. "You're looking kind of, I don't know, *sweaty.*"

"Food poisoning," Charlie said. "I ate some dubious-looking chicken earlier."

"There's a 7-Eleven across the street. I could run over there and get you something. What do you need? Bottled water? Tums?"

"No, no," Charlie said. "I'm fine. But I think I need to sit here alone, you know? I'm feeling a little too weak to keep talking."

"Oh." Rex looked hurt. "Sure, not a problem," he said. "I need to get to the Castle anyway. The bouncer from the other day is working again tonight. I want to see if he remembers anything." Rex hesitated, as if to gauge Charlie's reaction, but Charlie remained poker-faced, unmoved.

"Good luck," Charlie said.

"What took you so long?" Jainey crawled out of the trunk, gathered her belongings.

"Shhh. We'll talk about it later. Let's hurry."

"Are you okay? You look a little *green.*"

"I was getting worried about you."

"You were?"

"Shhh. Let's go."

Charlie repressed all thoughts of Jill. Instead, he tortured himself with memories of Petra. *Sexual* memories. Whenever Charlie was bored, his mind wandered to past sexual encounters. This happened to him on airplanes, too. Charlie would start each flight by reading all the crap stuffed inside the pouch in front of him—the safety tips, information about the *kind* of airplane they were on, the in-flight magazine with its tedious business advice, and, finally, the catalog that sold everything you didn't need, from a CD player you could hang in the shower to an autographed Mickey Mantle baseball. Since Charlie could usually dispense with all of the airplane's reading materials in about fifteen minutes, his mind would start to drift—first toward any attractive stewardess on the plane, and then toward memories of actual sexual encounters from his past. Usually he'd have to return the tray table to its locked position so that its subtle rising and falling from his own involuntarily twitching hard-on didn't frighten the unfortunate soul sitting next to him, and then he'd need a blanket or a coat to cover his lap. The memories were torturous in both their precision and repetition, the mind's ability to replay a single moment over and over. Had the moment really been *that* great? He certainly hadn't paused during the actual sex itself to savor it, so why did it come back now so forcefully? Sometimes it was a look the woman had given him. Other times it was something raunchy that was said, or maybe his partner's sudden intake of breath, or the way she looked at him and said, "Oh my God, Charlie." It wasn't as if Charlie had been any kind of Don Juan before he'd hooked up with Petra, but once you started breaking down even a few sexual encounters, you could divide them into a hundred specific moments, each one as intense as the other. And with Petra, there were thousands of such moments, and Charlie now felt himself getting sucked into the vortex of his own memories. It was as if someone inside his head had opened a door to a room, and inside that room were dozens of copulating couples, and Charlie, unable to resist, had walked inside only to discover, after the door had been shut and locked, that all of the couples were Charlie and Petra.

Charlie crossed his legs. He tried to shift his focus to Jainey's present dilemma, but his mind sailed toward a single, predetermined thought: *this girl sitting ten feet away from me has been having sex.* Charlie tried to smother the thought, but how could he? It was a fact, no less true than that Abraham Lincoln had been the sixteenth president of the United States. And what else could a man as bored as Charlie do but wonder what the girl was like in bed? What sorts of things did she like? What was her favorite position? How did she moan? Where did she draw the line between the things she would do and the things she wouldn't do? *Was* there a line? Did she keep her eyes open or did she close them when she came?

When Jainey looked up, Charlie feared he had asked the last question aloud.

"Hunh?" he said.

"I need to pee."

Charlie nodded.

Jainey blew into her cupped palms. "This place is colder than a witch's ice maker."

"Actually," Charlie said, "I'm kind of hot today."

Jainey looked at him like he was a madman, and Charlie had to admit, there was probably some truth to it.

"O'SULLIVAN," Jainey muttered. "O'Sullivan." She was standing in the "O" section of Deep Storage, searching for her own file. "Ah-ha!" she said when the first O'Sullivan file appeared, but her excitement quickly evaporated. There must have been a few million O'Sullivan files. "Shit!" she said. "You piece of rotting dog shit." There were times Jainey wondered if she had Tourette's syndrome, one profane word climbing atop another, until a pile of profanities lay before her, all writhing and moaning. "Rat fucks," she added to the pile. "Fuck-a-ducks."

Some files were mere manila file folders; others were thick and accordion-shaped. When she found hers, nearly thirty minutes into her search, she was disappointed. While not the thinnest file, it certainly wasn't one of the fat ones. She tucked it under her shirt. She was ready to walk back to the lobby—she'd found what she was looking for, after all—but then she noticed a door that was half the width of a normal door. Though there were no warning signs posted anywhere, something about the door was telling her to keep out. Naturally, Jainey opened it.

The narrow door opened into a narrow hallway. Overhead were exposed pipes and wires, silver ductwork. The floor was on a slope, and Jainey headed down it. There were sconces with lightbulbs hanging on the wall, but the farther she went, the greater the space between the sconces, and the darker it got. The darker it got, the colder she became. Soon, she was shivering. She turned a corner, and the floor's slope became steeper, the walls narrower. In a few places, she had to turn sideways to squeeze through. The ceiling was lower, too, and there were times she had to duck so as not to hit her forehead on a pipe. She hoped she wouldn't get stuck because no one would ever find her. It was like walking inside her own brain, where every passing idea had the power to suffocate. Until recently, Jainey had always believed that her state of mind—the low-grade depression and anxiety that she couldn't shake—was the result of her situation at home and school, that the desire to escape her own skin was actually a desire to escape her present set of circumstances, but she wondered now if maybe it wasn't chemical, too. A glitch in the brain. Was she clinically depressed? Was she manic? It wasn't something she'd ever considered before because the very idea of being depressed was depressing in and of itself, so why compound the problem if she *was* depressed?

Her skin was covered with goose pimples, and her teeth were chattering. When she breathed, she saw puffs of her own breath. At the sight of those steamy wisps, she remembered a movie she'd watched with her father when she was a little girl, *The Wolf Man*. There was a guy in it—Harry? Larry?—who turned into a wolf at the sight of a full moon. A lycanthrope! Why hadn't the movie occurred to her before now? Seeing her own breath in Deep Storage instantly brought back the scene in which the Wolf Man lopes through foggy woods while hunting his next victim. What she vividly remembered was that the Wolf Man still had on his shirt and pants, and when Jainey asked her father why he was still wearing a shirt and pants, her father said, "You're an odd little girl, you know." Jainey wasn't sure what her father meant—she was only five or six—but that was how she started to think of herself and that was what she eventually became: the odd little girl. It was as though she had been a normal girl until her father told her that she was odd, and then *poof*, Jainey was the odd girl. She retreated from other girls; she stayed out of the sun; she spent a lot of time staring at her own naked body in the mirror. For a while, whenever strangers introduced themselves to her, she would say, "You are what you eat," and whenever they asked what her name was, she would reply, "I am the walrus." Occasionally, she would overhear someone say to her mother, "She's an odd one," and Jainey would smile, remembering that day on the couch with her father, his arm draped over her shoulders, the Wolf Man lurking through fog, his mouth open, fangs bared. Why was the Wolf Man wearing a shirt and pants? The reason remained unclear, but one thing was for certain: Jainey was an odd little girl for asking.

Jainey's journey through the winding, downward-sloped corridor of Deep Storage ended at a second door made entirely of metal. The door was half her height and almost half her width. A thin layer of frost coated it. The knob was almost too cold to touch. Her skin stuck to it for a second, and when she removed her hand, it sounded like a Band-Aid peeling from flesh. This probably wasn't the best idea she'd ever had, but she couldn't resist seeing what was on the other side of the door. She'd come this far, after all. She had to lie on the floor and squirm to get inside. She wiggled, snakelike, and then she grabbed hold of the open door and pulled herself all the way in. *It's like a birth canal,* Jainey thought, and she almost heaved at the thought, connecting her present journey to the growing fetus inside her.

It was pitch-black on the other side of the door. She stood up and felt around until she touched a light switch. A series of fluorescent lights winked on, one after the other. It was a huge room with a single barrister's bookcase up against the wall. Behind the bookcase's glass doors was a lone leather-bound volume with a gold nameplate on its spine. Jainey felt like Alice in Wonderland—or did she actually feel more like Alice in Jefferson Airplane's *White Rabbit?* Was this book the magic pill? Or was she already hallucinating? She leaned in close to read the nameplate. George Walker Bush, it read.

Jainey's heart thumped harder. Shivering, she opened the glass door and reached inside. She pulled the file off the shelf. *So this is it,* she thought. *NTC's profile of our president.* She wanted to sit down and read it right there, but she suddenly felt off, hot and cold at the same time, perhaps from the stark contrast of the fluorescent lights after having spent so much time in the building's chilly bowels. It might have been the pregnancy at work, too, or the sheer strangeness of the moment. She ran her finger over the gold nameplate. *George Walker Bush.* Jainey laughed. An echo of her own laugh boomeranged back at her, and she was surprised at how crazy she sounded. Crazy and out of control. "I've got your number now, you little shit," Jainey said before stuffing the book down her pants, snug against her own file.

CHARLIE OPENED the door to Deep Storage and called out Jainey's name. Nothing. He started walking toward the restroom when he heard scrabbling in a row far beyond the restroom. Had someone been hiding in here? Had Rex sneaked back inside through an unmarked entrance? But Charlie didn't know of any such entrances. Now that he thought about it, the fact that the building had only one entrance was surely a violation of every conceivable fire ordinance, and if anything happened to block the sole entryway, he and Jainey would be doomed.

Charlie removed his pepper spray, the only weapon issued to him. He couldn't see where the intruder was, so he walked softly until he reached a cross-aisle that allowed him to see the length of each row. His shoes, however, squeaked regardless of how softly he stepped. Each squeak set off a physiological chain reaction: Charlie's heart would flutter, so he'd instinctively suck in air to stabilize the beating, but then his lungs, too full, would involuntarily decompress, causing Charlie to sigh heavily, expelling too much air too fast. Charlie'd take another step, and his shoe would squeak again.

"*Shit,*" he muttered, catching his breath.

In the final row, Charlie saw the culprit.

"Jainey!" he yelled. "What the hell are you doing?"

Jainey froze, then raised her hands. "Is that you, Charlie?" she asked.

Charlie walked quickly toward her.

"It *is* you," she said. She lowered her arms and clutched her stomach.

"What are you doing?" Charlie asked. "Are you okay?"

"I got lost," Jainey said.

"Lost?"

"What? You don't believe me?" Jainey asked.

Charlie hadn't said he didn't believe her—of *course* he believed her—and it killed him to hear in her voice the desperation to be credible.

"Of course I believe you," Charlie said. "I was just worried is all. You were gone a long time."

"You were worried?" Jainey said.

"*Yes,* I was worried."

Jainey said, "Can we get married?"

Charlie laughed, but it sounded more like a bark: *harf.* He put his arm around her shoulders. "Whatever you want," he said.

On their way back to Pompeii Inn, after Charlie had let Jainey out of the trunk and into the front seat, Jainey said, "What are we going to do?"

"What do you mean?"

"About me being pregnant."

"Oh." Charlie hesitated, thinking. He said, "I know a doctor who works at a clinic."

"Really? You do?"

"Akshay Kapoor."

"Akshay," Jainey said. "Is that Middle Eastern?"

"Indian."

"Akshay," Jainey repeated. "Akshay Kapoor." Charlie sensed that

Jainey had pivoted toward him, but he kept his eyes on the road. "You know what?" Jainey finally said.

"What?"

"You're like my guardian angel or something. I don't believe in any of that crap, and I think that people who *do* believe in that kind of crap are stupid, but if I *did* believe in it, which I *don't,* you'd be my guardian angel for sure."

"We'll see," Charlie said. "The jury's still out."

Turning into the hotel's parking lot, Charlie spotted a man across the street. He was leaning against a phone booth and looking at the motel through binoculars. *Rex,* Charlie thought. *Rex, you son of a bitch.*

He realized he should go over and put an end to this nonsense right then and there. He should pin the bastard up against the phone booth and demand to know what he was doing here, why NTC was tracking him, and when it was all going to stop, but he was too tired. He could barely keep his eyes open.

On their way to the motel's front door, Jainey shivered and said, "I don't feel too good."

"Don't worry," Charlie said. "You'll be okay." He opened the door for her. As Jainey crossed the threshold, Charlie turned and gave Rex the finger.

The binoculars lowered. The man's face was painted camouflage.

Only after the binoculars went back up did Charlie register that the man was dressed from head to toe in military gear. There had been two major drug busts at Pompeii Inn since Charlie had checked in. In both cases, policemen wearing paramilitary gear had dragged men from their rooms. Charlie had witnessed the aftermaths of the first arrest: the assailants wearing only briefs or jeans, nothing else, cuffed and dragged toward a squad car. Charlie'd read about the other arrest in the *Daily Southtown;* it had happened while he was at work.

Maybe it *wasn't* Rex across the street. Maybe Charlie had hastily flipped off the wrong guy.

Well, Charlie thought. It was too late now. The damage was done. Whoever the son of a bitch was, he'd just have to live with it.

August 3, 2004

DALE O'SULLIVAN HADN'T HAD ANY CONTACT WITH HIS family the entire time he was in the joint. Barbara had divorced him and then barred the two kids from coming to visit. He'd already planned on hanging up on Barbara, that cooze, if she answered the phone, but a man with a deep voice picked up, and it was at this point that Dale realized he hadn't thought any of this through. What if this was some jagoff Barbara was shacking up with?

"Who's this?" Dale asked.

"No," the man said. "You tell me first: who's *this?*"

"Dale O'Sullivan. Now, who the fuck is *this?*"

There was a pause. Then, "Dad?"

"Ned?"

They agreed to meet at White Hen Pantry on 79th street. He told Ned to look for a silver Ford Fairmont.

The Fairmont was the biggest hunk o' junk he'd ever driven. Not that Dale had any room to complain. Larry Two Fingers had asked his brother who ran a used-car lot in Plainfield to help Dale out, and Larry's brother actually gave the car to Dale. Just like that. Handed the keys to him. "No one'll buy it, anyway," Larry's brother had said, "so I figure, what the hell, why not just give it to you?"

That was the last kind gesture afforded him. Getting released back into the world proved to be a royal kick in the ass. Dale's parole officer helped him get a minimum wage job as a janitor at Chicago Ridge Mall. All day long Dale swept floors and cleaned toilets and picked up trash. No one looked at you. You didn't exist unless you proved to be an obstacle to someone's desire, as when Dale set up the chintzy CLOSED sign in front of the restroom door and placed an orange cone on either side of it. Then and only then would people notice the janitor's existence, but not as a living, breathing human being. What you became was a nuisance.

"Hey, you. When're you going to be done cleaning?"

Dale looked up. He calmly told them that there was another restroom at the other end of the mall, not to mention the various restrooms inside each anchor store.

"Yeah, but when's *this* one gonna be open again?"

Dale smiled. He wished he could walk up real close and say, *You know where I've been the last seven years? You know why I was there? You want a doctor to screw your skull back together? Is that what you really want? Because I'll make damned sure it happens, motherfucker.* But Dale suffered in silence, either ignoring the patron altogether or providing a specific time that was way beyond however long Dale would actually be there.

The job wasn't without perks. He could take frequent smoke breaks. He wasn't always under someone's watchful eye. And there were a lot of young mothers who came to the mall alone. Well, not *exactly* alone. They came with their strollers and babies. But alone enough. Enough alone, at least, so that Dale could easily daydream about what it might be like to spend an afternoon with one of the young mothers.

One morning, a young woman sitting in the food court next to a stroller noticed Dale looking at her and smiled. Dale smiled back, then turned away. Later, the woman approached and said hello, and what Dale learned was that the baby wasn't her baby, that she was merely watching it for the afternoon, that she was bored and wanted to go somewhere and get high. What Dale felt was how safecrackers must have felt listening to the tumblers fall into place, one after the other, only to get stuck at the last tumbler. For Dale, the last tumbler was this: His Life. He *couldn't* get stoned with her—it would be a violation of his parole—and they *couldn't* go back to his place, which was a room rented by the week at a dump on Cicero Avenue, the sort of place he wouldn't have been caught dead walking out of ten years ago. It was where junkies and whores spent their afternoons.

In the end, they made out by a row of lockers, like a couple of teenagers. The lockers, according to Dale's boss, had been permanently locked up since 9/11, the fear being that a terrorist might put a remote-control bomb inside one. Dale had wanted to say, *Oh yeah, that makes sense—the World Trade Center, the Pentagon, Chicago Ridge Mall,* but Dale kept his mouth shut. Apparently, every Tom, Dick, and Harry thought he was next in line to get blown up.

The woman's tongue was dry and tasted like Diet Coke, but her body was warm and felt good pressed up against him.

"Look," he said. "Come back tomorrow. Maybe I can work something out."

The woman sighed. Up close, he saw now that she was older than he'd first thought. Makeup covered crow's feet, and her chin had faint whispers of hair. Her skin was unnaturally porous, and for a second he was reminded of Tommy Tits and all those black market hormone pills the guy took so that he could look like a chick.

"You know what?" he said. "If you can't wait until tomorrow, then fuck you."

"What?"

"You heard me."

The woman reached for the stroller. The baby had begun to cry, which made Dale all the more incensed.

"What the hell kind of broad takes someone else's baby to the mall and looks for guys to make out with? Huh?"

By now, the woman was nearly at the end of the corridor, but she was having a hard time walking fast on high heels, and one of the stroller's wheels was stuck.

Dale shook his head. The world was full of crazy people. He had to remind himself of this sad fact every second of every stinking day, lest he fall in with the wrong crowd.

JAINEY'S LIFE had finally turned inside-out. She stayed awake all night, slept all day; something was growing inside her, presumably a baby; she was living in a hotel room instead of her own home, sleeping next to a man she didn't know but who made her feel safe; Mrs. Grant's death was still a giant question mark hovering over her life; summer was careening to an end, but there would be no school to go back to, nothing to do; the war in Iraq raged on, people were still getting beheaded, and although things were looking worse every day, life in Burbank, life in the United States, chugged right along.

It was possible that Mrs. Grant's death had sent Jainey tumbling into some dark netherworld of her own subconscious, and that everything happening to her right now, everything she thought was reality, wasn't really happening at all. This was a game she played when she was a kid: *pretend the whole world is a fabrication, and that the only thing that exists is Jainey and her brain.* But maybe it wasn't a game anymore; maybe it was real.

Jainey used to play all kinds of games, the goal of which was to psyche herself into believing that something was true that actually *wasn't* true. When she was ten, soon after her father nearly killed her gym teacher, she started pretending that she was capable of making herself invisible. Having achieved invisibility, she decided she was also insubstantial: she could walk through walls, ghostlike, or a bullet could pierce her without consequence. Nothing could hurt her. One day after school, while crossing 79th Street, Jainey stopped in the middle of a busy lane. An eighteen-wheeler was a block away, barreling toward her. Jainey stood waiting for the truck to pass through her, for her to appear on the other side of it, but the key was to keep concentrating on invisibility. She stood her ground, thinking, *I'm invisible, I'm invisible, I'm invisible,* but when the driver pulled the chain for the air horn, Jainey clutched her head and screamed. Brakes smoking, the truck squealed to a stop less than a foot from where Jainey, unable to move, stood. The driver got out and yelled at her, but she was so frightened by the close call that all she could concentrate on was the ghostly heat rolling off the engine and washing over, as if to say, *I'm what you're not.*

Jainey looked over at Charlie. His eyes were shut. He wasn't really asleep. He wasn't awake, either, though. It was Jainey's contention that Charlie had finally done the impossible. He was both wide awake and sound asleep at the exact same time. There was no longer any middle ground. His eyes twitched rapidly beneath thin lids, but if she were to ask him a question, he'd answer her without a pause.

Jainey had stowed George Bush's secret file inside her backpack for future examination, but she held onto her own. Her palms were sweating. Now that the file was in her possession, she wasn't sure that she should open it. *Should I or shouldn't I?* she wondered.

She opened it.

The first thing that struck her was the number of drawings all over the edges of her test booklets and work sheets. A doodle here, a doodle there. Even at six years old, Jainey couldn't stop drawing. There were a lot of cartoon dogs, too. Mr. Ditka, her bulldog, appeared several times. The drawings had caught her off guard, and she wanted to cry, but maybe what was making her want to cry was a surge of hormones, her body no longer sure what was genuinely sad and what wasn't.

Jainey flipped to the back of the file, the final projection. She took a deep breath. *So this is who I am,* Jainey thought. She had to remind herself to breathe out.

PROBABILITIES for Jainey Ann O'Sullivan

Political affiliation: `Radical`

Activism: `Probable`

Employment: Artist/Alternative Retail (Coffee Shops, Goodwill, etc.)

Earnings: Lower 10%

Marital Status: Divorced (multiple?)

Sexuality: Promiscuous

Religion: Buddhism

Threat to Self: Grave

Threat to Society: Moderate

Most Likely Crime to Commit: Suicide

Suicide. The word itself altered her body's physiology. The rest of the analysis seemed true enough, but *this* . . .

"Suicide," she said.

Charlie, eyes closed, said, "What was that?"

She put her hand on the top of his head and gently smoothed down his rabbit-white hair. It was how she had rubbed Mr. Ditka's big head when he came snuffling up to her. "Nothing." Charlie, probably not even sure who was touching him or speaking, grumbled his approval. Jainey shut her file. She took a deep breath. She eased off the creaking bed and stuffed the file into her already overstuffed backpack.

Earlier that day, Charlie had draped a white bedsheet over Osama W. Bush—"He kind of gives me the creeps," Charlie'd said—but Jainey wanted to take another look at him, so she yanked off the sheet, as smooth as a magician, and there he stood with his long, gray-streaked beard, arms wide open, as if he were about to say, *Come here and give li'l Osama some sugar.* Why hadn't Jainey noticed before that Mrs. Grant had created a benevolent-looking Osama?

An inviting Osama? Of course, Osama wasn't really Osama. Jainey yanked down his beard, popped off his fake nose, and lifted the turban. Where once there had been a kinder, gentler Osama now stood George W. Bush smirking at her. It was as if he were now thinking, *Look at you, you pathetic weirdo . . . what rock did you crawl out from under?* Jainey could almost see him chuckling at her, shoulders twitching.

"That's right," Jainey said to George W. Bush. "Keep on smirking, you bastard."

Charlie said, "Hunh? What was that?" His eyes remained shut.

"Nothing, honey," Jainey said. She tried sounding like someone he might have once loved, someone he'd have been pleased to find when he opened his eyes. She walked over to the bed, looked down at him. "Keep sleeping, sweetie," she whispered. "I'm right here." Charlie's sadness was as much a part of him as a Siamese twin. Separating him from it might be fatal. Even so, Jainey wished he'd stop being so sad. She crouched and whispered into his ear, "I won't leave you, baby." She kissed his forehead. "Ever," she said. "*Ever.*"

CHARLIE SAT UP, swinging his legs off the bed, his feet to the floor. The toilet flushed, and Jainey walked out of the bathroom.

"You're up!" she said.

"Was I asleep?"

"Kind of," Jainey said, "but not really. Hey, listen, I made a decision. I want you to take me to Akshay Kapoor."

The very name—*Akshay Kapoor*—was like a knife through Charlie's heart. He now regretted having suggested him. He'd done so only to reassure Jainey that he knew people and that a solution was at hand. But no: there was another motive for bringing him up. Who was he fooling? Charlie had wanted to see the bastard. He had wanted to size up his competition, but now he wasn't so sure. "You know,"

Charlie said, "there *are* other clinics and other doctors. Akshay isn't the only guy in town who'll do a, you know, an abortion."

"I know," Jainey said, "but I like his name. Plus, he wasn't born here, was he?"

"In Chicago?"

"No. This *country*," Jainey said.

"He was born in India," Charlie said.

"Good."

"Why should that matter?"

Jainey launched into a detailed report about Ruby Ridge, how the U.S. marshals had first killed the dog and then the boy, and how FBI sharpshooters were called in to shoot and kill the boy's mother while she held a baby—*"Blew her entire chin off!"* Jainey said, pressing the tip of her forefinger against Charlie's chin—and how later, when the sharpshooter who had killed the mother was being tried for the murder, the judge simply dropped the charges. "They protect their own," Jainey said.

"Who?"

"The government. Look at Waco. Same thing."

Jainey then laid out all the parallels between Ruby Ridge and Waco, of which there were many.

"I'm not saying that Randy Weaver at Ruby Ridge or David Koresh at Waco were *good* guys," Jainey said. "They probably would have hated me. But you can't raid someone's property and then, when one of your own gets shot, turn it into a war and kill everyone in sight. You can't do that! Get this. The FBI rewrote the rules of engagement before going to Ruby Ridge. Did you know that? Changed it on the spot."

"Whoa. Easy," Charlie said. "I'm not disagreeing with you."

"And then *this* man"—she thumped George Bush's head—"wonders why there are terrorists. Do you know why Tim McVeigh blew up the Oklahoma City federal building?"

"He hated the government, right?"

"Do you know *why* he hated the government?"

Charlie shrugged. He had probably once known the answer but didn't anymore. That's how most news stories came to him—as fleeting bits of information that didn't really warrant hanging on to.

Jainey was happy to explain: "Because of what the government did at Ruby Ridge and Waco. He was handing it back to the U.S. on a silver platter. And up until they fried his ass—and they *should* have fried his sorry ass—he stuck to the same story. He was saying to the Feds, 'You think you can do whatever you want, you think you can violate people's rights and get away with it, well, here's your own frickin' medicine.'" Jainey took a deep breath. "And now look what's happening in Iraq."

"*Iraq?*"

"Where were all those guys before? What do you call them—those guys blowing up cars?"

"Terrorists?"

"No."

"Insurgents?"

"Bingo!" Jainey wanted to know where all the insurgents had been *before* the U.S. started bombing their country. And where had all those people been who were now doing the beheadings? According to her own research, the United States had killed far more innocent Iraqis than Saddam Hussein *ever* killed when you took into account the first Gulf War and then the way the U.S. abandoned all those people during the uprising that followed—an uprising, Jainey noted, encouraged by the first George Bush. And then there were all those sanctions that didn't do anything to hurt Saddam personally; the sanctions only resulted in the starvation of innocent Iraqi citizens and their babies. And now there was *this* war. A hundred thousand Iraqi civilians had already been killed. *One hundred thousand!* "If the Iraqis didn't have a reason to hate us before, they sure as hell do now." Jainey started crying. "I think my hormones are on the blink," she said.

Charlie stood up, hugged her. "Easy, okay? You shouldn't be getting so excited."

"I'm not imagining all of this, am I? I feel crazy."

"You're not crazy." The crazy thing was, she *wasn't* crazy. Everything she'd said made perfect sense. "But here's what I'm curious about," Charlie said.

"What?"

"What does Ruby Ridge, Waco, and Iraq have to do with Akshay Kapoor?"

"I don't know anymore," Jainey said. Her eyelids were puffy from crying. "I don't know, but I want to go to him."

"Okay, okay," Charlie said. "I'll find what time he, you know, works. And then we'll set up an appointment with him."

"One other thing," Jainey said.

She took a step back, sniffled, and wiped her eyes. "I want to go in disguise."

"Disguise?" Charlie asked. "What kind of disguise?"

"Here it is," Jainey said. She pointed to a wig store. A train roared overhead. Shady characters shuffled along the sidewalk. Charlie checked his wallet, making sure it was still deep inside his back pocket.

"This is what you want?" he asked. "A wig?"

Charlie followed Jainey inside. An old Kool & the Gang song crackled over old speakers. There were a thousand fake heads inside, giving Charlie the macabre feeling he'd stepped into a morgue, or worse: a ghoulish chamber of horrors, like Jeffrey Dahmer's Wisconsin apartment.

The woman behind the counter said, "How's my Jainey?" She came around and gave Jainey a hug. When she saw Charlie, she narrowed her eyes. "You must be Tarzan. King of the monkeys."

"That's me," Charlie said, smiling. "Tarzan the Ape Man."

Mariah winked at him. The joke was clearly for Jainey's benefit, so Charlie didn't ask. What Charlie noticed, however, was how relaxed Jainey had suddenly become. For the first time since he'd met her, all the tenseness in her body loosened, allowing her features to soften. Her smile for Mariah was uninhibited.

To Jainey, but loud enough for Charlie to hear, Mariah said, "You didn't tell me you like the older men. My first husband, he was twenty years older. Had a heart attack one night when we were in bed getting all romantic."

"Actually," Charlie began, and he was about to clarify their relationship for Mariah but Jainey shushed him with a look.

"He's only a *few* years older," Jainey said. "He dyes his hair white."

Mariah squinted at Charlie. "Really? Looks more than a *few* years older."

"I haven't been sleeping well at night," Charlie said.

"Not sleeping well?" Mariah said. "A person eventually goes crazy if they don't get enough sleep. Happened to my third husband. Insomniac. Eventually jumped into a canal. Drowned himself."

"Is that true?" Jainey asked.

"Honey," Mariah said, "all stories are true for at least *one* person."

While Jainey wandered the store, Mariah joined Charlie at the display of silver bobs. The hair hung like Christmas tree tinsel off the dead-eyed mannequin heads. Mariah, who was shorter than Charlie, rose up and whispered into his ear, "I'll show you what your girl *really* wants." She led Charlie to a wig with long red hair—*real hair,* the tag said. *$412.00.*

Charlie laughed. "Whoa. That's a *lot* of money."

"For who? King o' the apes?" She nudged him. She sucked on her teeth. "Tell you what," she said. "I like your Jainey. She's got spunk. I used to have spunk, but she's still got it. I'll sell you this one for cost."

"And how much would that be?"

"Two hundred."

Charlie examined the wig, turning it inside-out. Two hundred bucks was still a lot of money—money he didn't have. When he touched the wig's *real hair,* the hair on his own neck rose.

"See how she looks with it on," Mariah said. "Go on."

Jainey, wearing an unflattering black mop, gasped when she saw which wig Charlie had in his hands.

"Try it on," Charlie said.

"Really?" Jainey replaced the cheap tarantula-looking wig with the expensive red one.

Mariah took a step back and said, "Why, look at you!"

Jainey, standing in front of the mirror to appraise herself, pouted her lips. She tipped her head back ever so slightly, then peeked over at Charlie's reflection. With sleepy bedroom eyes, she kissed the air, as if kissing him. As simple as that, Jainey O'Sullivan was no longer the wayward waif.

Gone was the punky little girl desperately trying to find herself. Gone was the paranoid political conspiracy theorist. What Charlie witnessed was something akin to the metamorphosis of Norma Jean Baker, the pale and freckled girl who grew up an orphan but ended up Marilyn Monroe, an international icon. The wig had turned Jainey into another *species.* It was that transformative.

Charlie walked up behind Jainey, put his hands on her shoulders. In the mirror, they could have been lovers, a kind of Sid and Nancy before Sid and Nancy had gone and gotten themselves all fucked up. "You want it?"

"It's too expensive," she whispered.

"I think I can work something out," he said.

"Really?" Jainey asked.

Charlie put a hand on top of her head. The wig's hair may have been real, but it felt like a dead girl's head. Charlie quickly removed his hand. He put both arms around her, a hug from behind, and said, "Why not."

John McNally

THE FAIRMONT stalled each time Dale O'Sullivan accelerated, a glitch that nearly killed him the first few times he tried making left-hand turns at busy intersections. Piece of shit though it may have been, Dale had to remind himself that it beat walking. Even so, Larry Two Fingers' brother could have picked out a better car for him. Every time Dale was stalled in an intersection with oncoming cars speeding toward him, Dale had half a mind to drive back to Plainfield and run the cheap bastard over.

When Dale wheeled into the White Hen, the Fairmont stalled again. Dale coasted into a space, braked, jerked it into park, and waited. It was dinnertime, and Dale's stomach growled a few times. He slapped his gut and said, "Easy, boy, easy."

Dale's fear was that Ned, who'd always veered toward the chunky side, was going to be a serious fat-ass by now. The boy had the propensity for it. Dale was waiting for a four hundred pound tub of lard to waddle up to his car when a soldier knocked on the passenger-side window. Dale leaned over, rolled down the window. The man, dressed head to toe in camouflage, had that lean, almost chiseled look that Dale had always admired. The man's head was shaved, too.

"May I help you?"

"Dad?"

"Ned? Is that you? Well, I'll be a son of a bitch." Dale opened the passenger-side door. "Look at you," Dale said after Ned was inside. "Are you in the military now or what?"

"Not yet," Ned said.

"You've . . . changed."

"I've had a vision," Ned said.

Dale nodded. Vision? What the hell did that mean? He said, "How's your mother? I'm sure she's still riding everyone's ass. That woman could ride an ass the way cowboys ride bulls. She was a first-class ball-buster, but I probably don't have to tell you that."

"She smokes too much," Ned said.

"Yeah? Well, who doesn't?" Dale said. "So tell me. How's my Jainey?"

"Let's go for a drive."

"A drive?"

Ned nodded.

"Okay. Sure. Let's go."

They parked across the street from the Pompeii Inn.

"So this *broad* actually has someone else's kid with her, and she wants us to go to a motel and get stoned and then, I don't know, probably ball all afternoon while the kid stays in its stroller and—"

"Shhhh. Look."

Dale narrowed his eyes at Ned. Was his own kid shushing him? What the fuck was up with *that?* But Ned wasn't even paying him any mind: his eyes were focused on Pompeii Inn.

Dale turned to see what the big deal was. What he saw was a hot piece of ass with long red hair going into the motel with some old white-haired dude. Did Ned think this was the first time he'd ever seen a hooker with a john? Hell, Dale should bring Ned over to *his* place. The sign outside advertised "two hour nap specials," for Christ's sake.

"There she is," Ned said.

"Who?"

"Jainey."

"*What?*"

"That's what she looks like now," Ned said. "She left home and moved in here. The hair's new, though."

"And who's the old fart?"

Ned shook his head. "I'm not sure yet. But they're sharing a room."

An irrational urge washed over Dale. He wanted to reach over and pop Ned. He knew it wasn't Ned's fault that his eighteen-year-old daughter was shacking up with some old pervert at the Pompeii Inn, and yet there was a good reason people always wanted to kill the messenger. If not for the messenger, there wouldn't be any bad news. Couldn't Ned have allowed Dale a few more hours of happiness? Couldn't they have talked about other things—*good things*—before Ned hauled Dale's ass down the street to this seedy gangbanger motel? Apparently not, and that's why Ned deserved a good pop.

"How long's this been going on?" Dale asked.

"At least a week," Ned said. "Maybe longer. It took me a while to find her after she left home."

Dale pulled a pack of cigarettes from his shirt pocket and started smacking it against his palm when Ned raised his hand and said, "No smoking."

"What? Hey! Whose car are we sitting in? Hunh? And who's the father here? You or me?" Dale started smacking the cigarette pack harder into his palm. He shook his head. Un-fucking-believable. Who did this clown think he was talking to?

While tearing open the pack with his teeth, Dale spotted a man sitting in a car in another parking lot. He, too, was watching Pompeii Inn, but he was taking photos. Dale nudged Ned and pointed. "What the hell is this? One big Peeping Tom convention?"

"I don't know him."

Dale opened the glove compartment, pulled out a .22, also from Larry's brother. Like the Fairmont, the .22 was a piece of shit. A cap gun. One notch above a BB gun. The good news was, Larry's brother had filed off the serial number. Dale could toss it, if need be, and that would be that.

Dale opened the car door. "When I come back," he said, "I'm going to smoke a fucking cigarette whether you like it or not." He shook his head again. The nerve!

Dale put the gun in his coat pocket and strolled over to the Peeping Tom. Dale knocked on the window, and the man, who was still looking through his viewfinder, jumped and clutched his chest. After catching his breath, the man rolled down his window.

"You and me," Dale said. "We need to talk."

The man said, "No offense, pal, but why don't you go fuck yourself, okay?"

"What?" Dale laughed. "*What* did you say?" Dale shook his head, then flashed his gun and said, "I think maybe we got off on the wrong foot. Hey, what kind of camera is that? Is that one of those digital jobs? Looks like it has a zoom. Hey, do you mind scooting over? There you go."

NED O'SULLIVAN'S father drove off in the other car and never came back. This alone was an odd turn of events, but then Jainey and the white-haired man didn't leave the motel when they normally did, either. The lights in their room eventually snapped off, but their cars remained in the parking lot. What this change in routine suggested to Ned was that something was brewing. What if their plan was to leave town early the next morning? What if they were going to drive someplace sordid, like Mississippi, and get married?

Well, Ned was going to be right there with them. The problem, however, was that he wasn't prepared tonight. He needed to go home and gather his things.

Ned drove his father's car home. He hurried past his mother, who was asleep on the couch. A cigarette still burned in a coffee cup. He bounded up the stairs, past Jainey's room, and climbed the ladder up into his attic. He quickly applied the camouflage makeup. He put on the rest of his father's military clothes. He gathered his duffel bag. Inside the duffel bag was his father's rifle, the very gun Ned had used to kill his first deer all those years ago. On his way out of the attic, he picked up his Bible. He slid it into the duffel, too.

Ned had read the Bible three times now, cover to cover. It was how he spent most of his time in the attic when he wasn't listening to Ratt or Motörhead, licking a forefinger to turn the tissue-thin pages, putting dots next to meaningful passages with a marker that bled through. Not that he was ever going to be one of those persons who walked around quoting Scripture, citing chapter and verse. Ned hated those people. He hated people who drove around with "What Would Jesus Do?" bumper stickers. And he especially hated those morons who said things like, "Hate the sin, love the sinner." Where in the Bible did they find such crap? God *hated* sinners. All anyone had to do was look at Psalm 5:5. *The arrogant cannot stand in your presence; you hate all who do wrong.* Well, Ned hated them, too. And unlike Jesus, who took the road of least resistance, Ned was going to do something about it. Ned was going to be the son God never had.

August 4, 2004

WHILE CHARLIE WAS BUSY BUYING THEIR BREAKFAST from a vending machine, Jainey accidentally gave herself a nasty paper cut. The cut was so deep it didn't even bleed at first, but when Jainey pulled the skin apart, she saw a deep and ugly cavern between her fingers. She felt, if only in passing, like puking her brains out. She glanced around the bathroom for Band-Aids but already knew more or less what was in there, so she opened Charlie's suitcase and rummaged through his belongings. She didn't find any there, either, but tucked inside the fishnet lining was what appeared to be an essay or short story: "Akshay Kapoor and the Russian Beauty: A Childhood in India. By Charlie Wolf." When the room's door started to open—Charlie returning with food—Jainey kicked shut the suitcase's lid and ran to the bathroom, locking the door behind her. *Akshay Kapoor,* Jainey thought. *What the fuck is going on?* She sat on the lid of the toilet and began reading:

Akshay Kapoor and the Russian Beauty:
A Childhood in India
By Charlie Wolf

When Akshay Kapoor was a little boy of seven, he dreamed of meeting a Russian beauty, but in India, in the tiny village of K___, the chances of meeting a Russian beauty were as slim as finding an oyster with a pearl inside, and not just any pearl, either, but one the size of his tiny fist. Nonetheless, little Akshay could dream, and dream he did.

One year ago, Akshay had found hidden inside his father's steamer trunk an old American movie magazine, and inside the magazine was a photograph of the Russian actress Vera Kholodnaya. She had intense dark eyes and jet-black hair, perfect and stark against her pale skin. She wore a string of beads around her hair. Her blouse, cut low, looked more like a bolt of velvet that had been artfully draped over her. Akshay could read English—it was his best subject, in fact—and according to the magazine, Vera had died in 1919 of the Spanish influenza epidemic. Every night, Akshay pulled out the old magazine and turned the brittle, brown pages until he found Vera, and every night, after carefully hiding the magazine, he would fall asleep thinking about the day he would meet his own Russian beauty.

The caste system, which had been in place in India for centuries, prevented little Akshay, who was lower caste, from mixing with children of the upper caste, but Akshay had big dreams for himself, the biggest of which was to leave his tiny fishing village far behind, never again having to look at wooden fishing boats or coconut trees or sand. Where Akshay lived was near the Benaulim Beach, which was one of the Goa beaches, and where, strangely enough, there were no jellyfish. There was a famous legend about the creation of Goa, and every child knew it. The legend went like this: While standing on the Western Ghats, the great warrior-sage Shri Parasurama shot an arrow into the sea, ordering it to recede. Where the arrow landed was the spot now known as Benaulim. Akshay would sometimes walk to Benaulim Beach at night, and he would meet with his good friend Mohan, who was the son of a rice farmer. One day, Akshay brought his copy of the old American magazine with the Russian starlet to show Mohan. He kept it tucked under his shirt, fearful that it would blow apart as he walked across Benaulim Beach. The magazine was his most treasured possession, this despite knowing that it wasn't even his to keep. Even so, Akshay treated it with the same care he might have treated some ancient and holy parchment.

"Mohan," Akshay said upon his arrival. "I must show you something. But you must promise not to tell anyone."

Mohan promised. He led Akshay to a place outside where no one was likely to find them, and then he lit a candle. Each gust of wind threatened to extinguish the flame.

"Look," Akshay said, and he turned to the page with the photo of Vera Kholodnaya. "She was a Russian actress," Akshay explained. "She died in 1919 of the Spanish influenza epidemic."

"Let me see," Mohan said. When he took hold of the magazine, he ran a great distance from Akshay and began singing, "Akshay's in love with a Russian! Akshay's in love with a Russian!"

"Mohan!" Akshay cried. "Please be careful with the magazine!" There was desperation in his own voice unlike any he'd heard before. Mohan walked closer to the water's edge, and panic bloomed inside Akshay's chest. "No, Mohan! Please, come back!"

"Akshay's in love with a Russian." Mohan was running backwards, holding the magazine over his head, when he tripped over a rock and fell. The magazine landed on the wet sand.

Akshay ran to Mohan and snatched up the magazine. There were creases where only a moment ago it had been smooth, and under the moonlight, he could tell that Vera Kholodnaya's face had been smudged by Mohan's reckless thumb. Akshay brushed the magazine off but to no avail. It was permanently damaged.

Mohan was holding his ankle, which he'd twisted when he fell. He asked for Akshay's help. "I don't think I can walk back to my house."

Instead of helping him, Akshay wanted to kick his friend, kick him hard in the ribs, but he merely walked away instead. Walking through sand was difficult and slow, a bare foot sinking deeper each time he lifted his other foot to step. He had to watch for glass and rocks. On other beaches he would have to watch for jellyfish, but not here. Why didn't this beach have jellyfish? Maybe it had something to do with the legend of Shri Parasurama, the great warrior-sage. Maybe little Akshay didn't know the whole story. He could hear Mohan crying out his name—"Akshay! Akshay!"—but it was a dim sound, like the groan of a sick animal, and Akshay was able to ignore it. He and Mohan would no longer be friends. Not after tonight. Mohan was too reckless, thinking only of himself.

By the time he reached home, Akshay's feet were burning as they always did after a long trek through sand. His father's feet, almost entirely callused, reminded Akshay of two crustaceans, a pair of prehistoric-looking sea creatures with hard shells. If Akshay never escaped the fishing village, his own feet would one day look the same.

"Akshay," his father said upon Akshay's arrival. "What's that under your shirt?"

Akshay's tiny heart began to pound. In his carelessness, Akshay had failed to tuck the entire magazine under his shirt, and a brown triangle's worth was now visible for all to see. "It's nothing, bap," Akshay said.

"Let me see, Akshay," his father said, standing and walking toward the boy. The other children—the ones old enough to understand what was happening—stood off to the side and watched.

What could Akshay do? He couldn't deny what was so obviously visible. He pulled up his shirt, removed the magazine, and surrendered it to his father.

"Why, what's this, Akshay? Is this what I think it is?"

Akshay nodded.

His father said, "Where did you find it?"

Akshay said, "I found it in your trunk, Papa."

His father nodded. Briefly, Akshay thought that this would be the end of it. His father was so calm upon hearing the news. Why had he been so afraid? What had made him so nervous? It was all seeming so silly now until Akshay's father took Akshay by the hand and led him to the steamer trunk where the magazine had been stowed.

"Please," his father said. "Open the trunk."

Akshay obeyed.

"Now, please. Remove all these other interesting magazines. They are interesting, aren't they?" His father smiled.

"Yes, Papa," Akshay said. "They are. But this is the only one I looked at."

"Shhhhhhhhh. Please. Remove the other ones, too."

There were hundreds of them, and Akshay could reach the ones that were piled high, but when the piles became too low to reach, Akshay told his father that these were all he could remove.

"Here," his father said. "I have an idea." He lifted Akshay into the air and placed him inside the steamer trunk. "There! Now, hand the piles of magazines to me, and I'll continue piling them on the floor over here."

Akshay did just that, handing stack after stack to his father. Akshay's fingers were black now from the smeared newsprint, and sweat dripped from his forehead onto the magazines below. When he handed the last stack to his father, he expected his father to lift him up out of the trunk, but this did not happen. "Sit, sit," his father said. "Let me give you this magazine. It's yours now." His father gave him the magazine with the beautiful

Vera Kholodnaya inside. "I want you to spend the night with your new magazine. In the morning, I want you to tell me what you've learned." His father began shutting the steamer trunk's lid.

Akshay begged his father to keep it open, but his father merely latched the trunk shut. "I won't be able to breathe, Papa," Akshay cried, but it was too late: Akshay was left in the darkest dark, clutching a magazine he could feel but not see. He heard his father's callused feet slap the floor's wooden planks, and then he heard a door shut.

Akshay Kapoor spent the first hour weeping. Why was his father being so cruel? Why was the punishment so extreme? But as the night wore on, Akshay decided to use this time to figure out the arc of his life. His time spent in the steamer trunk tonight would not be without purpose, for this would be good practice for the day he stowed himself in a similar trunk bound for America. Even as he thought this, Akshay found weak places in the trunk where the hinges weren't entirely flush, places he could place his mouth so as to suck in fresh air. This was good practice for when the ship took him away from this awful village that smelled always of dead fish and rotting wood. He would move to America and, eventually, become a doctor. What were the new diseases that, like the Spanish influenza, might sweep across a region, killing entire families? He would dedicate his life to saving people. But he would also find a Russian beauty, a girl as pretty as, or prettier than, Vera Kholodnaya. Akshay spent the remainder of the night conjuring this woman and his new homeland, filling in detail after detail until it had all become real enough to touch. Her name would be Petra Petrovich, and he would meet her in a cornfield in the heart of the heart of the country, and he would take her away from whatever life she might be living, from whatever man she was with, a life that wasn't worthy of her, and like the warrior-sage Shri Parasurama, Akshay would shoot an arrow into the air, and wherever that arrow landed, that's where he and Petra would go, that's where they would start their new and beautiful life together, and no one—<u>no one</u>—would ever stand between them.

"YOU READY?" Charlie stood outside the bathroom door, waiting for Jainey. She'd been in there for half an hour.

"Just about," Jainey said.

When she finally came out, she looked as though she'd been crying.

"It'll be okay," Charlie said.

"Why did I ever let Mr. Licks screw me after he'd been with Beth Ann Winkel?"

"What's his name?" Charlie asked. "Mr. Licks?"

"Alex," Jainey said, "but I call him Al Licks. *Mr.* Licks."

"You're a funny girl," Charlie said.

"You think? Because he never got it."

"If you ask me, that's a pretty reliable indication that he wasn't right for you. You don't want to date someone who doesn't get your sense of humor."

Jainey smiled at Charlie. "*You* get my sense of humor." She waggled her eyebrows at him. "Hm? What do you say?"

"You're flattering me," Charlie said.

"Maybe," Jainey said. "Maybe not." She put her cold palm on his face. "Before we leave, would you do me a favor?"

"Sure."

"Kiss me."

Charlie laughed, but his face was growing warmer. He knew he was blushing. How did he end up in a rat-trap motel with a pregnant eighteen-year-old girl with purple and green hair who wanted to kiss him? How had his life veered so far off course?

Jainey said, "*Really* kiss me, too. Don't kiss me like you're my grandfather."

"Okay."

Charlie cupped Jainey's face in his palms, and Jainey instinctually tipped her head back. She was a pretty girl with a small, almost childish nose. Her face was without a single blemish, nor did it appear as though a blemish had ever appeared on her. The only imperfection was a small mole on her cheek, which wasn't an imperfection at all. Her lips were barely parted.

Charlie moved in for the kiss. She simultaneously opened her mouth wider and shut her eyes.

"Don't shut your eyes," he said. Once their mouths had touched, he took a handful of her hair and squeezed. She pressed herself against him, but her face, which he was still trying to study, blurred into indistinguishable features. They kissed for a good five minutes before falling onto the bed and kissing for several more minutes.

"We should probably get going," Charlie finally said. He was out of breath. He brushed her hair back to get a good look at her.

"Whew!" Jainey said. "I needed that. Especially today."

"You and me both," Charlie said.

The clinic was in a building so nondescript it could have been an insurance company. It was on the far South Side, and nearly all the women in the waiting room were young and black—girls, really. A few of them looked up at Jainey, who was wearing her long red wig, but only one girl smiled. Another girl was talking into her cell phone, this despite a posted sign that said no cell phones were to be used in the waiting room.

The women probably assumed that Charlie was Jainey's boyfriend, the man responsible for this turn of events, the reason she was here. Curiously, he was the only man in the room. Where were the other men? It was possible, he supposed, that the other men didn't even know that the women were there.

"Jainey O'Sullivan."

It was a nurse calling Jainey into a back room. Charlie squeezed her hand.

"I'll be right here," he said.

The way Jainey headed toward the nurse gave Charlie a glimpse of what kind of child she must have been: the little girl gathering her courage to go somewhere she didn't want to go, barely lifting her feet, hands swinging heavily at her sides.

While the nurse held the door open for Jainey, Charlie tried to see if he could spot Akshay Kapoor at work, but Charlie couldn't see anyone but staff shuffling between the photocopy machine and the wall of files. Charlie picked up a magazine and mindlessly flipped through it. Not until he shut it did he realize that it was a copy of *Good Housekeeping.*

The woman sitting on the other side of the end table smiled at him. "Any good tips?" she asked.

"I'M DR. KAPOOR." He offered Jainey his hand, which was warm and moist in the otherwise ice-cold room. He was younger than Jainey expected. A few years ago Jainey had watched a special on PBS about India's Bollywood, the rising movie scene in India, and they interviewed some of the actors, all of whom were gorgeous with dark, intense eyes that could either kill you or bring you back to life. Akshay Kapoor could easily have been one of those actors, the kind of man who might visit a girl only while she slept, appearing in her deepest of dreams, but who would never appear in the real world. These actors were too beautiful for the gritty reality of cancerous sunlight and pesticides. And yet, miracle of miracles, here he was—Akshay Kapoor! Despite his intense, piercing eyes and Bollywood good looks, Jainey felt she already knew him. She knew, at least, the story of his childhood in a tiny and impoverished fishing village, and she knew about his improbable dream of marrying a Russian beauty.

Jainey said, "Do you think we could crank up the heat in here a bit?"

Dr. Kapoor smiled. "It *is* a bit chilly, isn't it?" But then he frowned, adding, "We must keep it that way. In heat breeds bacteria. I can have someone bring you a blanket, however."

Jainey said, "Hey. Guess what. I think you know my friend."

"Oh really?"

"Charlie Wolf," she said, hoping to see that smile of his again, but something dark crossed his face.

"Charlie Wolf did you say?"

"From Iowa," Jainey added.

Dr. Kapoor nodded. He gave Jainey a long, hard look.

"Is something wrong?" she asked.

"No," he said. "It's just that . . ." He looked pained, and Jainey wanted to tell him, *Forget I said anything,* but it was too late—the damage was done. "Well, then, I'll have to say hello, I guess. But it will have to wait."

Nothing was making sense. "One question before you go," Jainey said.

"Yes?" he asked, distracted.

"Did your father ever punish you by putting you in a steamer trunk for the night?"

Dr. Kapoor stared at Jainey a good while before shaking his head. "No," he said. "No, he did not." He left the room. Jainey expected someone to bring a blanket for her, but the blanket never came. Jainey's mentioning Charlie had clearly distracted Dr. Kapoor. Like that, the offer of the blanket had evaporated, and though Jainey knew it was only her imagination, the room seemed chillier now, and her teeth started to clack together.

CHARLIE WAITED nearly two hours before Jainey returned to the waiting room. She was pale and shivering, and a nurse was holding her arm. When Jainey saw Charlie, she put her arms around him and started crying.

"It's okay," Charlie whispered. "You did the right thing. It's over now."

Jainey let go. Her nose was running. Charlie hadn't realized until now that she wore makeup, but there were darker circles around her eyes where liner had smeared.

"I need to pay up here," Charlie said, "and then we can go."

Waiting for his credit card to clear, Charlie reached over the receptionist's desk and yanked free a handful of Kleenex from a box. "Here," he said. Jainey dabbed her eyes, then blew loudly into the wad.

Charlie put his hand on the small of Jainey's back as they walked outside and toward the car. A small band of protesters had gathered. They held up large photos of healthy babies and bloody fetuses. A woman shouted through a bullhorn, "Don't kill your baby! Let me take her!" A priest, hands clasped together, said a prayer. Charlie moved his hand up to Jainey's shoulder and hugged her closer to him.

"You're a brave girl," he said. "I hope you know that."

Before she could say anything, someone called out his name. "Charlie Wolf?"

Charlie turned. It was Akshay Kapoor.

"Yes?"

Akshay crossed the parking lot. "I'm Akshay Kapoor," he said. He was staring into Charlie's eyes. Was this a challenge? Charlie forced a smile. He tried to pretend that he didn't understand the import of who he was.

The woman with the bullhorn shouted, "Murderer! Murderer!"

Jainey stiffened at the sound of the woman's shrill, augmented voice, but then she said to Charlie, "I'm sorry. I told him you were here. I thought you two were friends."

Charlie shook his head. He coughed out a sad, little laugh. The ruse was up.

"Well then," Charlie said. "I guess this all must look kind of funny to you, given that you know who I am."

"More curious," Akshay said, "than funny."

"Murderer! Murderer!"

"Okay then," Charlie said. *"Curious."* He looked at his watch. It was twelve minutes after one.

NED CONCENTRATED on the simple mechanics. Trigger, he thought. Finger. It was all so simple, really, so long as he remained focused. Focus was everything.

Trigger. Finger.

Ned's heart pounded. He was conscious of the camouflage makeup on his face. The sky was overcast, but it was strangely muggy out, and the makeup made his skin feel as though it were melting. The doctor—the abortionist—stood between Jainey and her boyfriend. He looked Arab. An Arab man had aborted Jainey's baby. An Arab man had sucked the baby's breath out of Jainey. An Arab man had removed its tiny soul. Nobody was going to convince Ned that the Arab hadn't experienced satisfaction in doing so, either. *One more down,* the Arab had probably thought. *One less infidel.*

***OKAY,* CHARLIE** wanted to say, *we've met now . . . it's no big deal . . . let's wrap it up.* But Akshay Kapoor wouldn't leave. He was politely waiting for an explanation. There wasn't an explanation, though. Or maybe there was one, but it wasn't important now. The important thing was tending to Jainey, who was shivering and weak. Surely Akshay realized that this was not a good time for this discussion. Deep down, Charlie wished Petra could see her good doctor now. *See?* Charlie would say. *See how he's putting his own petty interests above the health and well-being of a patient? Is this the man you love?*

"Murderer!" the woman yelled.

MURDERER.

The sky was overcast in a way that always reminded Ned of grade school.

Mrs. Hendricks, his fourth-grade teacher, had walked up to Ned's desk on a day when snow had begun to pile up high on the blacktop, a day that meant school would be letting out early. She leaned forward, hands gripping the desk's edge, and said, "I don't understand, Ned. Why are you having such a difficult time? A *noun* is a person, place, or thing. A *verb* is the action *performed* by a noun. Why can't you remember that?" She handed back his paper.

What she didn't ask him—what no one ever asked him—was if he cared.

Murderer.

EVERY TIME a dark cloud blocked the sun, Jainey shivered, and each time the sun came back into view, shining down onto her bare skin, Jainey began to sweat. The wig was too hot on her head. An overwhelming urge to cry surged through her, but she didn't want to cry in the middle of a parking lot, and she didn't want to cry in front of the doctor or in front of all these crazy protesters. Especially not in front of them.

She shouldn't have said anything to Dr. Kapoor about Charlie. Only now did it occur to Jainey that she had no idea who Charlie Wolf really was or how it was that he had come into her life. Their meeting, hers and Charlie's, may not have been an accident, after all. Charlie Wolf may have been following her all along. But why?

Somewhere nearby a dog barked. *Striker,* Jainey thought. It was Striker's bark that had set off the chain of events on Ruby Ridge that awful day. A barking dog, and everything was put into motion: gunfire, deaths, a military buildup surrounding the Weavers' house, helicopters, tanks. A barking dog, and everything was suddenly irreversible—lives lost; the United States an embarrassment. "All of this for one family," someone at the scene had commented to a reporter. Jainey thought of the men who shot Striker, the Weaver boy, the wife. *Bullies,* she thought. *Bullies.*

"Murderer!"

MURDERER.

A big red "F" sat on top of Ned's answers. Ned wished he could see Mrs. Hendricks today because he'd tell her in no uncertain terms that he knew what a noun was. He knew what a fucking verb was, too.

Trigger was a noun.

Finger was a noun.

But *squeeze*—Ned's finger applied pressure to the trigger—*squeeze* was a verb.

In the end, when your life's calling brought you to the front line to fight all that was evil in the world, what did it matter if you knew the difference between a noun and a verb? This was where Mrs. Hendricks's imagination had failed her. Her vision of the world was too small. Ned's, on the other hand, had always been rather large.

Squeeze.

Squeeze.

Squeeze.

You had to be careful not to lose sight of the big picture.

Squeeze.

Squeeze.

Squeeze.

The devil, after all, was in the details.

Squeeze.

Squeeze.

Squeeze.

IT CAME OUT of nowhere, like those times people had thrown things at Jainey from their cars, an explosion of soda when she wasn't expecting it. Jainey's first thought was that something had fallen from the sky and hit her square in the face. She was momentarily blinded, eyes stinging, and after stumbling back against a parked car and wiping away whatever was causing her not to see, she looked down and saw that her hands were covered with blood. There was more noise—gunshots?—but Jainey wasn't connecting the noise to what was happening around her. People—the protesters—were screaming. Was her face bleeding? Had something cut her? Other than being stunned from the impact, she didn't *feel* hurt. A man was lying on the ground between herself and Charlie, his face an unrecognizable glob of flesh and blood. Then came more gunshots. This time, though, Jainey made the necessary connections between all the seemingly random details, and she screamed. The man was Dr. Kapoor; the blood that had blinded her was Dr. Kapoor's blood; the shouting she was hearing was Charlie yelling for her to get down, to roll under a car. She was about to tell him that everything would be okay, but then Charlie fell, too.

THE PAIN arrived first as an explosion of light, followed by pulsating brightness. It was as though someone had pinned Charlie down and then hit his shoulder with a sledgehammer. He was on the ground, but with his good arm he grabbed hold of Jainey's ankle and started pulling.

"Get down, Jainey. Listen to me. Get! Down!"

Jainey dropped to the ground. She scooted under a parked car. Akshay was dead, his face unrecognizable. Charlie had no idea where the shots were coming from. He was still trying to process what was happening even as he planned his next move. He and Jainey needed to reach a safe haven, but how? He yelled for someone to call 911. He yelled it over and over.

"9-1-1," he yelled. "9-1-1."

CHARLIE YELLED "9-1-1" over and over, and Jainey, shivering, thought Charlie was referring to 9/11. She wondered why he was splitting the eleven into two ones, and what did he mean by invoking the terrorist attack? Did he think that they, she and Charlie, were in the midst of another one? Did he think the clinic was going to explode, or that a plane was going to nose-dive toward them?

"It's not terrorists," she yelled. "It's my *brother.*" She yelled this again, but it was futile. Charlie wouldn't stop repeating "9-1-1" and Jainey started fearing that Charlie knew something that she didn't, that he was calling this out for someone else's benefit, not hers, the way the terrorists of 9/11 no doubt had their own secret codes they exchanged before taking over the airplanes and forcing them toward a destination not yet on fire, a world still intact.

FROM HIS NEW vantage point under an SUV, Charlie thought he saw the gunman across the street: a hefty man, roughly Charlie's age, wearing a black Windbreaker and baseball cap. But then another man, this one in camouflage, stepped into plain view from a thatch of woods, holding a rifle. The man in camouflage with the rifle hadn't yet seen the man wearing the Windbreaker, and Charlie realized that the two men were not together.

WHEN NED HEARD the gunshot, he looked down at his rifle, confused because his finger was no longer on the trigger. And then he felt it—the pain, the growing warmth in his own chest, the shortness of breath. He fell to his knees. This was not how the end was supposed to happen, but now that it had come, Ned was more than willing to embrace it. He had done God's work here on Earth, and he would continue to do so in the great beyond. Few people ever found their true calling. This wasn't the case for Ned. He had always sensed a larger purpose to his life, and after 9/11 he began to see the world more clearly, much as his own great president saw the world, in stark black and white. Here is good and here is evil. There were no shades of gray. There was no ambiguity. You're either with us or you're against us. It was that simple. Few people ever achieved that kind of clarity. Ned had. He was one of the lucky ones.

AS SOON AS the sniper dropped his gun and fell tumbling down the embankment, the man in the Windbreaker retreated into the woods. He weaved in and out of trees, growing smaller and smaller, picking up his pace. A flash of jacket or a glimpse of hand would briefly become discernible, but eventually even these bits and pieces stopped appearing. Soon, there would exist no proof at all of the man's existence, nothing save for a bullet in the sniper's heart.

THE DOG, which had barked throughout the shooting, stopped barking. Jainey shifted her focus to the oil slick next to her arm. Even under an overcast sky, Jainey could see the oil's various colors—*fish colors,* she thought—and she could see how the slick twisted ever so slightly, like a pinwheel, only in slow motion, or like a special effect in a movie, a transition to show that the main character was now entering the dream world, a world that, like Alice's Wonderland or Dorothy's Oz, would change her life forever, casting everything she looked upon in a new and brilliant light.

Part Four

The Lycanthrope

2004

Night had fallen over Tampico, Illinois, and Norris was tired of driving around and drinking alone. He kept circling the city, figuring sooner or later he'd see someone he knew, anyone. Maybe he'd see one of his co-workers from the Wal-Mart in Rock Falls, where he spent over forty hours each week stocking shelves and driving a forklift. Or one of his classmates at Sauk Valley Community College, where he was signed up for Bio 101 and Basic Algebra but actually spent most of his time in the parking lot getting stoned. If he saw anyone he knew, he'd pull over and tell them to hop in, and then he'd drive them to Tampico Memorial Cemetery or St. Mary's or Yorktown or Leon or Hume Cemetery, where they could look for familiar last names on tombstones and figure out how old people were when they died, and they could share a bottle of cheap wine. That's what he really wanted to do tonight—drink—but he didn't like drinking alone. He kept passing Casey's, expecting to see a familiar car in the convenience store's parking lot, but apparently everyone had stayed in for the night. Too bad. The forty-ounce bottle of Mickey's had grown warm between his legs, and each slug was more difficult to swallow than the slug before.

What Norris wanted was something larger—much larger—than what rural Tampico could possibly offer. In some ways, though, Norris figured that he was doomed for having grown up in a town that had already produced one of the country's greatest rags-to-riches story, that of Ronald Reagan. What were the odds of a single town the size of Tampico producing two Ronald Reagans? Norris already knew the answer to that one. Zilch. You never drove past an exit on I-80 advertising the home of two *famous people. And so, in many ways, Norris's fate was a foregone conclusion. If you were born and raised in Tampico, Illinois, you grew up under the shadow of the man responsible for the end of communism in Eastern Europe. In short, you were destined to be average. Ronald Reagan had made damn sure of that.*

Norris circled the town one more time before cracking open the Mad Dog. He'd bought it in anticipation of finding another lonely soul to share it with, but that wasn't going to happen. Not tonight, at least. Mad Dog was rotgut, pure and simple, and it looked eerily like radiator fluid, fluorescent green and practically glowing under the liquor store's lights, but it was a cheap and fast drunk.

By midnight, a thick fog had rolled into town. The moon, low and full, was orange. A harvest moon. There wasn't anything to do in Tampico. You had to go to Rock Falls or Sterling or Princeton or Dixon if you wanted to do something. Oh, there was the Good Times Tap on Main Street, but Norris was nineteen, still underage. Even Ronald Reagan ended up in Dixon and claimed, long after he was famous, that it was there where he had really found himself. And when you thought about it, what Ronald Reagan had said wasn't a compliment to Dixon, it was really more of an insult to Tampico. Tampico was so small, Ronald Reagan couldn't even find himself there! Of course, little Ronnie was only nine when his family had moved to Dixon, but still . . .

On his fifteenth or sixteenth circle around Tampico, Norris spotted a girl about his age, maybe a little younger. She had purple and green hair.

"Ho-ly shit," Norris said.

No one in Tampico had purple and green hair—no one Norris had ever seen. The girl was standing not very far from a house the Reagan family had once lived in. It wasn't the president's birthplace, which was in an apartment downtown, but rather a house they had moved into later when Ronnie was still a baby. The girl with purple and green hair was talking to a man with outstretched arms and a long beard. In his robe and funny hat, the man looked like some kind of prophet.

Norris took another swig of Mad Dog and circled the block. This time he drove slowly past, but his vision had started to blur, and he almost hit a parked car. He swerved at the last moment.

"Fuck," he said.

He circled again, honking this time. He rolled down his window and asked her if she wanted to go for a ride. He was sincere, but she gave him the finger.

"What the . . ."

Who was this girl? And what was she doing in Tampico? With her appearance, the night had shifted ever so slightly. It was as if the world itself had tilted a fraction of a degree or had begun to spin a half-mile slower per hour, but then maybe those weren't really slight shifts, maybe they were actually large enough shifts to wipe out life as Norris knew it. Norris didn't know anything about astronomy, except that an asteroid had once hit the Earth and killed all the dinosaurs.

By the time Norris had completed his third circle around the block, the girl was gone. The prophet, however, was still standing in the same place.

"No!" Norris yelled, stopping his truck. "Where did you go, goddamn it?"

Norris opened his door and nearly fell out of his pickup. He was drunker than he had realized, the Mad Dog kicking in suddenly and violently, everything spinning first one way and then, with a quick jerk of his head, the other way. Cautiously, he approached the man with the beard.

"Sir? Sir?"

The man's arms were spread wide, as if he wanted to hug whoever approached him, but he remained silent. Was he mute?

"Sir, could you tell me who that girl was that you were talking to?"

The closer he got to the man, the deeper his understanding that things were not as they seemed. The man looked familiar, for starters. When Norris realized that the man was Osama bin Laden, he took two steps backward and let out a high-pitched whimper. When he tried running in reverse, his knees buckled and he fell—hard.

"Ooof!"

For his part, Osama remained absolutely still. His eyes, surprisingly beady, glowed from the moonlight. Osama, Norris came to realize, wasn't a real man at all. He was some kind of statue.

"You son of a bitch," Norris said. The girl with the purple and green hair must have set him here on purpose, but why? And why would she set him in front of Ronald Reagan's boyhood home, of all places?

Norris stumbled over to Osama. "I'm not afraid of you, pal."

He took a lighter out of his pocket, flicked it a few times, then tried setting Osama bin Laden on fire. He held the lighter to Osama's robe, but nothing happened. The air was too moist, and the robe was damp. Norris tried the turban next but again met with resistance.

Norris walked to his truck, reached in, and found his bottle of Mad Dog—what was left of it. He carried the bottle back to Osama, then sat on the ground and soaked the hem of the gown with the wine. This time when he lit the cloth, the fire took.

"Die, you bastard, die!" Norris bellowed. The Earth had indeed tipped ever so slightly, for the night was taking on an entirely new dimension, one that Norris would never have been able to predict when he left his parents' house earlier that day eating a cold cherry Pop-Tart. "Die, die!" he yelled. He looked up at the moon and howled. "Ow-wooooo. Ow-wooooo!" Before long, the flames rose all the way up to Osama's beard, and Norris, leaning against a tree, watching through two barely open eyes, fell sound asleep.

"Get up," the voice said. This was followed by a club poking his ribs. "I said, get up!"

Norris opened his eyes. It was early morning. Too early. Norris blinked. He tried to focus. Two men stood over him. Cops.

"He's still got the lighter," one cop said. "The little shithead."

"You think he's one of those American Talibans?" the other cop said. "You know, like that guy they found in Afghanistan? You know. Whoseyface."

"John Walker?" the first cop said.

"Yep. That's the guy."

When Norris realized that they were associating him with the statue of Osama bin Laden, he cleared his throat. "No, no," he said. "You don't get it. I tried to burn *the son of a bitch. I set* fire *to him. I was making a statement, man."*

"We can see that."

Norris turned to look for himself. Osama bin Laden was nowhere to be seen; in his place was George W. Bush. What the fuck was going on? George Bush's suit, singed from the fire, was still smoking around the edges. The ground was wet. Norris was wet. A late-night rain must have snuffed out the fire.

"You don't understand," Norris said. "That's not really George Bush. That's Osama bin Laden."

The cops looked at each other. "Let's cuff him," the first one said, and together they restrained Norris, twisting his arms behind his back.

In the squad car, on their way to the station, the cop driving said, "I don't know what the charge is besides arson, but I know there's got to be something in the books about publicly burning a likeness of the president."

The cop riding shotgun nodded. "I'm sure he's in violation of the whatchamajig."

"The Patriot Act?" the other cop said.

"Yeah, the Patriot Act. That's what that whole law's about, keeping traitors like this one off the street."

"Hear that, boy?" the cop driving asked. "You'll be lucky if your ass ever sees the light of day again. Ten years ago you might have denigrated this fine country and gotten away with it, but no more. No sir. We lock hippies like you up and throw away the key."

The other cop turned around and smiled. "And who's gonna miss you besides your mama and your daddy? Huh? I'll tell you who's gonna miss you. Nobody. That's who."

Two Days Before Election Day

AFTER THE CLINIC SHOOTING, CHARLIE'S INSOMNIA returned in full bloom. He couldn't remember the last time he'd actually fallen asleep since that awful day. It might have been those few seconds in the shower two weeks ago, the soap falling from fingers gone slack, or that day one month ago when he backed into a parked car and then opened his eyes, not sure where he was. He was never *not* exhausted. Every time he moved an arm or a leg, he had to concentrate to achieve his goal. The very thought of lifting things, even objects that didn't weigh much at all, filled him with the darkest dread. *I can't,* he thought. He'd even quit pulling down the blankets on his bed. They *looked* heavy. When people spoke to him in passing, their words rarely made sense. "What?" he'd ask. "I'm not sure I understand." Mornings bled into nights and then bled back into mornings. One night he turned on the TV and couldn't stop laughing. What he was watching was a *Frontline* documentary about George W. Bush. Every time George Bush spoke, Charlie fell into hysterics. At one point, while Charlie was in tears, unable to breathe, someone knocked at the door. "Are you okay?" a man asked. Charlie, paralyzed by laughter, couldn't stand up to see who was speaking. The man knocked again. "I'm calling the front desk if you don't answer the door," he said. Charlie picked up a shoe and threw it. The shoe bounced off the door and hit a flower vase, which tipped over and broke. It was so damned funny, Charlie had to hold on to the bed to keep from sliding off.

According to the police, there were no leads for who'd killed Ned O'Sullivan. The more Charlie pressed, the less friendly the police became. Eventually, they quit taking Charlie's calls, and when Charlie showed up at the police station, they wouldn't let him talk to anyone.

Charlie wasn't sure why he cared. In fact, he shouldn't have pushed so hard; the mystery man, after all, had saved Charlie's life. But Charlie had begun to see his life as a pointillistic portrait—clusters of dots that represented something else—and yet he was always standing too close to see the bigger picture. He was convinced that if he could step back and see it from farther away, everything that had happened to him since Petra walked out of his life would start making perfect sense, but all he kept seeing were dots—nothing but dots.

Charlie was lucky: the bullet had missed bone by only a fraction of an inch. There was nerve damage, and the bullet had left two nasty holes in his shoulder, but things could have been far worse. A constant dull throb lingered, along with razor-sharp pain whenever he reached in certain directions. The doctor told him that his arm would never feel the way it used to, but why should it? That was the nature of trauma, physical or otherwise; it altered the way you lived your day-to-day life. The key was accepting the new conditions of your life and moving on. The people who couldn't accept what had happened to them were the ones who, barely able to make it from one day to the next, eventually self-destructed. Charlie had never much thought about the human body before his own had been ripped apart, but he had come to appreciate it as an amazing vessel. The fact that we could send men to the moon but were incapable of building a robot that could walk up a flight of stairs on two legs spoke wonders to the infinite complexity of the body's physics.

Charlie could accept the wound in his arm, but it was the deeper wound of Akshay Kapoor's death that he couldn't shake. On the one hand, it was easy to rationalize what had happened. Jainey's brother, Ned, would have killed *any* doctor who'd given his sister an abortion. On the other hand, Charlie had specifically chosen Akshay Kapoor for Jainey. Charlie had chosen Akshay because Akshay had chosen

Petra. Charlie had simply wanted to see the man face to face. He couldn't have said now *why* he wanted to see him, but that no longer mattered. The man was dead. That's what mattered. After Akshay Kapoor's death, Charlie wanted more than anything to call Petra, but he couldn't. He blamed himself, and maybe he could live with that, but Petra would blame him, too, and Charlie wasn't sure that he was ready to hear whatever she might have to say.

A new guard was working second shift when Charlie finally returned to work. He was an old man with a bald liver-spotted head who moved as though in the final clutches of arthritis.

"Where's Rex?" Charlie asked.

"Rex? Don't know any Rex. I'm Buster."

"Buster? Like Buster Keaton?" Charlie asked.

"Buster Crabbe," the man replied. He smiled. He and Charlie shook hands.

"I'm Charlie. Rex was here back in late July, early August."

"Oh. Well, I was out on medical leave. Ramsey Hunt."

"Ramsey *what?*"

"That's the name of what I had. *Ramsey Hunt.* Don't worry. I hadn't heard of it before, either. My face was paralyzed. Want to hear the other symptoms? Hearing deficit, severe pain, vertigo, blisters in the ear, nausea. Let me tell you. It's a pisser."

"So you don't know any Rex," Charlie said.

"Could have been a temp." Buster slid off the stool but grimaced when his feet touched the ground. Why had this man been hired to guard *anything?* He gave Charlie a little salute. "The ol' ball-and-chain's waiting at home," he said. "Not that I'm complaining. Not at my age."

After Buster had gone, it was as though Charlie had imagined him. His mind played tricks on him lately. The dream world and the real world sometimes blurred together, and more and more Charlie found himself asking, *Did I dream that or did it really happen?* His trip to the wig store downtown with Jainey, the way she stood on her tiptoes and kissed him while a train roared overhead, Jainey herself—it was all a dream now.

After the shooting, he had exchanged lives with Jainey. Sort of. He'd given her his car, and she'd given him the Turd. He'd already paid several months in advance on his apartment in Iowa, expecting eventually to return, but when he decided to remain in Chicago, he gave Jainey his key and told her to keep whatever she wanted. "Sell the rest," Charlie'd said. Jainey had needed a new life, a good place to live, a community where intellectual life was championed instead of scorned. He'd explained to her how to apply for student loans. He'd advised her on what courses to take her first year, which profs were worth studying with. She wanted to be an art major; she wanted to be surrounded by people who understood her. Charlie knew that a girl with purple and green hair would fit in perfectly in Iowa City. On the ped mall, Jainey might even be par for the course, nothing special, and that wouldn't be such a bad thing for her—for a while, at least.

"What am I doing here?" Charlie asked. "Jesus."

Charlie left his post. He walked into Deep Storage, pacing the aisles. He left the bank vault door wide open. There were millions of files here, and Charlie noticed that the floor sloped slightly downward. The further Charlie walked, the deeper into the Earth he went. Was he imagining all of this, a job that took him literally into the ground? No one would believe him, and yet here he was, walking so far that he was shivering. The deeper he went, the darker it got. He should probably stop walking. The upward slope was going to kill him. But down he went, further and further.

With his own private file from Deep Storage resting next to him on the seat, Charlie drove to Jill's. He needed to talk to someone, so why not Jill? She lived in an apartment behind her hypnotherapy clinic.

After pulling into the parking garage, though, Charlie hesitated. His paying Jill an unexpected visit at her home had all the markings of a bad idea, a slip in judgment. He'd never stopped by unexpected this late at night, but didn't their lover status count for something?

Using his cell phone, Charlie called Jill. He'd bought the phone after the shooting. If he'd had one at the clinic, maybe Akshay Kapoor would still be alive. The paramedics told him *no,* that Akshay was killed instantly, and Charlie could *see* that he'd been killed instantly, but that's how his mind had been working lately, always asking, "What if?" even when the obvious answer, along with all the evidence, lay before him.

Jill picked up on the second ring. "Yes?"

"It's Charlie. I thought maybe we could talk."

"Charlie?" There was a pause.

"Charlie," Charlie said. "Charlie *Wolf.*"

"Charlie Wolf? Did we have an appointment? What time is it?"

"Well, no, we don't have an appointment," Charlie said, "but I really need to talk, and I thought—"

But Jill cut him off. "Not today," she said. "I'm busy."

"You're busy?" Charlie thought about this for a moment, and the slow realization of what she might have been doing up there began to crowd his thoughts. "Who's up there?" he asked.

"That's confidential."

"Is it another *man?*"

"Charlie," Jill said. "I have other patients. You're not my only one."

Her words were a dagger rammed through the weak muscle of his heart. "It's four in the morning," he said and hung up on her. His breathing was labored. Sweat bloomed from his forehead.

You're not my only one.

"Jesus Christ," Charlie said. "What's the world coming to?"

Charlie peered at his folder. He hadn't yet opened it. He didn't want to be alone when he did. What if the news was bad? Then what?

He decided to call Petra. He needed to talk to her. He couldn't get through another day unless he explained everything to her. He turned on the car's dome light. His hands were shaking. He pulled from his wallet a tiny sheet of paper with her phone number on it. He was about to push the first number when the cell phone rang.

"Hello?"

"Charlie?"

"Yes? Who's this?"

"It's Rex."

There was a pause. Charlie's heart was pounding. He hadn't given his number to anyone.

"Rex," Charlie said. "Where are you?"

"Nowhere," Rex said. "But listen. Why did you take your file?"

"My file? What file?"

Rex said, "Charlie. You know what file."

"Oh yeah," Charlie said. "*That* file. Why? Is it a violation? I can put it back."

"Have you looked at it?" Rex asked.

"No. Nope. Net yet. I can put it back right now. There's no one on duty. I left early."

"Are you doing okay, Charlie?"

"I . . ." He wasn't sure he could say it; he hadn't even allowed himself to think it until now. "I don't think I'm doing so well. Lack of sleep, mostly. I haven't slept in over a month."

"A month? Jesus Christ, man, you should check yourself into a hospital. I'm not kidding. You need to take care of yourself."

"Why?" Charlie asked. "What's the point?"

"The point?" Rex said. "You *haven't* looked at your file, have you?"

"No," Charlie said. "I haven't." According to Jainey, the files gave profiles that assessed a person's threat to society, and Charlie had been assuming the worst, that he was a menace.

"Charlie," Rex said. "Are you still there?"

"Yep. Still here."

With the phone cradled between his good shoulder and his ear, Charlie opened the file. He held it closer to the dome light. His hands were shaking. He flipped to the final pages that listed a wide array of probabilities, along with a detailed analysis of what those probabilities meant, and it all added up to one thing: great things were in store for Charlie Wolf. Not just great things but *important* things. It was even possible, if the probable trajectory proved true, that Charlie's life would have a positive ripple effect, improving the lives of many others. *A life of value* was how the report summed it up.

"Charlie, talk to me."

Charlie laughed. "*You* killed the sniper, didn't you? You're the one who shot Jainey's brother." Charlie laughed harder. "I get it! Jesus Christ, I finally get it! You're not *after* me. You've been *protecting* me. Am I right?"

"I want you to go to a hospital right now," Rex said. "Can you do that?"

"I want to talk to Petra."

Rex said, "*I'll* talk to Petra, okay? I'll talk to her, and then *you* can talk to her. Right now, though, I want you to get your ass to a hospital. You need some sleep, *hombre.* You need to get your head screwed back on straight. You got a pen?"

Rex gave Charlie directions to a hospital; Rex promised to be there waiting for him. In return, he made Charlie promise not to blow him off.

"I won't," Charlie said. "I promise. But listen. I've got a question for you. Are you a spy for NTC? Jacob told me all about it. I thought he was full of shit. But you're one of those plants who watch people, aren't you? A mole?"

"Yes," Rex said. "And no." He cleared his throat. "I work for a grassroots political organization."

"What—the regional Democratic National Committee?"

"Christ, no," he said. "The DNC is a fart in the wind. Wusses. Dinosaurs. All but worthless. Fuck them. Don't even insult me." He sighed. "We're a guerrilla organization. We'll get nasty, if we have to. Our goals are long-term. Who's going to lead this country twenty years from now? That's what we're looking at."

Rex continued talking, but Charlie had begun to drift. It seemed like a dream now, the night Charlie and Petra had wandered into the old lodge, the mysterious animal adorning its walls, the antechamber, the George W. Bush piñata full of all those photos of dead servicemen. "Soldiers of Democracy," Charlie said. "Am I right? *That's* who you are."

Rex laughed. "Local chapter 4141," he said. "We're 220,000 strong now."

"That's a goddamn army," Charlie said.

"Exactly. You went to one of our meetings. I was there that night, watching on a closed-circuit TV from another room. We were all impressed. We couldn't stop talking about you for weeks. We knew we had to enlist you."

Charlie remembered the two-way mirror. It had been Rex's eyes he was staring into. "And NTC is part of this?" Charlie asked.

"NTC? Hell, no. They have their own agendas, but their agendas run counter to our own, which is why we keep a few men on the inside there."

"So what are you? Some kind of double agent?"

"A double agent," Rex said. "I like that." There was a pause. "This is all *entrez nous,* of course. You understand that, don't you? Everything I'm saying stays between us."

"So," Charlie said, "who do you have in mind?"

"For what?"

"For leading the country."

"How the hell should I know? We almost succeeded with one of our candidates, but then the bastard blew it. I mean, he royally fucked up. It hurt us. Set us back at least four years."

"Who?" Charlie asked. "Howard Dean?"

"Can't say. But listen: NTC had plans for you, but we've got plans for you, too, Charlie. Small ones at first. Then big ones. So get your ass to the hospital. I mean it. No more dicking around. We need you."

Charlie was starting to shiver. "Okay, okay."

"I'm not shitting you," Rex said and hung up.

The file was like a shot of adrenaline into his heart. The puzzle of his life, which until now had been a series of ill-fitting pieces, finally locked into place. The Big Picture came into sharp focus. *A life of value.*

On the Stevenson Expressway, a few hundred feet before the curve that merged onto Lake Shore Drive, a tire blew. Charlie took the curve with the blown tire at seventy miles per hour, causing him to veer to the right and nearly plow into the guard rail, but at the last second he managed to regain control and bring the car to a smooth stop in the breakdown lane. It was a terrible place to park, a blind spot for cars that hadn't yet reached the curve, but what else could he do? He picked up the file. It wasn't very heavy. He started to open it again but then stopped himself. *Everything's going to be okay,* he told himself. *Everything's going to be all right.*

With the hazard lights blinking, Charlie got out and popped the trunk. What he found instead of tools was a collection of miniature books, the tiniest books he'd ever seen. The smallest were the size of his fingertip. By the light of the trunk, he pushed the books around, searching for a tire jack, but then he found a book that was probably no bigger than one inch by one inch. It was Anton Chekhov's "The Lady with the Dog."

At the sight of the words—words so small he had to squint—Charlie could hear Petra's voice all over again, a voice that brought to mind cold nights outside the Kremlin, Siberian winds, and ominous

KGB codes. Charlie used his forefinger's nail to turn the itty-bitty pages until he found Petra's favorite passage in the story. Sitting on the trunk's bumper, Charlie held the book under the trunk's tiny bulb and read:

> *Experience often repeated, truly bitter experience, had taught him long ago that with decent people, especially Moscow people—always slow to move and irresolute—every intimacy, which at first so agreeably diversifies life and appears a light and charming adventure, inevitably grows into a regular problem of extreme intricacy, and in the long run the situation becomes unbearable. But at every fresh meeting with an interesting woman this experience seemed to slip out of his memory, and he was eager for life, and everything seemed simple and amusing.*

Anyone driving by would be able to see that Charlie was weeping, a grown man at four-thirty in the morning sitting on his bumper and reading the world's smallest book. He was weeping partly out of relief but also because he understood now that he must let Petra go. It was a realization that caused him tangible pain—in his heart, his lungs, his stomach, his brain. *Petra,* he thought, and the name alone caused everything to start aching. One night after reading this passage aloud, she had leaned over and whispered into his ear, "And of course you know who *I* am?"

"Who?"

"I'm that *interesting woman,* Charlie. And do you know why I'm telling you this?"

"Why?"

"So you can't say later that you haven't been warned." She slipped off her pajama bottoms and then took off her top. She wrapped a leg over him, curling up against him in the fetal position. Then she crawled over him, lying against his other side in the same position but, like a negative's image, in reverse now. She kissed his face a hundred times that night. At *least* a hundred. And despite having been duly warned only seconds earlier, Charlie fooled himself into believing that this would go on and on and on, and when Charlie shut his eyes for sleep that night with Petra beside him, he saw clearly their lives together, one day seamlessly unfolding into another—a world without end.

One Day Before Election Day

AT THE PED MALL, JAINEY SAT ON A BENCH AND WORKED on her final installment of Lloyd the Freakazoid. She planned to retire the cartoon for good, but this one was proving to be a tough nut. It was the one she'd started back at Pompeii Inn. Lloyd is appointed czar of George Bush's new education initiative, "No Child's Behind Left Untouched." After Bush makes the announcement in a grade school gymnasium, he and Lloyd start touching every child within their grasp. The frame that proved problematic was the fourth and final one. As it stood, the "No Child's Behind Left Untouched" banner is falling down but waving, flaglike, and though parents in the audience are yelling and children onstage are crying, George Bush and Lloyd the Freakazoid are having a grand old time—laughing, tears running down their cheeks.

Jainey liked the weird direction it had taken, but there was still something missing. She could almost see it, too, yet every time she thought she had it, the image dissolved.

"Fuck!" she yelled.

"You okay?"

Jainey looked up. It was a spiky-haired kid she knew named Rollo. His arms were covered with gothic tattoos, and his bottom lip was pierced three times.

"I'm fine," Jainey said. "Thanks."

A store was playing Coldplay's "Yellow." Before that, "The Rat" by the Walkmen. Nearby, two people were playing chess on a giant chessboard with pieces as big as their own legs. A crowd had gathered to watch. Jainey loved Iowa City. She had made a group of friends on the ped mall, friends with dyed hair and tattoos and fucked-up childhoods. Who'd have thought that they would all be here in Iowa? It was as if they had been waiting for Jainey to arrive, as if her arrival had been part of their grand plan, and now that she was finally here, they could all begin living life to the fullest. Jainey loved going to the Airliner to split pizzas with them. She loved going to the Soap Opera, a long and narrow store that sold every imaginable bath product. She loved going into Prairie Lights Bookstore, where Paul, a short man with suspenders who worked there, handed her piles of new books to read, telling her that she *must* read them, she *must.* How could she deny anyone so passionate? She always picked one or two from the stack and charged them with her new credit card. It was like living in some kind of Thornton Wilder play, where everyone knew everyone else. Jainey was going to enroll at the university for its spring term. Meanwhile, she worked at the co-op, selling organic vegetables and free-range chickens. *My Iowa life,* Jainey thought, and her heart swelled with gratitude.

Jainey used a pay phone to call her apartment. On her answering machine was a message from the Humane Society. They had a yellow Lab for her.

"Striker!" she bellowed. "Whoo-hoo!"

After calling her boyfriend, Maurice, and telling him that she couldn't make it for lunch but that she'd see him later that night at the rally, Jainey drove to the Humane Society. She liked the women who worked there. They were tough broads who looked like they could wrestle a pitbull and win. When Jainey first talked to them about adopting a dog, they didn't pull any punches. "Do you have any idea how much work owning a dog is?" one of them asked Jainey. "You can't stay out all night getting drunk. Your dog needs to do his business, just as you need to do yours. Imagine if your parents locked you in a room and you couldn't do your business until they came home and then they didn't come home." The woman, who reminded Jainey of a drill sergeant, shook her head. "That's not gonna wash, girl. You need to be there for your dog."

"I will," Jainey promised.

"And walks," the woman said. "You need to take your dog on walks."

"I will," Jainey said again.

But the woman wasn't done. There was more—much more.

Since Jainey had already been read the riot act, there were no more obstacles. The dog would be hers.

"Here he is," the drill sergeant announced.

The yellow Lab looked vacantly around before spotting Jainey, and then his thick tail started to wag and thump against the help desk. Jainey crouched, and the dog sauntered over.

"Hello, Striker," Jainey said and kissed its big nose. The dog licked Jainey's face once, then looked toward the door, as if to say, *There's the exit; let's go before anyone notices.* The dog, like Jainey, was eager to start a new life.

Jainey was already prepared with new bowls and toys and rawhides and a big bag of food from the co-op, but Striker curled up on the hardwood floor in the corner of the living room and fell sound asleep. Jainey sat in a wicker chair across the room and watched the rise and fall of the dog's chest. It was amazing, really, that a person could bring another species into her home, and that this species could fall so easily into place without question. *Oh, this is where I'll sleep, thank you.*

Occasionally, it was Jainey who felt like another species who'd come to inhabit the apartment—an *adult's* apartment—with all its books and notebooks, kitchen utensils, and extra sheets for the bed. Most times, though, the apartment couldn't ever have been anyone else's but hers. She pulled books randomly off the shelves and started reading them. Already she'd read the short stories of Guy de Maupassant, a history of Hollywood musicals, and *The Joy of Sex,* which was hidden behind a two-volume *Oxford English Dictionary* that came in a slipcase and had a tiny magnifying glass to read the microscopic print. But the book that surprised her was Sylvia Plath's *The Bell Jar*, the story of a young woman's descent into neuroses and attempted suicide. It was as though Plath had stepped inside Jainey's brain six months ago and started transcribing. Jainey didn't feel like that anymore—the circumstances of her life had taken a turn for the better—but the edge of the cliff was still in sight, and she knew that the potential for walking to its lip and peering over would always be there.

The phone rang, waking her up.

"Hello?"

"Where the hell are you?" It was Maurice.

"I fell asleep."

"Well, get your ass down here. You're late!" Maurice was like that: he'd yell, he'd swear, but he never meant any harm. The first thing he did each time he saw her was hug her, then kiss her forehead.

"I need to walk my dog."

"Dog? What dog?"

"I picked up my new dog today. Striker."

"Oh. Well, walk your damn dog then. And then get your ass down here."

"Okay, quit yelling."

"Am I yelling? I'm not yelling." Maurice hung up.

Striker was already awake, watching Jainey talk on the phone. When she hung up, he yawned.

"Okay, boy, let's go for a walk. You up for a walk?"

Striker fell back onto his side, but his tail thumped heavily against the floor. He liked being talked to.

It was election eve, and an anti-Bush rally was in full swing on the quad. The hope was that if enough students voted, Bush would be history, as would his policies of hate and destruction. Iowa was a swing state, and each time a candidate paid a visit, the polls would tip ever so gently toward the visitor before tipping back the other way, to the middle.

Jainey met up with Maurice at the Airliner, and together they walked over to the quad. Maurice was a grad student in art history, twenty-two years old. He was from New York City. Perhaps most notable—for Jainey, at least—was that he was black. Black people didn't live in Burbank—not many, at least—and although there weren't many black people in Iowa, there were *some* at least. Some was better than zero.

"Where's the dog?" Maurice asked.

"Home," Jainey said. "Sleeping."

Maurice shook his head. "Twenty bucks says he's eating your garbage. Probably has a pair of your nasty underwear in his mouth this very second."

"In other words," Jainey said, "the two of you have more in common than you first thought."

Maurice, stone-faced, said, "Ha-ha."

The rally was packed full of students wearing tie-dye, ski caps, and anti-Bush T-shirts. Jainey made her way to the center of the crowd. She imagined she was the beating heart of the rally, its pulse. She wanted to *feel* it. On her way there, she smelled patchouli, clove cigarettes, a whiff of pot. Someone was holding a sign:

SEPTEMBER 11 CASUALTIES: **3,189**

IRAQI CIVILIAN CASUALTIES
SINCE MARCH 2003: **100,000 +**

ARE YOU STILL NOT SURE WHY
THE IRAQIS AREN'T GRATEFUL,
MR. BUSH?

Upon seeing the sign, Jainey realized what her Lloyd cartoon needed. In the final panel, above the angry parents, above Bush and Lloyd, who are both laughing and groping, above the falling "No Child's Behind Left Untouched" banner, Jainey would add the ghosts of dead Iraqi children, a dozen boys and girls looking mournfully down at the scene below, with one dead child, the group's representative, holding a war-torn sign: A CAST OF THOUSANDS.

Jainey wanted to hug everyone all at once. She wanted to say, *I've been waiting for you my whole life! Where've you been?* She tried picturing Beth Ann Winkel here, but she couldn't. The last time she'd seen Beth Ann was at Osco the night she'd bought the pregnancy test. She wasn't even sure she could see Al Licks here. She certainly couldn't see him here in his Brookfield Zoo uniform, smelling like someone who'd just stepped in a pile of rhino poop.

Maurice said, "What are you thinking?"

"You don't want to know," Jainey said.

That was one of the things she loved about Maurice: he could read her body language. He knew that her mind traveled—and often. He was always there, ready to rein it back in, if need be. They had met outside a tobacco shop on the ped mall the day after she arrived in town. She was a wreck: rattled from the drive, disoriented, not sure whom she could trust. The first thing Maurice had said to her was, "*The Perils of Pauline.*" He narrowed his eyes, and she thought for a minute that she was going to disappear. "That's who you look like," he finally said. "Someone at the end of a silent movie cliffhanger." They stayed up all night talking—first on the ped mall, until a cop told them to move along, and then back at his apartment on Lucas Street. He was the one who convinced her that she should start seeing a therapist. "It's good to talk to someone you don't know," he had said. "I don't know *you,*" she said. He nodded. "True," he said, "but you will."

At the rally, she raised up and kissed him.

"You," he said, "are one big-ass kook."

"What do you mean?"

He shook his head. *Kook* was his highest compliment.

"You're always thinking," he said. "You never turn that brain off."

"If I turn my brain off now," she said, "who knows what'll happen? I might just vote for Bush tomorrow."

"Better keep it on then," he said. "But after you vote, turn it off."

When the rally was over, Maurice tried talking Jainey into spending the night at his place.

"I can't," she said. "I'm a responsible citizen now. I own a dog."

"Shit!" Maurice said. "That dog's already come between us." He shook his head, but then his eyes widened. "Hey, now, wait a minute. What's stopping you from inviting *me* over?"

"The dog," Jainey said. "He needs to get used to me first. *Then* you."

"Damn," Maurice said, but there was no malice in his voice. He was smiling. "A girl and her dog," he said.

Striker barked until she opened the door and he saw her, and then his tail started swinging. She tended not to believe in the mystical, but she hoped that the soul of the original Striker, the Striker who was killed by that worthless sack of shit Arthur Roderick, had found a new host in Jainey's Striker. It was possible, wasn't it, that her Striker was the reincarnation of Ruby Ridge's Striker?

She took Striker for a good long walk. When they returned, she gave him a rawhide to chew on, and he curled up with it in what appeared now to be *his corner.* In her bedroom, she slipped off her clothes and put on a pair of girl's flannel pajamas she had found in one of Charlie's dresser drawers. *Charlie,* she thought. *Poor Charlie.* She had tried calling him at Pompeii Inn, but he had moved on without leaving any forwarding information. Charlie Wolf had saved Jainey's life. His giving her his car, his apartment—his *life,* really—was no different from someone donating a vital organ to keep the blood flowing, the lungs pumping, her heart beating. White-haired and sleepy, he came to her often in her dreams. She would've married him. She would have. It was possible, she supposed, that she would still marry him. Not this year or next, but what if they met again a dozen years from now? What if their lives were such that they could drop whatever they were doing and run away together? Where would they go? Morocco? Costa Rica? It was possible that her plan would come to fruition, but it wouldn't happen anytime soon: Charlie was a ghost now in a city full of ghosts. It was possible, though, that he'd float so far away from her life, she'd never see him again.

Jainey's entire past was becoming more and more dreamlike. Jainey finally accepted that Mrs. Grant had indeed killed herself. Not that Jainey was letting the government entirely off the hook. Their policies had put undue burden on the poor woman, and she had seen no way out, no hope. Jainey still thought about her all the time. Every day. As for her own mother, she came to Jainey in visions obscured by clouds of cigarette smoke, and each time she thought of her, the smoke grew thicker, making it harder to see her. And Akshay Kapoor: Jainey saw him every time she was alone and shut her eyes. He wanted something from her—an explanation, an apology. The look he always gave her said, *Why?* Everything that had come before—Jainey's old life—was almost too much to bear.

The only person Jainey kept up any correspondence with was Mariah. Last week Jainey sent her a postcard featuring a giant ear of corn with IOWA written across it, and yesterday a heavily perfumed letter arrived from Mariah. The tiny note said simply, "Don't go turn Amish on us, you hear? Love, Mariah."

Jainey flipped on the portable heater and rolled it over to her bed, but she pulled it too close and the plug came detached from the socket. Crouched by the wall, about to plug it back in, she spotted a thick leather-bound file poking out of her camping backpack. It was George W. Bush's file from Deep Storage.

"Oh my God," she said. She hadn't looked at it yet. With all that had happened, she had pushed it out of her mind, but how was that possible? Maybe she was afraid that whoever was watching her would want to know what she knew, that they would drill holes through her teeth and force her to speak, like they did to Dustin Hoffman in that movie she had watched with her father late one night years ago, the two of them on the couch sharing a bowl of popcorn. Whatever the reason, she hadn't looked at it, even though the only person who had been following her, Ned, was dead. His ever-present eye was no longer on her. She was finally, blissfully, alone.

Jainey removed the file. She carried it to bed and slipped under the covers to read it. Like her own profile, Bush's began with pages of old standardized tests and scores, filed chronologically, from kindergarten through his senior year of high school, but the psychological analysis that followed Bush's was much longer and more complex than Jainey's, with dozens of charts and graphs that made no sense whatsoever.

Jainey flipped past all of these until she reached the "probabilities" page—the projected future for George Bush. What initially surprised her was its accuracy.

PROBABILITIES for George Walker Bush

Political affiliation: `Conservative`

```
WARNING: Predisposing personality factors
and levels of vulnerability may enhance
said person's continued vulnerability and
susceptibility while in this group.
```

Activism: `N/A`

Employment: CEO

Earnings: Upper 10%

Marital Status: Married

Sexuality: Heterosexual

Religion: Christian

WARNING: Predisposing personality factors and levels of vulnerability may enhance said person's continued vulnerability and susceptibility while in this group.

Threat to Self: None

What scared her about its accuracy had little to do with George W. Bush and more to do with her own file. The predictions NTC had made for Jainey were grim, and while it had been easy to categorically sweep them aside as being mere hypothetical suppositions, it was unnerving to see how accurate they could in fact be.

Jainey turned to the last page. There, she found the final two predictions for George Walker Bush.

Threat to Society: Grave

Most Likely Crime to Commit: Genocide

Jainey's breathing became shallow. *Genocide.* She wanted to call someone, but who could she call? Furthermore, who would believe her? Why hadn't someone stopped this man? What was the point of conducting a massive nationwide psychological profile if nothing was going to be done to stop the most serious of all threats?

Jainey turned out the light. There was nothing she could do. She was one person, one vote. And if the last election was any indication of the way the system worked, it was possible that her vote wouldn't be counted at all. In the end, she was utterly helpless. The election, like so many other things in Jainey's life, was a foregone conclusion.

That night, while Jainey slept, Striker loped into her room and climbed into bed with her. He pressed his spine against the backs of her legs and sighed. Jainey didn't notice. She was dreaming that she convinced George W. Bush to send his twin daughters, Jenna and Barbara, to Iraq to fight, and although both girls are crying—crying so hard that their pleas to their father are garbled, unintelligible—the president says that he's doing the right thing. *Not* sending them would denigrate the troops; it would convey the wrong message. And George Bush knows, this war is too important. The stakes are too high. His heart is full of love and faith. He believes in God. And there is nothing new about human sacrifice. It's in the Bible. It's a test. The ultimate test. A helicopter is already waiting outside. Jainey can hear the blades. Jainey, too, is crying. She says to the girls, *I'm sorry, but it's not my fault, it's* his *fault,* and she points to their father. And it *is* his fault. He's the one who wanted the war. But Jainey likes the twins, Jen and Barb. She likes them in this dream, at least. They aren't that much older than she is. "Please, Mommy," they cry. "Do something. Help us." Laura Bush, their mother, is crying now, too. She's yelling at George for making her daughters go to war. She's pleading with him to change his mind. Jainey doesn't like to see Laura Bush begging. It reminds her of her own parents arguing. *Why are you doing this?* Laura keeps asking. Laura must know deep down that her daughters won't make it back alive, as so many others haven't made it back alive. *Why, why?* she wants to know. But there is no other choice. There are no other options. The president is resolute. The girls must go.

Election Day

FROM THE MOMENT DALE SET FOOT BACK INSIDE JOLIET, Larry Two Fingers wouldn't let up riding his ass. "You weren't even gone long enough for them to get me a new cellmate," Larry said. "What'd you do—shoot the first person you saw when they opened the door?" When Dale didn't answer, Larry said, "I realize you missed me, but really Dale, I'd have written. You didn't have be such a dumb sack of shit and get thrown back into the can." On and on it went. Riding Dale's ass had always been a favorite pastime for Larry, but lately it had become a fixation, the only way Larry knew how to pass the day. For Dale, it was like being married all over again. Worse, actually.

"Larry," Dale said one day, backing Larry into the corner of the cell. "How'd you like to wake up one day with a shiv sticking out of your fucking navel?"

"Hey, hey, hey. Look who the sensitive one is!" Larry said. "Look who can't take a little ribbing!"

Dale let him go, but later that week he bought a stainless-steel butter knife on the black market and, using one of Jainey's teeth, started sharpening it. The tooth made a piss-poor sharpening tool, but what Dale had learned about jail was that everything required patience. There were times when the tooth became sharper while the knife's blade grew dull, but eventually the situation would reverse itself, and the tooth would once again sharpen the knife. It was a yin-yang relationship. Sometimes the knife was yin and sometimes it was yang. *Patience,* Dale told himself. *Just be patient.*

On Election Day, Dale lay on his bunk, trying to conjure up the split-second image of Jainey heading into the Pompeii Inn with the white-haired guy. He wished now that he had done things differently, since it was likely he would never see his daughter again. Instead of going over to see what the guy with the camera was up to, he should have gone to a pay phone and called Jainey's room. He should have tried talking to her. But Ned had put him in a bad mood with that smoking comment. Shit, Ned had put him in a bad mood *bringing* him to Pompeii Inn in the first place. When all was said and done, it was all Ned's fault. If not for Ned, Dale would never have sauntered up to the man with the camera, but he needed to get away from Ned before he reached over and smacked him a good one. And when the man with the camera told Dale to go fuck himself, well, what was he going to do then? Ignore it? Hell, no. He was going to poke a gun in the jagoff's ribs and tell him what was what. A few miles away, though, Dale realized that there was no place to go, especially since the man wouldn't say who he was or what he was doing there. At that point, Dale decided to put the s.o.b. inside his own trunk to buy a little time and figure everything out. It was shortly after this when the shit hit the fan. The man, whose name he learned later was Rex, detached the wires for the rear lights, including the brake lights, and it was *this*—faulty brake lights—that prompted the cop on Roberts Road to pull Dale over. Dale had to give Rex his props. The man had had the presence of mind to think it all through: yank the wires free, wait until a cop pulled the car over, and then start pounding like hell on the trunk. And once the cop had pulled him over, Dale's fate was pretty much sealed.

The memory of Jainey walking into Pompeii Inn triggered no emotions for Dale. For one thing, she didn't look like Jainey. She was so much older, for starters. Older and taller. And what was with the long red hair? Dale kept freezing that image in his mind, hoping for a physiological reaction to follow—a shortness of breath, a speeding up of his heart—but nothing happened. He felt exactly the same.

"Mail for O'Sullivan!"

"What?" Dale slid off the bunk, walked to the bars. "Mail? You shitting me?"

The man delivering the mail said nothing. The letter, as it turned out, was indeed for Dale O'Sullivan. It was from the U.S. Army.

"Look who's the popular one!" Larry said. "You had enough time to make a friend while you were out?"

The letter had already been sliced open—all incoming mail was read and censored before being handed over—but nothing in this one had been blackened out. The letter, which was on official U.S. Army letterhead, was an order for Dale to report for duty in Fort Jackson, South Carolina, to begin training. According to the letter, Dale O'Sullivan was still an active member of the Individual Ready Reserve.

Dale couldn't help grinning. He felt a surge of patriotism, the likes of which he hadn't felt in years. "Goddamn," he said.

"Who's it from?" Larry asked. "Mommy?"

Dale said nothing. No sense sharing the good news that he might be on his way out of this shithole, after all.

Later that night, while on laundry duty, he decided to show the letter to Walker Three Hundred. Walker Three Hundred had stabbed the man who was sleeping with his wife three hundred times. He was a tall black dude with arms as thick as tree trunks. No one screwed with Walker, and if you wanted to talk to him, you tiptoed up to him and asked him politely. In most regards Walker was a model citizen—the perfect inmate—but it was hard to ignore the fact that he'd stabbed a guy *three hundred times.*

Dale kept his shiv with him, just in case. You never knew when you might need it. "Walker?" he said.

Walker, startled, turned quickly around. "Man? You scared the *shit* right out of me. You like doing that? Walking up to people when they're not expecting you?"

"I'm sorry. Hey, look, you were in the Army, right?"

Walker nodded slowly. Talking to the man was turning out to be a really bad idea. Dale hadn't ever really said much to Walker before, especially about the Army. The room was steamy from the hot dryers, and Dale was having a difficult time breathing. He pulled the letter from his back pocket and showed it to him.

"What's this?"

"Letter from the Army. I've been called back to duty."

Walker didn't take the letter. He turned around and resumed folding sheets. "Your point?"

Dale didn't want to reveal his true feelings about the news. Dale's time in the military had been the happiest of his life. He had been in killer shape; his life had had purpose it otherwise lacked; he'd gotten laid in damn near every whorehouse in Germany. Clearly, though, Walker's experience in the first Gulf War hadn't been quite as positive. Still, Dale wanted to know if the letter was legit.

"When I left the Army," Dale said, "I retired. So I guess I'm wondering how they can call me back."

"You an officer?"

Dale nodded.

Walker said, "You retired from the Army, but you probably never resigned from your officer commission. The Army, that's their loophole, and they'll bring you back anytime they need it." Walker grinned. He said, "But why *you* worried? Your limp pecker is locked up."

"If you were me, what would you do with this letter?" Dale asked.

"Wipe my ass with it, then throw the motherfucker away."

"Oh."

At dinner, Tommy Tits was getting all kinds of shit from two new guys, guys who didn't like men with tits. "You're not really a guy and you're not really a chick," one of the guys said, "so what the hell are you?"

Under different circumstances, Dale would have gathered together a few of the men, and they would have made it clear, in no uncertain terms, that riding Tommy would only result in pain and misery, but Dale couldn't worry about Tommy tonight. He had other things on his mind.

Maybe Walker was right. Maybe the Army wasn't serious about calling Dale back to active duty since he was in prison. Surely, though, they made distinctions. Of *course* they wouldn't want some crazy fuck who'd stabbed a guy three hundred times. A guy like that, you couldn't really talk to. He was clearly a lunatic. Dale, on the other hand, had only cracked one guy over the head with a bat and then, many years later, put another guy in the trunk of a car at gunpoint. He didn't even *hurt* the second guy. Surely that showed Dale's capacity to be reasonable. One might even view it, in a certain light, as a textbook example of grace under pressure.

Dale was trying to think everything through, but Larry wouldn't stop talking. Larry was asking everyone who, given that it was Election Day, they'd have voted for. "Me?" Larry said. "I like the guy who's in there now."

Smokes Too Much glared at Larry. "Bush?" he asked, then spat into his green beans. "Tell me you're kidding me. You'd vote for *Bush?*"

"Why not!" Larry said. "And I'll tell you what I like about him, too. He's just a regular guy. Like you and me."

Smokes wouldn't drop it. "You'd really vote for that jackass? Tell me you're not serious."

Larry nudged Dale. "Hey! What about you? Who would you vote for?"

"Actually," Dale said, "I don't give a shit who's in office."

"What do you mean you don't give a shit?" Larry asked. "Hey, everyone, get a load of this. My cellmate is a communist! I'm sitting next to Castro here." He was throwing out his lure, hoping someone would bite, but no one wanted any of it. "Pinko Dale O'Sullivan," Larry continued. "Where's McCarthy when we need him?" Larry laughed, and Dale was thinking that Larry was winding down, but then Larry went on some more. There appeared to be no end in sight.

Dale reached down, touched the handle of the shiv in his sock. He was *this* close to pulling it out, reaching over, and stabbing Larry. *This close!* But then Smokes leaned forward and said, "Yo, Ann Coulter. Shut your trap before I reach under the table and cut your fucking dick off, you hear?"

Larry glared at Smokes Too Much a minute, then let it go. "Aw, to hell with it," he finally said. "To hell with all you guys."

Dale was glad Smokes had intervened. After all, there was no sense in Dale screwing up *his* future. The letter from the U.S. Army had given him a renewed sense of purpose. He now had obligations. Serious obligations. He had to report for duty at Fort Jackson, South Carolina. He had a country to defend. And he was more than willing to go. Didn't make a difference where or why, either. When your country called, you answered. It was that simple. And why not? America was number one in his book. *Numero uno.* And when you thought about all the other dumb-shit places in the world to live, like Canada or Mexico, you had to admit, America was still the best, bar none. The cream of the crop. The top of the heap. It really was. Fuckin' aye right.

Acknowledgments

Thanks to Wake Forest University for generous Archie Grants and a Junior Faculty Leave. Their financial support provided valuable time to work on this book. Thanks to the Christopher Isherwood Foundation for awarding a generous Thomas Williams Fellowship. I'd like to thank Jenny Bent, Wylie O'Sullivan, Dominick Anfuso, and Martha Levin. Thanks as well to the behind-the-scenes team at Free Press. My gratitude to Stephanie Kuehnert and Katie Corboy for hounding Columbia College–Chicago to invite me back to campus. As always, thanks to the fine folks at Columbia College for indulging me. Joe Caccamisi provided surveillance on (and useful digital photos of) a few Burbank landmarks. Thanks to Ted Genoways, friend and editor of *Virginia Quarterly Review,* and to Mary Anne Andrei, a wonderful science writer, for their continued support. Thanks to Judy Slater and Gerry Shapiro for their generosity. As always, Scott Smith is my word-of-mouth man. A heartfelt thanks to Bill and Sue Humphrey of Duke's Italian Beef Drive-In (8115 South Harlem Avenue, Bridgeview, Illinois) for providing the best publicity I could ask for. My father allowed himself to get roped into house- and pet-sitting duties in North Carolina so that I could flee to L.A. Finally, thanks to my wife, Amy Knox Brown, for taking time away from her own writing to read my stuff over and over and over. If I missed anyone, I'll catch you next time around.

I used Constance Garnett's wonderful translation of Anton Chekhov's "The Lady with the Dog."

I consulted Jess Walter's fine book *Ruby Ridge* to guide Jainey's understanding of the events.

The Iraqi civilian death toll figure of over 100,000 was taken from a study conducted by an international team of public health officials and published in the *Lancet*, a British medical journal.

The chapter titled "The Lycanthrope" first appeared in a slightly different version in *Sleepwalk*, a free Chicago magazine edited by three fine writers: Joe Meno, Megan Stielstra, and Lott Hill. My gratitude goes out to them for their support.

America's Report Card is a work of fiction. NTC does not exist in Iowa City. Though I've borrowed the actual names of some real-life locations, they are fictionalized versions of those places and should not be confused with their namesake. Any historical inaccuracies in this book are my characters' fault, not mine. I tried to tell them, but they wouldn't listen.

About the Author

JOHN MCNALLY is author of *The Book of Ralph,* a novel, and *Troublemakers,* a story collection. In the 1990s, John scored standardized tests for $8.10 an hour. More recently, he has been the recipient of a Chesterfield screenwriting fellowship (Paramount Pictures) and a Thomas Williams Fellowship in Fiction (Christopher Isherwood Foundation). A native of Chicago's southwest side, he presently teaches at Wake Forest University. He and his wife live in Winston-Salem, North Carolina. Visit www.bookofralph.com for more information.